If the walls of Stockwell Mansion could talk...

we'd welcome dear Madelyn and Brandon home at long last! To have the Stockwells' mother and uncle back in the family fold after all these years of thinking them dead...well, we're overwhelmed with happiness. Years ago, fueled by an unfounded inferno of jealousy, Caine Stockwell had cast out his own wife and brother—and falsely announced them drowned. Caine's deception lasted for decades, and robbed the Stockwell siblings of their mother's love— and a *sister?* It seems Madelyn had been pregnant at the time of her exile, and that child, Hope LeClaire, should have arrived in Texas to meet her clan days ago!

What could have detained Hope? We have a very ominous feeling about this, for the newspapers were splashed with her picture and the two-inch headline, *Stockwell Heiress Found,* making her a target for trouble. We can only hope she's not in harm's way, but nestled in the arms of a strong Texan hero....

Get caught reading Silhouette.

Dear Reader,

May marks the celebration of "Get Caught Reading," a national campaign the Association of American Publishers created to promote the sheer joy of reading. "Get Caught Reading" may be a phrase that's familiar to you, but if not, we hope you'll familiarize yourself with it by picking up the wonderful selections that Silhouette Special Edition has to offer....

Former NASA engineer Laurie Paige says that when she was young, she checked out *The Little Engine That Could* from the library fifty times. "I read it every week," Laurie recalls. "I was so astounded that the library would lend books to me for free. I've been an avid reader ever since." Though Laurie Paige hasn't checked out her favorite childhood storybook for a while, she now participates in several local literacy fund-raisers and reads to young children in her community. Laurie is also a prolific writer, with nearly forty published Silhouette titles, including this month's *Something To Talk About*.

Don't miss the fun when a once-burned rancher discovers that the vivacious amnesiac he's helping turns out to be the missing Stockwell heiress in Jackie Merritt's *The Cattleman and the Virgin Heiress*. And be sure to catch all of THE CALAMITY JANES, five friends sharing the struggles and celebrations of life, starting with *Do You Take This Rebel?* by Sherryl Woods. And what happens when Willa and Zach learn they both inherited the same ranch? Find out in *The Ties That Bind* by Ginna Gray. Be sure to see who will finish first in Patricia Hagan's *Race to the Altar*. And Judith Lyons pens a highly emotional tale with *Lt. Kent: Lone Wolf*.

So this May, make time for books. Remember how fun it is to browse a bookstore, hold a book in your hands and discover new worlds on the printed page.

Best,

Karen Taylor Richman
Senior Editor

Please address questions and book requests to:
Silhouette Reader Service
U.S.: 3010 Walden Ave., P.O. Box 1325, Buffalo, NY 14269
Canadian: P.O. Box 609, Fort Erie, Ont. L2A 5X3

The Cattleman and the Virgin Heiress

JACKIE MERRITT

Silhouette®

SPECIAL EDITION™

Published by Silhouette Books

America's Publisher of Contemporary Romance

Special thanks and acknowledgment are given to
Jackie Merritt for her contribution
to the Stockwells of Texas series.

SILHOUETTE BOOKS

ISBN 0-373-24393-6

THE CATTLEMAN AND THE VIRGIN HEIRESS

JACKIE MERRITT

is still writing, just not with the speed and constancy of years past. She and hubby are living in southern Nevada again, falling back on old habits of loving the long warm or slightly cool winters and trying almost desperately to head north for the months of July and August, when the fiery sun bakes people and cacti alike. Even Jackie's cat, Tige, doesn't go outside during the summer. Tige is Jackie's pal, her friend, her pet. He's an orange-striped tabby, neutered, of course, and too cute to accurately describe. She loves dogs, as well.

Silhouette Special Edition is delighted to present

Stockwells of Texas

Available January—May 2001

Where family secrets, scandalous pasts and unexpected love wreak havoc on the lives of the infamous Stockwells of Texas!

THE TYCOON'S INSTANT DAUGHTER
Christine Rimmer
(SE #1369) on sale January 2001

SEVEN MONTHS AND COUNTING...
Myrna Temte
(SE #1375) on sale February 2001

HER UNFORGETTABLE FIANCÉ
Allison Leigh
(SE #1381) on sale March 2001

THE MILLIONAIRE AND THE MOM
Patricia Kay
(SE #1387) on sale April 2001

THE CATTLEMAN AND THE VIRGIN HEIRESS
Jackie Merritt
(SE #1393) on sale May 2001

Available at your favorite retail outlet.

Silhouette®

Visit Silhouette at www.eHarlequin.com

Chapter One

She was on a road, the only thing she knew for sure in the nearly blinding rainfall. On a road in the black, black night, drenched to the skin and running. Running as hard as she could and still managing to breathe. Her chest ached from the gasping for air she'd undergone for...oh, Lord, how long had she been running? How far away was she from that terrible place?

And was *he* behind her in the dark? Fear made her take another look over her shoulder. She saw nothing but rain and darkness. Easily he could be toying with her, staying just beyond her scope of vision, knowing that he could reach her with a short sprint whenever he got over his perverted sense of fun.

Panic seized her again, and she forced her exhausted legs to run faster. She needed desperately to stop and rest and catch her breath, but she didn't dare, not for a minute. Would it help her plight if she knew precisely where she was? she wondered as her mind frantically sought salvation from the most horrifying experience of her life. She had a general idea of her location, but this whole area was frighteningly unfamiliar.

If only someone would come along. A police car would be perfect but far too much to hope for when she hadn't seen even one vehicle of any kind since her flight began.

And then, so suddenly that it sent a shock wave of fortifying excitement through her system, she saw a light. It wasn't close and it appeared to be wavering in the torrential rainfall that was nearly drowning her and blurring her eyesight, but she felt confident that it was a light. A yard light, perhaps. Indicating that someone lived out there, someone who might be kind enough to open his or her door to a soggy, scared-to-death stranger and let her warm up, dry off and calm her wildly beating heart.

Without hesitation she headed for the light. In moments she realized that she was running in prickly brush that tore at her clothes and skin. Her chest felt as though it were on fire, her right side was aching badly, her legs screamed with pain and still she didn't dare stop. Added to that list of miseries, she nearly fell down several times, as the ground had turned to slippery mud under her feet.

But the light gave her hope. Shortly she realized that she was crossing a road—a different road than the one she'd been on earlier. Even in the rain and darkness she could tell it was a different road, and gratitude flooded her heart. "Thank you," she whispered as her pulse leapt tumultuously over this additional proof that she was approaching inhabited territory.

But on the other side of that road was a rise in the terrain, and it was muddy and slicker than ice. She couldn't let it defeat her and she started up it. She lost her footing and fell backward. Grasping at anything to break her fall, she inadvertently twisted around, and when she hit the ground her head collided with a fence post.

She knew no more, and the rain mercilessly pelted her limp form and muddy face.

Matt McCarlson had heard the rain all night. At daybreak it was still raining, and Matt grimly got dressed and left the house to see what damage this powerful storm was wreaking. Wearing a yellow slicker and a wide-brimmed hat low on his forehead, he saddled his horse, Dex. Inspecting the ranch on horseback made sense. Storms of this magnitude and duration washed out roads, flooded creeks and created puddles the size of small lakes. Mounting Dex, Matt rode from the barn.

It was as bad as he'd suspected. Where water wasn't actually standing because of runoff to lower ground, it was so dangerously slippery with mud that Matt had to watch every step Dex took. The trees around the house had lost branches and limbs, and the debris was scattered far and wide. Leaving the compound, Matt checked the creeks that wound—normally at a lazy pace—through his land, and just as he'd known in his gut would be the case, every single creek had overflowed its banks. It was a spectacle of flash flooding and nature's formidable power, and it wasn't at its worst yet because it was still raining.

Shaking his head disgustedly, Matt directed Dex for home. There wasn't much he or the men working for him could do today. He'd tell Chuck Crawford, his foreman, to give the crew the day off. They could hang around the bunkhouse or try to get to Hawthorne, the closest town, if they wanted, though Matt doubted that the roads would be passable.

Matt was almost back to the barn when he remembered that he hadn't picked up yesterday's mail from the mailbox at the end of the ranch's driveway. He decided to do that before holing up until the rain at least slowed down some. Yesterday's mail delivery might be the last one for a week, he thought wryly as he approached the end of the driveway and the mailbox. He'd seen this kind of storm before, and if he managed to pull his ranch out of the financial doldrums into which it had descended this past year and he continued his life as a Texas cattle rancher, he would undoubtedly see it again.

Thinking of his financial problems pulled down his mood, which wasn't the best to begin with. There wasn't a place on earth that didn't need regular rainfalls, but storms of this nature were downright depressing.

"Hell," Matt muttered as he rode. Matt was just about to reach into the box for the mail when he spotted something strange. Turning his head, he gasped and mumbled, "What the hell?" He felt bile rise in his throat and an increased pulse rate. He saw a person lying in muddy water, resembling a pile of wet rags.

Was the person breathing? Heaven help him—he could be looking at a dead body.

Matt's stomach turned over. He scanned the area for a car and saw none. Fearful conjecture created horrifying images in Matt's brain. How had this person gotten here? The McCarlson ranch was miles from Hawthorne and almost that far from any other ranch. Was he looking at a victim of foul play?

With a suddenly bone-dry mouth and jangling nerves, Matt urged Dex over to the mud-streaked, soaking-wet, bedraggled creature. Sliding from the saddle to the ground, Matt blinked twice in genuine shock. It was a woman!

He could hardly believe his eyes. A woman! Where had she come from? Her face was unknown to him. Who was she, and what chain of events had delivered her to *his* doorstep? Was it something as simple as a flat tire or a disabled vehicle on the main road?

Well, he couldn't just stand there and speculate, even though he was almost afraid to find out if she was alive or dead. This sort of thing wasn't his forte, not even close. He was a rancher, not a medic.

And then he caught sight of something that made him grit his teeth and do what had to be done—there was blood in the watery mud next to her head. Obviously she had a head injury, a cut, a gash, some sort of wound that was seeping blood. Matt forced himself to kneel beside her. He removed the glove from his right hand and then took her wrist and felt for a pulse. He found one and breathed an enormous sigh of relief.

"Ma'am? Miss? Can you hear me?" he said, hoping that the sound of his voice would rouse her. At the same time he wondered how he would get her to the house if she didn't come to.

One option was quickly eliminated. Lifting her onto his horse when she was unconscious wouldn't be wise. She could have more than one injury and laying her over the saddle like a sack of potatoes could exacerbate her medical situation.

He hated leaving her alone while he went for one of the four-wheel-drive trucks—the only vehicles on the ranch that might make it through such heavy, clinging mud—but that really was his only choice.

"Miss, I'm going to be gone for a few minutes, but don't be afraid, okay? I'll be back in a flash. I just need to get a truck to—"

Her eyes opened, startling him, but the intensity of his relief momentarily weakened his knees.

"Hello," he said gently. She stared at him and said nothing. "Hold on, maybe I can make you a little more comfortable." Standing, Matt took off his slicker and laid it over her. She couldn't possibly get any wetter than she was, but maybe the slicker would warm her a little. Kneeling again, he leaned over her and looked into her eyes. They were a beautiful blue color, but so dull and lifeless that he felt another jab of fear.

"Can you hear me?" he asked. "Does your head hurt? Do you feel any pain anywhere else?"

"No," she whispered.

"Your head doesn't hurt?"

"Uh, maybe a little. In back."

He'd never seen such a blank expression in anyone's eyes before, but he had no idea what it meant. "Are you sure you have no pain anywhere else? The reason I'm asking is that I want to get you out of the rain and into the house, and I don't want to make matters worse by moving you if I shouldn't."

"No pain," she whispered, and closed her eyes again. "Please, just let me sleep."

"No! You need to stay awake," Matt said sharply, causing her eyelids to flutter open again. "You have to stay awake until I can get you inside, do you understand?" He didn't have to be a doctor to know that she should not be seeking sleep in this unholy situation; it was just common sense. She was obviously weak and probably chilled to the bone. She needed to get warm, she needed dry clothes and a doctor, and she needed those things now, or as close to "now" as he could manage them.

He made a decision then. The fastest, most efficient method of getting her to the house was for him to carry her there. Him, not Dex, not a truck.

"Don't be alarmed," he said. "I'm going to slide my arms under you and pick you up so I can carry you to the house. Please just lie still and let me do the work."

Once again he received a totally blank stare, almost as

though she didn't comprehend speech at all, and yet she let him pick her up and slip and slide to his feet in the mud without any sign of objection.

It was slow going. He estimated her weight to be around 110 pounds and thanked the good Lord it wasn't more. By the time he reached the house, however, it felt as though he were carrying a ton. His whole body ached, especially his arms and back. During the entire struggle, she had not uttered one sound, though he'd glanced down every so often to make sure that her eyes remained open.

"We're here," he said, gasping the message because he was out of breath and tired. Even so, he managed to hang on to her and still turn the doorknob.

A minute later, walking down the hallway to the bedroom area of the house, he felt renewed strength; it was almost over. There were three bedrooms, and he entered the first one he came to and strode to the bed. Laying her down on it, he straightened his back and groaned silently. It wasn't that he was physically out of shape—far from it—but carrying another person for a good quarter of a mile wasn't a common occurrence for him. Hell's bells, was it a common occurrence for anyone?

Standing there, looking at her, he realized what a mess he had on his hands. She was injured, soaked through and muddy from head to shoes. Along with her worrisome physical condition, there was her listlessness, and the uncaring tone of her voice the few times she'd spoken. Shock, Matt thought. She had to be in shock. Her head injury was the most probable cause, but how had she gotten hurt in the first place? And way out here, on his ranch, to boot? It didn't add up.

Regardless of so many questions without answers, she was here, in his house, and other than the ranch hands— who were probably wondering why he wasn't at the breakfast table with them—there was no one else to help her. He was it, and he wished to high heaven there was another woman on the place, because someone was going to have to help her get out of those filthy, wet clothes.

"Okay," he said under his breath, dreading that prospect. "Let's take care of first things first. Miss, I'm going to call a doctor, Doc Adam Pickett. He's a good doctor and a good friend, so don't you lie there worrying. Stay put, all right? I won't be long." Matt took his slicker away from her and replaced it with a warm down comforter. "Try to relax, but don't fall asleep." He hurried from the room and headed for the kitchen telephone.

His heart sank when he put the receiver to his ear; there was no dial tone. The phone lines were down and who knew when they would be repaired?

"Damn!" he exclaimed, and tried the wall switch for the ceiling light. It came on, so the electricity was still working. "For how long, though?" Matt muttered as he left the kitchen.

Walking back into the bedroom, he saw that she'd either fallen asleep or passed out. *Or died?* No! he thought frantically. She hadn't been hurt that badly, had she?

Hurrying over to the bed, he again felt for a pulse. Surprisingly it was a little stronger than before. Standing straight again, he rubbed his mouth with the back of his hand. What should he do now? Check her head wound and hope to God it was something he could take care of with antibiotic cream and a gauze bandage?

The mud in her hair was already beginning to dry and cake. He would have to clean her hair in some way before dressing the injury. Cautiously he pulled back the comforter a little. If she were a man he wouldn't hesitate for a second to take off those wet clothes, even if he had to cut them off with a pair of scissors or a knife.

Her gender really didn't matter, did it? She was a person in distress, a human being like himself, and she was

alone and injured. Would he care if a strange woman undressed him under similar circumstances?

Of course not. He was being silly. He had to help her
the best he could until he could get hold of Doc Pickett.

Matt strode purposefully from the room to get a pan of
warm water and some clean towels and washcloths. He
would also bring the first-aid kit back with him.

An hour later Matt was in the kitchen, staring broodingly out the window over the sink. He had a stressful
knot in his gut, caused by Ms. X in his guest room. Before
undressing and bathing her, his thoughts had been strictly
impersonal. Certainly he hadn't considered her an attractive female, and she was. She was young and pretty and
her body was...well, it was perfect, that was the only
word for it. Ripe, full breasts, a tiny little waist, long legs
and a shapely but firm behind.

He hated the way his mind was working now. He had
no right to admire that woman's sensual good looks. She
was reasonably clean now, there was medication and a
bandage on the gash he'd located in her thick, dark brown
hair, and he'd managed to dress her in a freshly laundered
sweat suit of his. It was miles too big—he was six feet
three inches tall and she couldn't be more than five-five—
but at least she wouldn't wake up naked, and it would
warm her chilled flesh through and through.

"Hell's bells," he mumbled and shot the telephone a
dirty look. The lines were still down, and God only knew
when the ranch would have phone service again.

The questions in his mind regarding his mysterious
guest just kept piling up and getting more urgent. Who
was she? Where had she come from? How had she gotten
to the ranch last night? How long had she been lying out
there in the rain? And what about the chafed bruises on
her wrists, as though her hands had been tied to something

with a rope? Damnation, all he'd heard in the night was the storm. No telling what had occurred on his own land—and not that far from the house—and he'd been completely oblivious to it. Good Lord, was it possible that one of his men had brought her out here with the intention of forcing himself upon her, and she'd gotten away from him? As discomfiting as that idea was—Matt hated thinking that any of the men living at the ranch and working for him were capable of such a heinous crime—it made as much sense as any other conjecture. After all, that woman hadn't just materialized with the storm, and with those rope burns on her wrists Matt felt pretty certain that she was a victim of some sort.

But if any of that speculation had credibility, wouldn't she be grateful that he'd rescued her, at least from the elements? Or was she the type to become hysterical when she realized she was in a strange house with a strange man? A man who'd undressed her and washed the mud from her naked body?

Matt sighed heavily. He was out of his league here. *Way* out.

Still staring out the window, he spotted Chuck heading for the house, wearing a rain slicker and dodging the deepest puddles. He was carrying something, and when he saw Matt at the window, he raised a hand in a casual salutation.

Then he walked in through the kitchen door. "Hell of a morning," he said by way of a greeting.

"Hell of a storm," Matt replied. "Phone's out, and probably the electricity will go next. What've you got there?"

"A woman's purse. Here's the mail and yesterday's newspaper, too."

Chuck laid the mail and paper on the table, but handed

the purse to Matt. "Where do you suppose that came from? It's got a whole bunch of stuff in it."

"It does?" Matt opened the purse, saw numerous items and took out a wallet. Flipping it open he found himself looking at a Massachusetts driver's license photo of the lady he'd rescued. "Her name is Hope LeClaire," he said quietly.

"Whose name is Hope LeClaire?" Cluck asked with a curious expression.

Matt returned the wallet to the handbag and set it on the table next to the mail and newspaper. Then he looked at his foreman and told him what had taken place that morning.

Chuck was fifty years old, a lifetime cowboy, fiercely loyal to Matt and a kindly man. But he was an observer of mankind and its foibles, and not too much that passed between heaven and earth surprised him. The only thing that really bothered him about the story he'd just heard was that there were red marks—quite likely rope burns— on Hope LeClaire's wrists.

"This could be serious business, Matt," he said soberly.

"I'm sure it is. Chuck, we can only guess at what happened to her last night, but how in hell did she end up way out here, on foot and during one of the worst storms we've had in years?"

"Have you asked her?"

"The few times she's said anything at all she seemed to be disoriented. I attributed it to shock and didn't press her for any answers."

"Well, you're looking pretty damned gloomy about it, so I think the next time she opens her eyes you should ask those questions." Chuck walked over to the outside door. "The men are hanging at the bunkhouse. Anything you want done?"

"Not in this downpour. Tell them Mother Nature gave them a day off. If they can get to town, which I doubt, they might even enjoy the free time."

Chuck shook his head. "They won't be going anywhere. The road's totally gone in some places and flooded in others."

"You checked it on horseback?"

"Rode as far as that right-angle turn near the dam."

"You didn't happen to see a vehicle that might have broken down last night, did you?"

"No, sure didn't. She's going to have to tell you how she got here, Matt. It might not be a pretty story, but she's the only one who knows it. Among the three of us, at any rate. See you later." Chuck left the house.

Matt wandered restlessly for a while, then looked in on Hope LeClaire. Her eyes were wide-open and she looked back at him.

"Hi." For her benefit he spoke cheerfully. Entering the room, he approached the bed. "How are you feeling?"

She hesitated, as though she really didn't know how she was feeling. "I think I'm all right," she said slowly, "but where am I?"

"I'm Matt McCarlson, and you're at my ranch."

"Which is...where?"

Matt frowned. "In Texas, of course."

"Do we know each other?"

"Considering the fact that I only set eyes on you a few hours ago, I couldn't say we're fast friends," Matt said rather dryly. He was getting a peculiar sensation in his gut, a premonition, actually. "By any chance are you having trouble remembering some things?" Premonition or not, he did not expect what happened next.

Her big blue eyes got teary, and she whispered, "I—I can't remember anything. Not even my name."

Matt's initial reaction was to wonder whether he should

believe her. First of all, he was thirty-seven years old, certainly no wide-eyed kid to be taken in by a con game. Second, since the awful experience of his marriage with its tragic demise, he was cautious around the opposite sex. Even enormous blue eyes and a drop-dead body weren't going to make a sucker out of him.

He remembered the woman's purse and wallet in the kitchen and knew he had the upper hand. "Hold on a second," he said a bit smugly, because confronted with such irrefutable evidence of her identity, her con—if that really was what was going on here—would crumple. "I've got something you should see. Be right back."

Hurrying away, he returned in a minute with the purse, which he laid on the blanket near her right hand. "I presume this is yours?"

Hope picked up the purse and looked at it front and back. It was black leather and quite attractive, but it rang no bells. Was it hers? Was there something inside that would tell her who she was?

"Check the wallet inside," Matt said gruffly.

Hope raised her gaze from the purse to Matt Mc-Carlson. For the first time she really saw him. He was very tall and well-built, a ruggedly handsome man with chestnut hair and brown eyes. If they didn't know each other, why was she here, in bed at his ranch? Very easily she could panic and fall apart, she knew. She was teetering on the brink of hysteria, terribly frightened and confused because her mind was such a void. But there had to be some answers somewhere, and if she gave in to panic, she might never find them.

What puzzled her, though, was Matt McCarlson's reluctance to take her seriously. She'd told him that she remembered nothing, not even her name, and he didn't seem to believe her. Well, pray God there was something in the wallet he'd mentioned that would trigger her memory.

Dropping her eyes to the purse again, she opened it and took out the wallet. She studied the driver's license, especially the photo, but realized that she had no idea what she looked like.

"Is this a picture of me?" she asked.

"You're kidding, right?"

Hope could feel her heart harden. What she needed right now was someone who cared that her mind was a terrifying blank.

"If you think I would kid about something so...so ghastly, then you have an extremely warped sense of humor," she said coldly. Peering under the blankets and sheet, she saw how completely she was clothed, then threw back the covers. "There's a mirror over there. I'm going to get up and see myself, *for* myself."

"Stay put," Matt growled. "I'll bring you a hand mirror."

"Why on earth should I stay put?"

"Because you might fall flat on your face if you got up, that's why." He hurried from the room.

Hope frowned. Why was she in bed at all? Well, her head did hurt a little, so maybe she'd already taken a fall. Gingerly she felt the back of her hair and encountered a bandage.

Fear suddenly gripped her, and she put her hand over her mouth as her eyes wildly searched the strange room. She'd only been here a few hours, according to Matt McCarlson. Where had she been before that? The driver's license was from the state of Massachusetts. What was she doing in Texas, if Massachusetts was home? In particular, how had she ended up on a ranch?

She breathed deeply several times, got her emotions

under control and was studying the license photo again when Matt returned and handed her a mirror.

Looking into it, she saw blue eyes and dark hair. It was the face in the photo, though heaven knew that snapshot wasn't a flattering likeness.

"It's me," she said, and bit down on her bottom lip. "I'm Hope LeClaire." She paused, then murmured, "Hopeless would be a more appropriate name."

"Knowing your name doesn't help your memory?" Matt realized he was beginning to believe her, and it didn't make him happy. What did the medical profession do for amnesiacs? As a layman, what could *he* do? He'd been in prickly, uncomfortable situations before, but none of them compared to this one.

"No," she said quietly, though blood was rushing through her veins at a furious pace. "It doesn't help." What would help? she thought. Certainly this man, this acquaintance of only a few hours, couldn't help. Maybe there was more information in the wallet and purse. She pulled some cards from the wallet. "There are credit cards, and this. It reads, 'In case of emergency, please notify Madelyn LeClaire, mother, and there's a telephone number."

"The phone's dead because of the storm."

"There's a storm?"

"It started yesterday and is still going on."

"Then I guess I can't call Madelyn, can I? But if she's my mother and my last name is LeClaire, then I'm not married."

"There could be exceptions to that rule. A career where you prefer using your maiden name, for instance."

"Please don't cite exceptions when I deduce some information about myself," she said sharply. "How would you like to know absolutely nothing about who you are and then when you think you've come up with one tiny piece of data, somebody punches holes in your theory?''

Unaccustomed to chastisement of any kind, Matt felt his spine stiffen defensively. ''Forget I said a word. How about something to eat. Are you hungry?''

Hope thought about it. ''Yes, I think I am.''

''Bowl of soup and a sandwich sound okay?''

''Anything.''

''Glass of milk or a cup of coffee or tea?''

''Hot tea, please.'' She watched Matt McCarlson leave the room, and she sighed, because she felt totally miserable in her ignorance. Truth was, she felt like bawling her eyes out, but what good would it do?

She pulled out the other items in the purse with anxious fingers. Knowing her name was a plus—and her mother's, who would certainly be able to tell her all about herself—but maybe there were other clues in the purse. To her disappointment, all she found was a small assortment of cosmetics, an unopened chocolate bar, a pocket-size book of crossword puzzles and a pen.

Lying back, she stared at the ceiling. *I'm Hope Le-Claire and I live in Massachusetts. So what in heaven's name am I doing in Texas? And why am I in the bed of a man who, by his own admission, has known me for only a few hours?*

That was when the trembling started…and the tears…and the panic she'd been battling so hard.

She could no longer keep a lid on the all-consuming fear that had been threatening her sanity, and she turned to her side, buried her head under a pillow and wept.

Chapter Two

In the kitchen, Matt set the teakettle on the stove to heat water for tea, then started putting together some food for Hope LeClaire. Glancing out the window he could hardly believe it was still raining so hard. He took a moment to try the telephone again, and put down the dead instrument with an impatient grimace.

His gaze fell on the mail and newspaper on the table, and he picked up the paper to check the weather report. But he never got past the front page. In large print the headline read, Newest Stockwell Heiress Missing.

Quickly he read the article and felt his blood pressure rising. The missing heiress's name was Hope LeClaire, and she had allegedly disappeared from the Grandview, Texas, airport after deplaning. Airline personnel were positive she'd used her ticket to get to Grandview, but no one could recall seeing her in the airport after the arrival of her flight. The Stockwell family had announced a fifty thousand dollar reward for information that would lead authorities to Miss LeClaire, and the newspaper would print a photo of the missing heiress in the next edition.

"Well, isn't this just great?" Matt mumbled. "Just what I need, another rich woman mucking up my life."

His attitude was based on his marriage to a woman who had been born and raised to wealth. She'd gotten tired of playing rancher's wife after only a short stab at married life and had wanted to get back into Texas society. She was about to leave Matt for the son of a rich Texas banking family, but she was killed in a freak accident. Matt had been helping her load her car with her worldly possessions, and they'd been arguing. A Jeep had come flying down their private road, and it had been filled with drunken, joyriding kids. Matt had tried to pull his wife out of the way, but one of the kids shot his leg full of buckshot and he'd fallen before he could pull Trisha to safety. The Jeep crashed, the kids had all been killed, and so had Trisha. Matt had never stopped feeling guilty for their argument and breakup. He had learned to live with community censure, but he'd vowed many times to never get involved with a woman again—especially a rich one as Trisha's lifestyle had left a bad taste in his mouth.

But he was involved with one now, wasn't he? She was occupying his guest room, and he was waiting on her hand and foot. And he could only shudder and guess how long they'd be stuck there in his house with the storm still raging and the roads already impassable, plus no phone service.

Not that he couldn't use fifty thousand bucks. Hell, with that much money he could bring his mortgage payments current with the bank and even catch up on his vendor accounts, all of which were past due. The only bills he paid faithfully every month were his utility bills, and it was a scramble most of the time to do that. His present crew, including Chuck, was about half the number of men he used to have on the payroll, and they were mostly working for room, board and loyalty.

The McCarlson ranch had been a successful operation until a fast-moving virus had spread through the area's cattle population only last year, financially crippling at least half of the ranches. The owners of those hard-hit operations were struggling to survive, just as Matt was doing. Times were tough now, make no mistake, and Matt worried almost constantly about how much longer he could hang on.

So yes, he could use that reward, but before he told anyone anything about Hope, he had to uncover what happened to her last night. Right was right, after all, and there were a lot of things he wouldn't do for money. For instance, maybe she didn't want to be found. Maybe her amnesia was a deliberate ploy to avoid the Stockwell family. Maybe she'd slipped out of the Grandview airport, and…

"Aw, hell." He could come up with "maybes" until doomsday and never know the truth until it came from Hope's own lips. But it was possible that her reading this newspaper article and realizing that everyone in the area—including the Stockwells—were on to her disappearing act would bring about a miraculous recovery.

With a wry little shake of his head Matt folded the paper and laid it on the tray he was preparing for Hope. He quickly made a sandwich and warmed a can of soup. The tray was laden with a good lunch—including the hot tea Hope had requested—when Matt carried it to the bedroom she was using.

He stopped at the threshold. Hope was sobbing so hard her back and shoulders were heaving.

If she was faking amnesia she must have a reason, and if she wasn't, she was in no shape to be reading newspaper articles about herself. He balanced the tray against the wall enough with one hand to remove the paper and drop it in the hall, out of Hope's sight.

Then he walked in and set the tray on the bureau. "Hope?" Obviously she couldn't hear him over such intense sobbing, and he sat on the edge of the bed and placed his hand on her shoulder. "Come on, dry your eyes and face whatever it is that's got you bawling. Not that a good cry doesn't help one's disposition at times. Relieves some of the tension that we humans have been fortunate enough to be blessed with."

Hope felt his big warm hand on her shoulder and found it strangely comforting. She didn't know him—she knew next to nothing about anything, for that matter—but this man, this stranger, was offering comfort, sympathy and even a bit of cynical humor, and the awful loneliness within her became just a little easier to bear.

Turning over, she wiped her eyes and whispered hoarsely, "I'm sorry."

"Do you have something to be sorry for?"

"I'm intruding in your home, aren't I?"

"This bed was just sitting here not doing a thing, and since I'm the only occupant of this house, nothing in it gets much use."

"Hardly a reasonable excuse for your taking in strays," Hope murmured. The corners of her lips tipped slightly in an effort to force a faint smile, because it was apparent that he was trying to ease the weight of her situation and he deserved some sort of appreciative response. "May— may I ask some questions?"

Matt got up for the tray of food. "Stack the pillows behind your back so you can sit up and eat. As for questions, ask away, but don't expect too many answers."

Hope bunched the pillows behind her and sat up. With

the tray on her lap, she realized how hungry she was, and she began eating at once.

Matt took a chair and watched her. "A good appetite is a good sign," he told her.

"It's the sign of an empty stomach," she retorted.

He grinned. "Yes, but if you felt lousy otherwise, you probably wouldn't even notice hunger."

"I suppose," she conceded. "You said your name is Matt?"

"Matthew McCarlson. Everyone calls me Matt."

"And this is what, a cattle ranch?" Matt nodded. Hope added, "In Texas. Where, in Texas?"

"The closest large city is Dallas. The nearest town is Hawthorne. Ring any bells?"

"None. You said you've only known me for a few hours. Did I knock on your door?"

"You don't even remember this morning?"

"My very first memory is of waking up in this bed," Hope said, speaking so quietly that a chill went up Matt's spine. He believed her now, though he wasn't sure exactly why he did. Maybe because she had wept so convincingly, or because she seemed so sincerely unconnected with her present reality? Whatever the reason, he felt certain that this was no con. Hope LeClaire was as clueless about her past as he was. In fact, because of that newspaper article he knew far more about her than she did.

"No," he said gently. "You didn't knock on my door. I found you lying in mud near the mailbox this morning. Haven't you noticed the rain? Well, it rained all night and it's still coming down." The shocked expression on her face made Matt feel bad, but he hoped what he was telling her was enough of a shock to jar her memory. "I carried you to the house and put you to bed. Then I tried to call a doctor, but the phones aren't working. The storm must have brought down some lines."

"Uh, wait a minute. *You* put me to bed? Oh, my! These sweats can't possibly be my own clothes. Did—did you undress me, or did some woman do it for you?"

"There's not a woman anywhere on the ranch. Sorry, but your own clothes were soggy tatters, and I felt it was urgent to get you warm and dry. I didn't have a choice and neither did you, so don't be embarrassed."

Hope put down her soup spoon and pressed her fingertips to her temples. Her forehead was deeply furrowed. "This is some kind of nightmare."

"I'm sure it feels like a nightmare to you," Matt said softly. "But I told you the truth. You were unconscious, soaked to the bone and lying on the muddy ground. You also have a deep cut on your head, which probably is the cause of your amnesia."

Hope swallowed hard. "Amnesia?" she whispered.

"That's what I would call your memory loss, yes. Of course, Doc Pickett might have another diagnosis. When the phone is working again, I'll call him."

"Please take the tray away," Hope said dully.

Matt hesitated a moment, then got up and did as she'd asked. "I'll take this to the kitchen," he told her.

"Before you go…do you have any idea how I got here? Did you hear a car in the night? Did you see one this morning? I'm very confused on that point."

Matt looked at her sorrowfully, unable to conceal his true state of mind on what seemed to be the pivotal question of her dilemma. "So am I, Hope, because, no, I neither heard nor saw a car. I have absolutely no idea how you got to this ranch." He walked out.

Hope lay there for a few moments, then folded back the covers. Sliding to the edge of the bed, she got to her feet. Her head was swimming and the muscles of her legs and lower back were surprisingly sore, as though she had overexercised after a long period of immobility. "Odd," she said under her breath, frowning over another barrage of questions without answers.

That wasn't an accurate summary of the situation, of course. There were answers to everything she wondered about, she just didn't know what they were. If she could remember, all the answers would fall into place. She was suddenly impatient with herself. *Dammit, if you could remember, you wouldn't have a bunch of questions eating holes in your already damaged brain!*

The word *damaged* caused her to shudder, and, fighting debilitating frustration, she steadied herself for a minute then walked over to the window and pushed the curtain aside. Indeed it was raining, and everything outside looked nearly drowned, but what made her heart almost stop beating was the vast expanse of open country she could vaguely make out through the downpour. Beyond the house and other buildings was…nothing. Nothing but huge, soggy, empty fields and enormous puddles.

"My Lord," she whispered in a shaky little voice. "How *did* I get here?" Someone must have driven her to this ranch, then…then…? Hope came close to crying again. Surely someone hadn't driven her to this isolated ranch and then thrown her out of the car. But why on earth would anyone do something so awful?

But there was another possibly, she realized, one that was reinforced by the soreness of her body—she could have walked!

But walked from where? Maybe Matt would have some ideas, she thought, and closed the curtain. Leaving the bedroom she peered up and down the hall and figured out which direction to go.

When she appeared in the kitchen doorway, Matt looked first surprised then uncertain. "Are you sure you're strong enough to be out of bed?"

Hope waved her hand, a gesture that indicated she considered that particular question to be trivial. "I'm physically all right," she said. "A slight headache and some sore muscles, but that's about it. May I talk to you?"

Matt went over to her, took her arm and led her to a chair. "You can talk all you want, but you're barefoot and I'm going to get you a pair of socks to wear." When she was seated, he hurried out.

Hope glanced around the kitchen, which was roomy and pleasant. The appliances were white, but the countertops, flooring and curtains were an attractive shade of yellow, and the color brightened the atmosphere of this gloomy, gray day. She felt much more at home in the kitchen than she had in the bedroom, which might have made sense if she had any sense, she thought drolly.

In the next instant, however, nothing seemed even remotely amusing, and she had to blink back self-pitying tears, which made her angry. She'd cried enough. Matt McCarlson was her one and only link to the rest of the world and her own past, and maybe he knew something that even he didn't realize.

Matt returned with some warm wool socks. He knelt down in front of her and slid them on her feet before she could voice an objection, so she merely murmured, "Thank you," when he stood up again.

"You're welcome. Would you like another cup of tea or anything?"

"No, thank you. Matt, I was thinking that maybe I know someone around here and was visiting him or her. I can't begin to guess what occurred last night to bring me here, but it's only logical to assume that I'm in Texas for a reason, perhaps a very uncomplicated reason. Do you know any other LeClaires? They could be ranchers, like you, or even live in that little town you mentioned."

Matt shook his head. "Hawthorne."

"Yes, I believe that was what you called it."

He could see the expectation on her face, and thought again of the newspaper article that would at least create a foundation of knowledge that she might build upon. But dealing with an amnesiac was a complete mystery to him, and Hope seemed calmer now than she had before. What if giving her that much information caused her another panic attack? He would much rather keep her calm until he could speak to Doc Pickett.

"I'm sorry," he said quietly. "There are no LeClaires around here that I know of." It was the truth. He'd honestly never known anyone by that name.

Hope couldn't conceal her disappointment. "And you know most of the area's residents?" she asked, obvious in her hope that he would say, "No, I only know a few."

"At least by name. Hope, I was born and raised on this ranch. This is a rural community, and you don't have to be friends with everyone to know their names."

"Even in Hawthorne?"

"It's a small town."

Hope bit her bottom lip. "I suppose." Her gaze met Matt's. "Do you have any theories about how I came to be lying in your mud this morning? Does Hawthorne have a hotel? Is it any kind of tourist spot? I mean, does the town attract...tourists?" Her voice trailed off, giving Matt the impression that she was grasping at straws and instinctively knew she hadn't visited Hawthorne, Texas, as a tourist.

"It has a couple of motels, and if the phone was working it might even pay to give them a call and ask if you were registered. But the phones *aren't* working, and there really isn't anything either of us can do about it."

"How about driving to town? I hate being even more of an imposition than I already am, but—"

Matt broke in. "The road has been washed out by the storm. Everyone on the ranch has no choice but to *stay* on the ranch until the storm passes and things dry out. Even then we'll probably have to do some road repair before it's usable again.''

'' 'Everyone on the ranch?' There are other people here?''

"The men who work for me…the ranch hands. And the foreman, Chuck Crawford.''

"Where are they?''

"At the bunkhouse, which is also where they take their meals.''

"But none of these people are women.''

"No, they're not.''

Hope fell silent and thought for a few moments. Then she said excitedly, ''The clothes I was wearing when you found me—where are they?''

"In the trash. They were tattered and torn, and—''

"Why would they be torn? I want to see them.''

"Hope, I cut them off of you so I wouldn't have to jostle you more than I had to. I was still uncertain about the extent of your injuries, and—'' He saw the determination in her eyes and gave in with a faint sigh. "I'll go and get them, though all you'll be examining is a pile of wet rags.''

"Rags! Is it your opinion that my clothes were rags when I put them on?''

She seemed so affronted by that prospect that Matt realized grimly that even with amnesia she knew she wore the best that money could buy. The Stockwells weren't just comfortably well off, they were superrich. Looking at her pretty face and anxiety-filled eyes, he found himself wishing that she were just a common, ordinary citizen, which was quite an unusual wish for him to be making. He really couldn't remember the last time that one particular woman stood out in his eyes, and the whole concept was deeply unnerving.

Spinning on his heel, he muttered, "I'll go dig 'em out. You can figure it out for yourself."

Hope frowned at the tone of his voice. Why, he'd sounded almost angry. Remorse hit her very hard. She was an intrusion in the man's life and routine, for heaven's sake. Why wouldn't he be irritated over a request that obviously had sent him back out into the rain?

But she couldn't go back to bed and do nothing, she just couldn't. In the first place there was no reason for her to act like an invalid. Sore muscles and a bit of headache certainly weren't anything to cause alarm.

Hope's eyes narrowed slightly as she pondered that conclusion. Perhaps sore muscles and a headache weren't cause for alarm, but what if they were clues to last night's events? And maybe her clothes were also clues. No, she hadn't been wrong in asking to see her things. If Matt had taken umbrage over it, then he'd either have to get over it, or not. Did it really matter to her how he or anyone else she might meet took anything she did or said when she felt so hopelessly adrift in a completely unfamiliar, even alien world? She had to follow her instincts; they were all she had.

Matt walked in with an armload of dark green fabric, which he placed on the table in front of her. "Have at it," he said gruffly. "I think I managed to save your shoes. I'll get them."

Hope began taking apart the many pieces of fabric. Matt returned with a pair of black leather shoes, and she took them from his hands and frowned.

"They're very...bruised," she murmured.

"Scuffed," Matt said.

She looked up. "Pardon?"

"People get bruised, not shoes. Yours are badly scuffed and the leather is gouged in places. Rough usage, I'd have to say."

"Like maybe I had walked over some very rough terrain?"

"Yeah, that'd do it, but not if it was only a short walk. Then, too, these could be old shoes. They might have walked many miles before last night."

Hope had no grounds for disagreement, although she somehow felt that the condition of her shoes was immutably connected to whatever had brought her here in the night.

She began looking through the pieces of wet fabric, and almost immediately noticed something strange. "It's terribly snagged."

"I told you it was tattered and torn."

"Yes, there's a tear right here. But there are so many snags."

"Like what?"

"Look at the piece I'm holding. See all those little— uh, bumps, I guess you'd call them, where a thread has been pulled by something?"

Matt bent over for a closer look. "Do those snags mean anything to you?"

"If you're asking, do I remember how my clothes got so badly snagged, the answer is no, they don't mean anything to me. But what would cause such devastating wear and tear on one's clothing?"

Matt shrugged. "Beats me. Unless you fought your way through a bunch of prickly mesquite brush."

"Is there some of that around here?"

"Lots of it. Also scrub cedar and oak, and both of those can scratch the living daylights out of a person dumb enough to tangle with them."

She shot him a dirty look. "Other reasons beside stupidity might have caused me to tangle with some prickly plants, you know."

Her flare of defensive temper surprised him. "I wasn't even talking about you," he retorted.

"Who were you talking about then, the man in the moon? Let me ask you this. Wasn't I wearing underwear or were you too squeamish to bring it back inside with the rest of this mess, which I might add, was mostly caused by your scissors?"

"Women's underwear does *not* make me feel squeamish," he said coldly. "For your information, I took a brassiere and a pair of panties off your wet, shivering body, and once you were bathed, dressed in my sweats and warming up under the best blankets in the house, I rinsed the mud out of your delicacies and hung them in the laundry room to dry."

Hope's jaw dropped. "You *bathed* me?"

"Don't you dare use that indignant tone on me, lady. You were covered with mud. I suppose I should have put you to bed in that condition?"

Heat suffused Hope's face. "Bathing someone is just so—so intimate."

"Under this morning's conditions, it wasn't even close to being intimate." It was a lie but Matt managed to sound totally and innocently sincere.

Hope tried to steer this uncomfortable conversation in another direction. "I knew these huge sweats I've got on had to belong to someone very tall." *And very handsome?* He *was* handsome; it was simply a fact of her present limited life. Not that she wanted to expand on that fact. Goodness, she could be married, or engaged, or living with a man she loved madly.

"I rolled up the legs, but I could cut them off, if you prefer," Matt said.

"I wouldn't hear of it."

"Suit yourself, but I can see that you're swimming in loose material."

"Which is just fine for now."

"Are you finished with those pieces of cloth?"

"I guess so. Oh, wait a sec. I see a label." Hope studied the label of a hunk of fabric, then sighed because it meant absolutely nothing to her. "I was hoping…" she said in a husky little voice.

"Look, I'm going to go down to the bunkhouse and see how the men are making out. I'd feel better about leaving you alone if you were in bed again."

"Fine," Hope said dully. Matt was instantly at her side to help her up from the chair, and he held her arm all the way back to the bedroom and the bed. She told herself to forget that he was a tall, deliciously sexy, good-looking man—who seemed to get better looking every time they talked—but his big hand clasped around her arm made that impossible to do. She was glad when she was finally under the covers again and Matt had left the room.

She heaved a long, helpless sigh. This was not a game, and she really must be demented to be noticing a man's good looks under such trying circumstances.

But then, maybe that was the kind of woman she was. Maybe she slept around. Maybe any sexy guy was fair game. Maybe she was a—a tramp!

Tears rolled down her temples. Matt McCarlson had not only undressed her, he'd given her a bath. Maybe she should be worrying about what kind of person *he* was. After all, she had been unconscious and entirely at his mercy!

Matt stayed away from the house for a couple of hours. He talked to the men at the bunkhouse and they weren't a bit shy with their complaints.

"Danged if we ain't out here trapped like rats in their hole."

"We can't hardly stand to look at each other anymore, Matt."

"Hell, I'd take backbreaking work over being stuck in this bunkhouse with these yahoos any day of the week."

"Matt, have you been listening to the radio for weather reports? The radio out here ain't working worth a damn. We've been getting mostly static, probably because of the storm."

"It's the same in the house, Joe, but I did manage to catch one weather report and it looks like we're in for more rain."

The grousing went on, and Matt drank a cup of strong bunkhouse coffee and let them vent. They had a right, he felt. Cowboys were used to being outdoors. The bunkhouse probably felt like a prison to them, just as the house would've felt to Matt if his time and thoughts hadn't been so taken up by Hope LeClaire.

It occurred to Matt then that no one had said anything about her. There'd been no teasing comments and no tongue-in-cheek innuendo, which wasn't at all like a bunch of cowhands, particularly cowhands with nothing to do but gripe about the weather.

He caught Chuck's eye and could tell then from the foreman's expression that there'd been no conversation between him and any of the men about the ranch's unexpected guest. Giving his head a slight nod at Chuck, he indicated appreciation of his reticence. Chuck nodded back, and that was the end of it.

The bunkhouse had a kitchen and a bunch of tables and chairs. Most of the men could cook a little—a pot of chili or beef stew, red beans and rice, fried steak and potatoes—plain fare but filling, and there was a big pan simmering on the stove today. Matt rinsed his cup at the sink and noted that the men might be edgy as a hive of bees, but they planned to eat well that evening.

That thought raised the question of what he would feed Hope for dinner. Alone, he would come out here and eat whatever the men had cooked in that big pot, but not today. Like it or not, he had a responsibility in his guest room that he could not ignore.

He was suddenly irritated and exasperated over fate playing such a dirty trick on him as to actually deliver a Stockwell almost to his front door, and to do it in a storm that isolated the ranch and everyone on it from the rest of the world. His hands were tied as far as Hope went. He couldn't even phone someone—the doctor, Hope's mother or any of the Stockwells—and get rid of her through one of those avenues.

He was as stuck as the ranch hands were, he thought disgustedly, only all they had to worry about was being cooped up with each other until the storm passed. *His* worries could be measured in miles, and that road seemed to be getting longer with each passing day. Wearing a disgruntled expression, he told the men he'd see them later and then braved the rain once again to trudge through the mud for the return trip to the house.

He didn't look in on Hope. Instead, after kicking off his muddy boots, he walked stocking-footed to the living room, plopped down into his favorite old recliner chair and pushed it back. The gray light in the room bothered him almost at once, and he reached out to turn on the lamp next to the chair. The switch clicked, but nothing happened.

Cursing a blue streak, Matt leapt to his feet and tried other lights. None came on, and for a moment Matt felt like tearing out his own hair. Now the ranch was without electricity, and just how long would that inconvenience go on?

"This miserable damn storm," he muttered as he went to a window and looked out at the bunkhouse. The lights that had been on only minutes ago were no longer burning.

Matt walked back to his chair and sank onto it. The loss of electricity seemed like a final straw. There would be no heat, no cooking, no lights.

Plus he had an amnesiac on his hands. How in hell was he going to deal with it all?

Chapter Three

The room had an inert, pewterlike quality that dulled distinctiveness and distorted perspective. Worse for Hope was its frightening unfamiliarity.

Her heartbeat was so hard and fast that she could hear it. She had just woken up, and not recognizing the bedroom she was in was so terrifying that she felt paralyzed. In the next instant she came fully awake and remembered the hours before she'd fallen asleep, and while the paralysis relaxed its grip on her system, the fear did not.

The house seemed eerily quiet. Where was Matthew McCarlson? Light, she decided as her pulse rate kept time with her pounding heart. Some light in the room might help calm her nerves. Reaching out to the lamp next to the bed, she located and then pushed the switch.

"Oh, no," she whispered when no light came on. Was the bulb burned out? Her hands clenched into fearful fists as she forced her bewildered and disoriented brain to concentrate on the problem. Maybe the lamp wasn't plugged in. Or maybe it was plugged into one of those outlets that required the use of a wall switch.

But she would have to get out of bed to find out. The room seemed to be getting darker by the minute, and she couldn't tell if there were wall switches anywhere.

She could hear rain; it was still coming down. And, obviously, night was falling. She'd slept away the day. She must have been exhausted, or maybe it had simply been easier to sleep than to stay awake and face her situation.

Her situation, she thought with a heavy sigh that was a combination of fearful desperation and incredulity. How could so many awful things happen to one person at the same time? She was in a strange place in a stranger's home and knew nothing about herself except for the little information she'd gotten from a purse—her purse, even if she didn't recognize it.

On top of her amnesia was the storm, which had isolated this ranch to the point of no possible means of communication with the rest of the world. It was all so...so bizarre...so Hollywoodish. More like a plot in a movie than a real-life experience.

Or was it? Hope frowned in the deepening darkness. Since she knew nothing about herself, perhaps this sort of adventure—or misadventure—was the norm for her. She sighed again over such a repugnant prospect, and then felt slightly better because the idea of living on the edge of a precipice *was* repugnant.

And then she gulped uneasily and wondered if amnesia altered victims' personalities so drastically that they became different people than they'd been. Maybe the way she saw things now wasn't even close to her normal point of view on anything and everything. Moaning in anguish over that horrifying possibility, Hope whispered, "God help me."

After lying in a heap of utter misery for a while, she realized that the more she pondered her plight, the worse she felt. It would be very easy to just let go and scream her throat raw, but would it change anything? Would the telephone suddenly start working—or the lights? That was the problem with her lamp, of course. The storm had wreaked havoc with the area's electricity.

Screaming would accomplish nothing. Neither would crying herself sick. What she needed to do was to get out of this bed.

Wouldn't a shower feel wonderful? Or a long soak in a hot-water bubble bath?

Hope slid off the bed and made her way to the door in the pale shards of daylight still available. But the hallway was much darker than the bedroom, and the house suddenly felt ominously silent. Her nerves began jangling.

Standing with her hand on the frame of the door as though it were some sort of safety line, she called, "Matt?" Almost immediately a light appeared at the end of the hall and began growing in intensity. In a moment she saw the dark silhouette of a man behind the glowing light of a lantern, both of which were coming toward her. "Matt?" she repeated, because she honestly couldn't tell if the silhouette was him or someone else.

"I'm here. You had quite a sleep."

Relieved that it was Matt and not another stranger to deal with, she answered. "Yes. Apparently the electricity is off now, as well as the phone."

"In a nutshell, yes."

"I was hoping for a shower or bath. Guess that's out of the question."

"Not necessarily. The hot water tank is full, and I'm sure the water in it is still hot. If the power stays off all

night it won't be hot by morning, so someone might as
well use it. Are you sure you're up to it, though?''

"I'm very sure." She wanted to wash her hair in the
worst way—naturally she would be careful about the cut
on her head—and soap every inch of her. She didn't even
want to think about Matthew McCarlson bathing the mud
from her nude body, so she certainly wasn't going to
question him about the method he'd used to undress and
cleanse an unconscious woman. Anyhow, whatever his
technique, it hadn't been all that adequate because she felt
more gritty than clean.

"If you're that certain, then fine. Take this lantern with
you. I have others. Leave the bathroom door unlocked, in
case you're not as strong as you think you are and need
some help. Don't let modesty prevent you from calling
for me if you get into trouble. When you're done, you'll
probably want some supper. I've already set up my propane camp stove on the back porch and can do a little
cooking on it. We'll decide later what sounds good.''

He was holding out the lantern, and Hope took it from
him. So, she thought, he would rush to her rescue again,
should she call out from the bathroom. Was he hoping for
another peek at her bare skin, or hadn't her nudity before
bothered him? Maybe he'd barely noticed. Maybe her
body wasn't worthy of notice. For some reason that idea
stung Hope's pride. She hadn't taken inventory of her
figure yet, but she would, she decided.

Ignoring his offer of help, she said, "After all you've
done for me, I shouldn't have the gall to ask for one more
thing. But these sweats I'm wearing are uncomfortably
large and I was wondering if you had some old ones that
you wouldn't mind my cutting inches off the legs and
arms.''

"As a matter of fact I do. I'll get them and bring them

and the scissors to the bathroom.'' He walked off, vanishing in the darkness right before Hope's eyes.

Her stomach turned over. She didn't like being alone in the dark in this strange house, even with a lantern in her hand. It threw light, but it also created shadows, and Hope wondered if she'd always been leery of the dark or if this was just another perturbing side effect to amnesia.

Making her way to the bathroom door, she went in and set the lantern on the sink counter. Leaning forward until her nose was only a few inches from the mirror, she peered at her face in the lantern's glow. She realized after a few moments that she had no base of information on which to judge her own looks. Was she pretty or plain? Her eyes were blue—quite a vivid blue, actually—but she'd noticed that Matt's eyes were brown, and perhaps brown eyes were considerably more desirable than blue eyes.

Her dark hair might be appealing when shiny clean and curled—or something. How did she ordinarily wear it?

Hope had left the door open, and Matt walked in without preamble. ''Here are several things you can cut up,'' he said while placing a stack of clothes on the other end of the counter from the lantern. ''Sorry I don't have anything smaller, but I haven't been your size since I was in the fifth grade.''

''You are…quite tall,'' Hope murmured.

''Six foot three.'' Matt walked to the door, but didn't leave immediately. ''Remember what I said about calling out if you need any help. In fact, if you'd leave the door ajar an inch or so, I'd feel a lot better about hearing you.''

''I…guess that would be all right.'' She could detect the hint of an amused grin on his lips in the lantern light and became defensive. ''Maybe I'm accustomed to bathing with the bathroom door open, but something inside me rebels at the idea so I can't help doubting it," she said sharply.

Realizing that no part of her predicament was funny to Hope, Matt erased all signs of amusement from his expression and said solemnly, "I doubt it, too. Take your bath and don't worry about me peeking through the crack of the door. In the first place, I wouldn't see anything I haven't already seen, and in the second, I'm not in the habit of preying on healthy women, let alone one who's in such sad shape." He walked out, and pulled the door shut, leaving about a three-inch opening.

Hope's jaw had dropped in painful surprise. Why, he'd practically come right out and said she was a pitiful specimen of womankind! No wonder he'd been able to undress and bathe her without emotion.

Oh, the shame of it, she thought, completely mortified over being so utterly undesirable. She hurried through a bath and a cautious shampoo, and never once really looked at her body. After all, why would she or any other woman want to inventory something so—so pathetic?

Later, Hope and Matt dined on grilled cheese sandwiches—prepared in an iron skillet on his propane camping stove—and small bowls of canned fruit. The lantern light softened Matt's features, Hope noticed, and wondered if it did the same with hers. Not that his features needed softening. In spite of the constant concern gnawing at her over her long list of personal grievances, she admired Matt McCarlson's masculine good looks. It seemed almost insane to be aware of a man's looks under the circumstances, but Hope really couldn't help herself.

Not that she expected or even fantasized anything coming of her admiration. She was, after all, so out of Matt's league in the looks department that even if she was a hundred percent healthy, with a perfect memory and some decent clothes that actually fit, he would be no more affected by her than he would be by a great-grandmother sharing his house and table.

Hope sighed quietly and spooned a bit of canned peach to her mouth. Something flashed through her mind, something about peaches that she couldn't hold on to or read clearly.

"You're very quiet," Matt said. "Are you feeling all right?"

"Yes, and I think I just had a glimmer of a memory."

"You did? What was it?"

"It was nothing earthshaking, so don't get excited. It had something to do with peaches."

Matt sat back. "With *peaches?* Why in hell would your first memory be about peaches? I doubt there arc very many peach trees in Massachusetts."

"Didn't I tell you not to get excited?" she said dryly. "Believe me, if I had any say in the order in which I might recall my past, my first memory would not have been about peaches. Besides, it wasn't even a full memory. I mean, I don't know if I was eating peaches, buying them or picking them off a tree." Hope paused for a short breath and added, "Maybe I was throwing them at someone, possibly an irritating man."

Matt's eyebrows went up. "So you think I'm irritating."

"Did I mention you?"

"Since I'm the only man you know at the present, you didn't have to identify who you'd like to throw peaches at."

"Don't be ridiculous," Hope muttered.

"You're angry. Not only that, you're angry with me. What happened? What'd I do?"

Hope fell silent, did some thinking and realized that he was right. She was hurt and so angry that she would love to throw something at him. Yes, he'd rescued her from the storm—and only the good Lord knew what else—but then he'd found her so unappealing, so unattractive, that she might as well have been a mangy stray dog instead of a woman.

But she could not explain herself on that score, and she resorted to a lie. "Sorry, but you're dead wrong. I'm not a bit angry with you. Why would I be? You probably saved my life, pathetic as it apparently is."

Matt frowned. "Why would you think you have a pathetic life?" Should he go and get that newspaper article for her to read? The information in it sure didn't read to him like Hope LeClaire led a pathetic life. An heiress to millions, possibly billions of dollars? And she was no slouch in the looks department, either. In truth, he'd never seen a more perfect body. Full, rounded breasts with gorgeous rosy nipples that looked as though they'd been created specifically for a man's mouth. Oh, no, Hope's assets weren't all in banks or safes, not by a long shot.

"Have you seen anyone out here looking for me?" she retorted. "Wouldn't you think your life was pretty pathetic, too, if no one gave a damn about where you were, or what horror might have befallen you?"

"No one can get out here. I told you that. It might be days after the rain stops before the roads are repaired enough to drive on."

"But if someone I cared about was missing, I wouldn't leave a stone unturned to find him or her, *and* I wouldn't let a storm or washed-out road stop me," she snapped.

Matt was beginning to hear a note of hysteria in Hope's voice, and the last thing he needed in the isolation everyone on the ranch must bear until things returned to normal was a hysterical amnesiac. No, he would *not* show her that article. In fact, he would do anything he could think of to get her thoughts away from her own admittedly wretched situation.

"You didn't eat much of your sandwich. Would you like something else?" he asked.

"You deliberately changed the subject," she said, suddenly weary of it herself. "It's okay, I'm bored with my problems, too. Scared spitless, let me add, but harping on the same old know-nothing theme is nothing but wasted energy. You know, I bet that you'd give anything you own not to have found me today."

You've got that right, baby! "Don't be silly," Matt said out loud in a soothing tone of voice. "Tell you what. You sit there while I clear these dishes away, then I'll walk you back to your bedroom."

"Fine," she said listlessly. Could he say or do anything that would take away her blues? Her self-pity? Lord above, what was she even doing in Texas? Was her mother, Madelyn, worried about her, or had Hope left Massachusetts for an extended trip, gotten in this mess somehow, and *no one* was worried about her?

Watching Matt move from table to sink, it struck Hope that he was all she had. Until she regained her memory—she *would* regain it, wouldn't she?—Matt McCarlson was the only person she knew face-to-face in the entire world.

And yet she had snapped at him, admitted anger at him—if only to herself—and pretty much blamed him for this mysterious fiasco. Well, it wasn't that she blamed him for everything, but one would think a rancher living miles and miles from civilization would be better prepared for a damn storm.

So *that's* it, she thought with narrowed eyes. She blamed him for living a lackadaisical lifestyle that didn't include emergency communication.

"How come you don't have some way to contact…uh, the town, for instance…in case of an emergency?" she asked.

Matt heard the distinct disapproval in her voice, the

judgment, and it raised his hackles. "I'm like a lot of ranchers," he said flatly. "I'm not particularly fond of people, especially city dwellers, and I'd rather wait out a storm by myself than have a horde of do-gooders descending on my land under the guise of neighborly generosity to rescue me, when I never needed rescuing in the first place."

"And I suppose the men who work for you feel the same?"

"My men are seasoned ranch hands. They know the table stakes and when they're dealt a bad hand, they take their lumps without complaint."

"As you do."

"Have you heard me complaining? Let me say it like it is, Hope LeClaire. You're the only person on this ranch who's done any complaining about being landlocked, so to speak. Now, I have to concede your right to a few complaints, but—"

Hope broke in. "How big of you," she said with drawling sarcasm. "I wonder what you'd do if you woke up in a strange place with no memory." She got to her feet. "I'm going back to bed, and I don't need your help in getting there, so please just let me leave without offering the support of your big, manly arm."

"Hey, my arm *is* big and manly, and your sarcasm doesn't make it any less than it is. Take the lantern so you don't fall flat on your ungrateful face!"

"Ungrateful? *Ungrateful?* How would you like me to express my gratitude, by kissing your feet? I've said thank you repeatedly, which you've either obviously forgotten or were too dense to register at the time."

"I'm not dense, lady," Matt growled. "And since you are, I would think that *dense* is a word you'd try real hard to avoid."

"You jerk!" she shouted, then turned herself around,

plucked the lantern from the table and did her best imitation of royalty sweeping from a room filled with ignorant peasants.

"Yeah, I'm a jerk," Matt mumbled while lighting another lantern for his use. "And you're just as spoiled and overbearing as every other pampered princess I've known."

Matt went to bed about an hour later. Lying in the dark he listened to the rain, which had slowed to a barely discernible drizzle. The storm was passing, but at this stage it was hard to forecast its final gasp. It could drizzle and mist like this for days, it could start pouring again at any time, or it could stop completely without a dram of warning.

And when it did stop, the work would begin. Cleaning up after a storm like this one was an enormous job. Washed-out roads, flooded creeks and mud everywhere. Yeah, every rancher in the storm belt and even some townsfolk were in for a lot of backbreaking labor.

Matt was visualizing the ravages to his land and worrying about the cost of restoring everything to its prestorm condition when a bloodcurdling scream made his hair stand on end.

Jumping out of bed, he ran down the hall to Hope's room. His first thought had been that someone had gotten into the house and was trying to throttle her. But since she'd left the lantern burning on low, he could tell at once that she was only having a dream.

She was thrashing around in bed, not screaming anymore but making almost inhuman sounds that all but curdled Matt's blood. No one deserves a nightmare that terrifying, Matt thought and hurried over to the bed where he lay down next to her.

"Hope...Hope..." he said as he pulled her into his

arms, held her tightly against himself and stopped her from throwing herself around. "It's only a dream, Hope, just a dream. I've got you now. You're safe."

She opened her teary eyes and heard Matt's quiet voice. His arms were around her, and her face was nestled against his bare chest. She felt warm and comforted and, as he'd just told her, safe, and she did nothing to alter their positions.

"I had a nightmare," she whispered tremulously. "An awful nightmare."

"I know. I was in my room and you screamed so loudly that I thought a monster was gnawing on your big toe."

She smiled weakly. "You're trying to make me feel better."

"Did it work?"

"Something's working."

Something was "working" for him, too, but it wasn't a corny joke. It was Hope and the fact that she was plastered against him and his body could feel every delicious curve of hers. He shut his eyes and groaned inwardly. It was only natural for a man to become aroused while holding a beautiful woman, but this particular woman was not one he should be fooling around with. He'd sworn an oath to never again get involved with a woman who had more money than he did, which, at the present time, pretty much eliminated the entire female population of Texas. Thus, it was a rare day—or night—when he so much as paid for a lady's hamburger or movie ticket. In truth, he hadn't done any real dating since Trisha's death, and he'd never felt as though life was passing him by because of it, either.

However, things were starting to look a little different to him. Lying in bed with a luscious lady wrapped around him sort of took the guts out of that well-intentioned oath, which, he realized, should probably make him resent the hell out of Hope. He had enough worries and problems with the ranch without piling on the heartache of an intimate relationship that couldn't possibly go anywhere. Still, regardless of commonsense arguments against any such liaison, he was about to toss that earthshaking oath over the edge of the bed when she said, "The man in my dream had tied me up and he was...he was—"

"He was what?" Matt prompted when she left him hanging and he already had some bad feelings about what that dream had really been about.

"How strange," Hope murmured uneasily. "I don't know if he was trying to seduce me or I was trying to seduce him. Wouldn't you think I'd know the difference?"

"Uh, seduction comes in many disguises." Even the word *seduction* increased the aching desire Matt was suffering. He had to get out of this bed and back in his own. If he didn't he was going to do something he'd be sorry for when he regained his senses. "Are you okay now? Is it all right if I leave?"

Sudden panic nearly choked Hope, and she lifted her arms and locked her hands behind his head. "Please don't leave me alone...please!"

Matt knew that she was not offering him anything to stay with her; she was only clinging to him because she was panicky and scared out of her wits.

Gritting his teeth, he tore his thoughts away from sex. "I'll stay," he said, "but I need a little more room."

"Oh, I'm sorry. I'll move over." Hope released her death grip on him and moved over about two inches. "Is that better?"

"That's...fine." Her head was still on his arm and her hand on his chest. He slid his other arm away from her waist and laid it down his side on his own torso. "Let's try to get some sleep now."

"Yes, of course." But after a moment she said, "I think that dream was symbolic of something that really happened."

"Symbolic?" He was trying to get sleepy by pretending he was in his own bed and not lying close enough to Hope to feel the warmth emanating from her body. A state of pretense would be much easier to achieve if she would stop talking.

"I'd hate to think it wasn't just symbolic. I mean, what if some horrible man really did tie me up?" Hope's hands were free now, and she absentmindedly rubbed her wrists. "Matt, my wrists have rope burns! I was tied up!"

He'd seen the marks on her wrists, and wondered about them, but he couldn't add to her horror by telling her about his own misgivings concerning those bruises.

"You shouldn't let your imagination run wild," he said flatly, keeping even compassion out of his voice and telling himself that it was for her own good. Until she recalled everything about herself *for* herself, speculation on her part and suggestions from him or anyone else who might eventually get wind of this drama would only make her more fearful, and she was scared enough already.

"These sore spots around my wrists are not imagined, Matt. And the man in the dream wasn't conjured up by a troubled mind, either. He's a real-life, flesh-and-blood person who wants to do me harm." Hope paused to ponder her own conclusion. "But why?" she murmured, speaking more to her confused inner self than to Matt.

Her determined logic startled Matt. After all, she hadn't gotten so far off the beaten path all by herself. Someone must have brought her here, or, at least, brought her to a spot within walking distance. *And then what'd that someone do, throw her out of his car? Or had she made a run for freedom and her first opportunity for escaping some warped bastard had happened on McCarlson land?*

Maybe the guy didn't know the area well and hadn't realized he was on private property.

But the theme of that newspaper article was that Hope was missing. Maybe she'd gone off with a boyfriend and he hadn't been the nice guy she'd thought he was. This whole muddle of facts and guesswork could be nothing more than a romantic tryst getting out of hand. And if Hope hadn't lost her memory for some damned reason then there wouldn't be anything at all mysterious about her delivery to this part of Texas.

"Can you remember what the guy in your dream looked like?" Matt asked, because now he was thinking that if there was a man involved with the fright she'd received last night, she just might know him.

A shudder passed through Hope's body. "No, but I know he was a horrible person."

"How can you be so sure about that, Hope? I'm not trying to be cruel, but without memories to back up your assumptions, can you be certain of anything?"

She hesitated a few moments, then she raised herself to her elbow, looked down at him and said, "I guess I'm relying on basic instinct, which we all have, don't we, memory or no memory?"

Her eyes, even in the soft glow of lantern light, were as blue as Texas bluebonnets. She wasn't just pretty, she was sexy. At least she was making him *think* of sex again. She had on an old shirt of his, and coincidentally it was almost as blue as her eyes. She was as enticing in that worn-out old shirt, with her head of thick, lustrous dark hair in appealing disarray, as any woman he'd ever seen.

"Instinct is…uh, usually a good barometer to, uh, to go by," he stammered, making a stab at reassurance when his mind was stuck on the ache in his groin. He almost told her about it. He came very close to saying, "Hope, if I stay in this bed for the rest of the night, I'm not going to be able to keep my hands off you. Can you deal with that? Are you having similar ideas about me?''

Hope couldn't read his mind, but there was something in his eyes that made her heart beat faster. *You're letting your imagination run wild! If the man thought of you as attractive, you'd have sensed it before now. Good Lord, go to sleep before you make a complete fool of yourself!*

She lay down again and turned her back to him. ''I'm suddenly very tired. Good night,'' she said.

Matt heaved a quiet sigh of relief. Things would be better in the morning, he told himself, praying it would be true. Once the phones were working again, he could let the Stockwells know that Hope was safe. She wasn't so sound, true, but with the Stockwells' money they could hire the best specialists the medical profession had to offer to cure her amnesia.

As for him, he'd get over the yen he had for her, that itch he didn't dare scratch. What choice did he have but to get over it?

Hope's eyes simply would not shut. She hadn't deliberately lured Matt into her bed, but that's where he was, and every cell in her body was aware of it. He was, after all, wearing nothing but undershorts, and the sensation of being held in his arms, pressed tightly to so much masculine bare skin, would not leave her. Her skin seemed to tingle every time she thought of it, and, much to her dismay, she kept thinking of it until she could just barely manage to breathe without Matt hearing her. She would be humiliated beyond words if he should catch on that she was lying there pining for…for…

Hope frowned. What, exactly, was she pining for? Some kisses? Being held by strong, manly arms again? For some reason, even with that erotic ache in the pit of her stomach, she couldn't envision herself under a man and making love. Why not, for heaven's sake? She had no trouble recalling ordinary things, such as eating, bathing and dressing. And even kissing.

So how come she couldn't recall the act of lovemaking? Her lips pursed almost angrily. *Say it like it is, dodo, how come you can't recall sex? It's not because you're a cold fish, by any means, not when you're lying here sweating and yearning for Matt McCarlson to touch you!*

Chapter Four

The Stockwells, Hope's Texas family, and her Massachusetts family tried not to think the worst, but as time
passed with no word of Hope's whereabouts, the "worst"
gradually became everyone's greatest fear. Kate, in particular, could not stay off the phone with her mother, Madelyn. In the first place, just having a mother to talk to
about anything was a miracle for Kate. She'd grown up,
after all, believing the story that her mother ran off with
her brother-in-law and they'd drowned on Stockwell property. Then, when her father, Caine, had lain dying just a
short time ago, he'd told his four children the shocking
truth—that he didn't know their mother's current place of
residence, but he'd been certain she was still alive.

Kate and her three brothers, Jack, Rafe and Cord, had
been deeply shaken by their father's confession. They had
decided to find their mother, and they'd been successful
only recently, which had resulted in a trip to Massachu-

setts for a reunion. That was when Kate and her brothers had met their baby sister, Hope. Caine's will was scheduled to be read when they got back to Texas, and they had convinced Hope to attend the event. There was proof that she had left Massachusetts for Texas, but then the seemingly impossible had happened: Hope had vanished without a trace.

And so Kate and Madelyn ran up huge long-distance bills by talking to each other at least twice a day, even though most of their conversations covered the same ground.

"Mother, she used her plane ticket to Grandview, so she has to be somewhere in Texas."

"Unless someone else used her ticket," Madelyn replied.

It was that possibility that gnawed at reason for Kate and Madelyn. Hope's long trip from Massachusetts had included several stops and plane changes. How could they conclude unequivocally that whatever had befallen Hope had taken place in Texas?

Kate had some worries that she hadn't yet expressed to anyone, but she knew that she couldn't keep such basic concerns to herself for long. Was Hope, the sister Kate had only recently met and just barely knew, the kind of woman to disappear for a week or so, perhaps with a man, and not give a whit what anyone might think about it?

"Mother, would Hope decide to...to, uh, take a little side trip without...without informing anyone?" Kate posed the question as tactfully as she could, but embarrassment over broaching their mother with a query that cast Hope in a bad light caused Kate to stammer.

"Hope has always been a very considerate person. I could never believe that she would do anything to hurt or worry her family," Madelyn said quietly.

The cold wind of reality that had been almost constantly buffeting Kate since Hope's disappearance washed over her again. Her throat suddenly filled with tears and prevented an immediate answer.

"No," Madelyn continued, "wherever Hope is, she's not there by choice. Not her choice, at any rate."

"Then, someone else's choice?" Kate said hoarsely.

"It's the only thing that makes any sense, Kate. Hope has been kidnapped."

Kate gasped. "Oh, Mother, if that really is the case, why hasn't anyone been contacted for ransom?"

"Kate, the only reason I'm staying in my own home in Massachusetts instead of hightailing it to Texas is that Hope's kidnappers could try to contact me. Brandon and I are financially well off, but our wealth is peanuts compared to the Stockwells' fortune. I've thought so much about it, Kate, and there are so many possibilities, and perhaps Hope's kidnappers are from these parts and don't know about the Stockwells. My name and photo are often in the art section of the new England and New York City newspapers, and an idiot inclined to get something for nothing could easily think that Brandon and I are fair game.

"Anyhow, that's the reason I'm sticking close to my telephone. But in case I'm miles off the mark, you and your brothers should be alert to any possibility. The culprit could very well be from my side of the country, but he or she could also be from Texas. Be particularly cautious with the children."

Kate froze. "You think the kidnapper might strike again?"

"I don't know what to think, Kate. Just be careful. All of you."

"You, too, Mom," Kate whispered. She needed to talk to her brother Rafe, who was a U.S. Marshal, and get his professional input on Hope's disappearance. The whole family was concerned, Kate already knew that, but maybe their concern was more confused than focused.

Yes, she definitely had to talk to Rafe. He would know what they should all be doing.

Hope awoke to the steady patter of rain on the roof. It seemed to her to be a softer, gentler rainfall than before, but even without its former fury, Hope felt weighted down by the determination of this storm to never end.

Her thoughts abruptly moved from the storm to last night, and she recalled that terrible nightmare and then how she'd snuggled against Matt and begged him to not leave her alone.

"Oh, no," she groaned as her mind dredged up some very personal details of his comforting embrace and her clinging method of expressing gratitude for his understanding. "What must he think of me?" They hadn't kissed, nor had there been intimate caresses between them, and yet, lying together, with bodies tightly interwoven and arms around each other, hadn't there been quite a lot of unnecessary movement that could only be described as a type of sexual foreplay?

Matt had known it, too, because he'd asked her for more room. In other words, Hope thought miserably, he'd known where that much togetherness could lead and didn't *want* it to go there. *You should have known yourself what was really going on, you dolt! That wasn't a cucumber you felt—and enjoyed feeling—in his shorts!*

And you hardly know the man. How could you behave so…so imprudently? You could already be involved with someone you can't remember, someone who this very minute could be walking the floor and worrying himself sick over your disappearance.

Hope stared at the ceiling and wondered what time Matt had gotten up and left her bed. She heaved a sigh. Maybe she'd behaved badly last night, but at least she hadn't felt so alone and lost while Matt was holding her. And if there was a man somewhere—more than likely in Massachusetts—who loved her enough to worry about why she was out of touch, he would understand and even thank Matt for taking care of his beloved.

That perfectly logical conclusion made Hope's mouth get dry. He *would* understand, wouldn't he? Matt had probably saved her life! And her memory loss certainly wasn't anyone's fault, especially Matt's.

Moaning in misery, Hope turned her face to the pillow and wept. Why couldn't she remember anything? What if there was a man somewhere that she loved with all her heart? Would her body respond to another man if she *was* in love with someone else? Why was she thinking even now how incredible it had felt to lie in Matt's arms last night?

"You have got to stop this," she said out loud, angry with herself for dwelling on things better ignored. She got out of bed and realized that she felt much stronger. Except for her amnesia and just the barest amounts of stiffness in her muscles and joints, she was in good condition.

"Great!" she exclaimed, meaning it wholeheartedly. First she went looking for her underwear and shoes that Matt had told her were in the laundry room. Then, in the bathroom, she received a very pleasant surprise: the electricity was back on. She had pushed the light switch without thinking and the flood of electric lighting in the small room seemed to be a miracle that no one should ever take for granted.

After a shower, she got dressed in the jeans Matt had given her and she'd cut off to fit the length of her legs, along with a blue T-shirt that was much smaller than she'd expected. *Probably shrank in the wash,* she decided. From the small cache of cosmetics in her purse, she heightened the color of her cheeks with blusher and applied a light coating of lipstick. Her hair, she realized, was straight when wet and slightly wavy when dry. Except for some wispy bangs, she brushed it back and tucked it behind her ears. She was still cautious around the cut on the back of her head, but it really didn't seem to be a problem.

Hope then searched drawers and cupboards until she found a piece of heavy twine that she wound through the belt loops on the jeans. Satisfied that the makeshift belt would keep the jeans in place, she went to the kitchen for something to eat.

The small amount of food in the cupboards and refrigerator surprised her, but after thinking about it she reasoned that the men working on this ranch must eat elsewhere and Matt probably took his meals with them.

Accepting that explanation and almost immediately letting it slip from her mind—it was hardly significant to her, after all—she took eggs, butter and cheese from the refrigerator. After looking for and locating a few other ingredients in the cupboards, she set to work making her breakfast.

She was eating when Matt came into the house. He shed his slicker and hat in the coatroom off the kitchen, then walked in. Seeing her sitting at the table and lighting up the room with her natural glow of feminine beauty, he stopped in his tracks and stared, wondering if he'd ever seen a prettier woman. And look what she was wearing. Obviously she was one of those rare people who didn't need glamorous clothes to be outstandingly beautiful. Anyone would notice Hope just as she was.

He stared so long without saying something that Hope became uncomfortable. Obviously there was some ice that needed breaking here, and her interior become hot with embarrassment.

She cleared her throat. "Good morning."

Matt came back to earth. "Good morning. I see you're aware of the electricity having come back on."

"Aware and glad," Hope answered.

Matt's stare became a deliberate, rather doubtful scrutiny. "Are you sure you're feeling well enough to be up and around like this?"

"I feel fine." She quickly added, "Physically. Nothing's changed in the memory department."

"Oh, too bad. I mean, I'm glad you're feeling good physically, but it's too bad your memory…" He ran his fingers through his hair. "Oh, hell, you know what I mean. What're you eating there?"

"An omelette."

"You made it? How come it looks so…puffy?"

"It's fluffy, not puffy. It's a fluffy omelette. It's made differently than a regular omelette. Would you like some of it? I've only eaten a little of this one end and you could have some from the other side."

He grinned, and he looked so handsome that Hope felt a rush of heat race through her system. *Good grief, get hold of yourself! He only grinned, for Pete's sake! What would you do if he really turned on the charm, become a gibbering idiot?*

"I doubt if I'd get ptomaine if I ate off the same side of the omelette that you did," he said with a slightly teasing tone to his voice. "And yes, I'd like to try it." Matt got a small plate and a fork and brought them to the table. "Just give me a small piece. I had breakfast a couple of hours ago, but I'm positive I've never eaten that kind of omelette before and it looks especially good."

Hope cut a portion off her omelette and put it on Matt's plate. He took a bite and declared it to be the best omelette he'd ever put in his mouth. "Where'd you learn to cook like this?"

Every cell in Hope's body froze. "I—I don't know."

"Let me get something straight. You made this omelette without remembering how it should be done?'

"I...just did it.''

"Without thinking about it.''

Hope nodded and felt as though she'd functioned in the twilight zone since entering the kitchen. How on earth could a person without a memory cook anything, let alone a fluffy omelette that she knew in her soul had turned out perfectly?

Matt frowned slightly. He finished his portion of the omelette in two bites, then said casually, "The cupboards in here are pretty bare. I wonder what you'd be able to cook up with more ingredients."

"I honestly don't know.''

"Do you want to find out?''

"And how would I do that?''

"I'd bring some groceries over from the bunkhouse. It has a kitchen and ever since the cook quit a while back the men have been fixing their own meals. They have a good supply of food on hand over there, and if I brought some of it to the house, you just might enjoy, uh, cooking up some dishes that—''

Hope broke in with a flatly stated, "You need a cook.''

"Not necessarily. No, don't get me wrong. It's best to have one person doing the cooking, of course, but we've been getting along pretty darned good without one. But I see your cooking this omelette as a crack in the amnesia blocking your memory.''

"Really,'' Hope said dryly.

"Yes, really, and don't sound so suspicious. Do you think I would butter you up just to get a little free cooking while you're here?''

"What gave you the idea I'd cook for a bunch of men for free? Assuming I could actually do it, of course.''

Matt sat back and looked at her. ''There's a pretty common phrase, which you probably don't recall, but it goes like this. I scratch your back and you scratch mine.''

"Oh, I get it. You've already scratched my back by saving me from the storm, and now it's my turn.''

"I wouldn't dream of expecting payment on any scale for taking you into my home and saving you from God knew what fate.''

How can you say something like that and still look as innocent as a newborn babe? "But you would gladly accept a tradeoff,'' she said with exaggerated sweetness.

"I'm a Horse trader from way back.'' He flashed another grin, before adding, ''Besides, neither of us knows if you're a real cook or not. Maybe fluffy omelettes are it.''

"Maybe they are,'' Hope agreed and picked up her fork to finish hers. It was incredibly delicious, and she had to wonder just how much she did know about cooking. Wouldn't experimenting in Matt McCarlson's kitchen be a better way to pass the time than lying in his bedroom? Goodness, much more of that bedroom and she'd be climbing its walls!

"Okay, fine,'' she said with a lifting of her chin. "Bring over the groceries. I don't know what you have at the bunkhouse, but I'll give it a try.''

"Good. I'll go and get a load right now.'' Matt got up, and just before leaving the table, sent her a smile that nearly melted her internal organs.

After he was gone, she put her head back and groaned out loud. Had a man's smile always turned her to mush, or was this a special case?

She rose from her chair so abruptly that it fell backward to the floor. Muttering to herself, she quickly righted the chair and then cleared the table. If only she could phone Madelyn, her mother, according to the wallet card. Or even that doctor Matt had mentioned.

Were things ever going to return to normal?

And for her, Hope LeClaire, what in heaven's name was normal?

"Rafe, Mother thinks Hope's been kidnapped, and so do I. You're a U.S. Marshal. Has that possibility occurred to you?"

"Yes, it has, but there's not a dram of evidence to support that theory. Kate, the police have interviewed the Grandview airport's personnel. No one remembers seeing her. Airline records indicate that her tickets from Boston to Grandview, Texas, were used exactly as specified. That's the sum total of information law enforcement has been able to gather on her. It's not much to go on."

"And no one's contacted any member of the family for ransom," Kate said with a ponderous sigh. "That's more frightening than if there'd been a dozen calls demanding a fortune in ransom."

"I know," Rafe said quietly. "I've even wondered if she left the Grandview airport to stretch her legs and get a breath of air before the chauffeur could pick her up for the drive to the Stockwell compound, even though it had already started raining when her plane landed. But suppose she likes to walk in the rain, and suppose she wandered far enough away from the airport that day and got lost."

Rafe stopped talking to shake his head. Then he said, "Kate, the police are looking for her and her picture's been published in the area's newspapers and on television. The best advice I have for you and the rest of the family is to try not to think the worst."

Kate got to her feet. "I know you're right, but I can't stop worrying."

Rafe walked her from his office to the front door of the

federal building that housed the U.S. Marshal's head-
quarters in Dallas.

"Still raining," he said after a look outside. "There's
already some flooding in outlying areas, and it's going to
get worse if this storm doesn't let up." He planted a quick
kiss on his sister's cheek. "Chin up, Kate. And drive carefully. The roads are slick."

"Talk to you later, Rafe. Bye."

Matt quietly slipped into the bunkhouse via the back
door and began loading a large box with food from the
pantry. Sooner or later the men would catch sight of
Hope—especially now that she was up and around—but
for some deep-down unexplainable reason Matt would
rather they not find out about her just yet. For one thing,
those cowboys would assume all sorts of things going on
in the house that were not going on.

Not that Matt hadn't visualized those very scenarios
himself last night while holding Hope in his arms, but
he'd be a damned fool to deliberately get involved with
a Stockwell. There'd been times in his past when the title
of Damned Fool had fit him like a crown, and he didn't
intend to wear that particular hat again, certainly not now
in his more mature years. He was, after all, thirty-seven
years old, not some wet-behind-the-ears kid, and if he
decided on a hands-off rule with a woman, then that's
how the old ball would bounce.

And the minute that telephone service was resumed,
he'd call Doc Pickett and unload the burden of caring for
an amnesiac without the slightest idea of what kind of
treatment was best for her on the good doctor. Matt figured that since the electricity was working again, phone
service couldn't be too far off. Yes, things would be getting back to normal in the not too distant future, and Matt
felt it couldn't happen soon enough for him. Of course, it

would take some time to repair the roads, but once the rain stopped and things started drying out, a four-wheel-drive vehicle would be able to get to town by cutting cross-country. It would be an immense relief to drive Hope LeClaire to Hawthorne and deposit her on Doc Pickett's doorstep.

Matt stopped to frown over that image. It would be a relief, wouldn't it? Hey, he wasn't getting silly over a woman that could only mangle his nerves *and* his heart, was he?

"No way," he muttered grimly, and continued filling the box again.

"What has you talking to yourself, the storm or your house guest?" Chuck Crawford asked as he walked into the room

"Both."

Chuck eyed the box of groceries. "What're you doing?"

"Taking food to the house. Hope did some cooking this morning with practically no ingredients, and so I'm providing her with the wherewithal to keep busy, which every person on this ranch would be better off having. Chuck, after I deliver this box to the house, how about you and me saddling our horses and taking a ride to check the water damage to the fields?"

"I already did that, Matt. Just got back, in fact, which is the reason I came looking for you. Lawana Creek is flooding worse than I've ever seen. Probably worse than you've seen, too, but we've got two fenced fields out there, each with about forty head of cattle, and they've got no place to go to avoid the rising water. We have to move 'em, Matt."

Matt nodded in agreement. "I'm going to get some things from the refrigerator and freezer for this box, then

I'm gone. You tell the men to get off their butts and into their rain gear. We'll all meet at the barn in ten minutes.''

"Right."

Chuck left and Matt raced to the huge refrigerator and then the freezer for the final items for the box. Loaded down, he hurried outside into the seemingly never-ending rain and to the house. Walking in, he set the box on the kitchen table.

"Would you mind putting this stuff away?" he asked Hope.

She gaped in surprise at the amount of food he'd brought. What did he think she was, a trained and experienced chef? How dare he presume *anything* about her? She was about to ask him that very question when he said, "The men and I are all going to be gone until late afternoon. We've got to move some cattle from a couple of flooded fields to higher ground."

Learning that some of his animals were in danger of drowning sort of took the wind out of her sails. At least, her indignation over his presuming she knew how to cook huge amounts of food for a bunch of hungry men noticeably deflated.

"Oh," she said weakly. "All right, fine. I'll put away this food. Don't worry about it."

Matt closely watched her as he worked a pair of leather gloves onto his hands. "Are you going to be all right by yourself for several hours?"

"Yes."

"Are you as certain of that as you sound?"

"Would you rather that I fell to the floor and hung on to your leg so you couldn't leave me all alone?"

Matt scowled. "Sarcasm doesn't become you."

That biased observation irritated her. "No? Well, maybe I dote on sarcasm. Maybe I live for opportunities to put other people in their places with barbs of needle-sharp sarcasm.''

''And maybe not,'' Matt snapped. ''See you later.''

''Yeah, later,'' she mumbled under her breath when he'd gone. After a few minutes of angry pacing, she set to work emptying the box of food.

Matt and Chuck rode together. The other men weren't far away, but they rode in twos or threes and talked amongst themselves. Complained more than talked, actually. None of them liked the weather. They were dryland Texas cowhands, and Seattlelike skies and rainfalls made them grouchy. Still, everyone agreed that they couldn't leave herds of cattle trapped in fenced fields with ''ol' Lawona Creek'' on a rampage.

''Ms. LeClaire must be feeling better if she was doing some cooking this morning,'' Chuck said, speaking quietly so the others wouldn't hear him. ''And she must be remembering—''

Matt broke in. ''No, she's not remembering anything, or so she says. But does it make any sense to you that a person who claims to remember nothing about her past would know how to cook?''

''Do you think she's putting on an act? Why would she do that?''

''Damned if I know,'' Matt muttered. A moment later he exhaled a sigh. ''I don't really think she's acting, Chuck, but she's rubbing my nerves raw. Not all the time, but memory or no memory she can sure hold her own in an argument.''

''Why in hell would the two of you be doing any arguing?''

''Good question, Chuck. *Damned* good question. Like I said, she rubs me wrong at times, and it seems that I do the same to her.'' After a few moments of silence, Matt said, "Chuck, there's something you don't know about Hope," he said, almost under his breath to keep this conversation private.

"What's that?" Chuck sent his boss a curious glance.

"It was in the newspaper you brought in with the mail and her purse. She's a missing person."

"Missing?"

"Apparently she was traveling from Massachusetts to Texas and just disappeared. Chuck, she's a Stockwell. The newspaper article states her name clearly, Hope LeClaire, and she's one of Caine Stockwell's daughters."

Chuck whistled softly. "A Stockwell? Hell's bells, Matt, she's probably richer than old King Tut. Uh-oh, that's the problem, isn't it? You're feeling that she's too much like— Uh...sorry, Matt, I know you don't like talking about, well things."

"You're right. I don't like talking about things, and we both know that in this case the word *things* is a substitute for two other words, *my marriage*." Matt looked broodingly off into the distance. Chuck very seldom brought up the past and Matt was usually even more closemouthed on the subject of his marriage.

But Hope was the first woman to stay in Matt's house since his marriage ended, and even for Chuck, a man who minded his own business and blatantly, sometimes rudely, suggested that other people do the same, the whole thing was just too weird to ignore completely. Especially the fact that Hope was a Stockwell and undoubtedly loaded with dough. Money had destroyed Matt's first marriage. Was it going to cause him further misery, even though all he'd done was to carry an injured woman into his house with the very best of intentions?

"Well, I don't normally ask questions, Matt, but I'm pretty darned curious about how Hope took hearing who she really is when she can't remember it for herself."

"I didn't tell her."

"You didn't. Any particular reason why you didn't?"

"I don't have the slightest idea how best to deal with a person with amnesia. Should she be told every little thing that other people know about her, or is it best for her to uncover her past for herself? If the damned phone ever starts working again, the first call I'm going to make is to Doc Pickett. Even if he can't get out here right away, I'm sure he'll be able to give me a few pointers."

"In that case, if I run into her I should keep my mouth shut?"

"For the time being, yes. It's inevitable that the men will eventually catch on to her presence, but just let them think what they want and act like you don't know any more about Hope than they do."

"Well, I'm not positive that keeping information from her is the best course of action, but we'll do it your way, Matt."

"I'm not positive, either," Matt said flatly. "But yes, we'll do it my way. For now," he added. And then after a few seconds he said, "There's the first field up ahead. Let's get to work."

Hope had just finished putting everything away—except the fresh vegetables, which were in the sink to be washed—when the lights went out again. She gaped at the ceiling fixture in dismay, then realized how dismal the kitchen was without lights. It was the gray sky and rain outside causing the gloom inside, of course, and other than lighting a few lanterns, there was nothing she could do about it.

She went to the laundry room, which was where she'd seen the lanterns on a counter, then stared at them with a sinking sensation because she didn't have the slightest idea how to light them.

"With a match, obviously," she intoned dryly, examining one of the lanterns more closely. So, she thought, how did the darned thing come apart so it could be lighted? She hadn't seen Matt actually light the lanterns, and she felt absolutely stupid because they looked so complicated and probably were simple enough for a child to use.

After ten minutes of self-disgust over her helplessness, she strode back to the kitchen and began washing the vegetables in the pale, dim light. Working fast, she made quick work of her chore and soon had the cleaned vegetables in the refrigerator.

Then she went to the living room and sat in a chair next to a window so she could look out. It wasn't long when she realized the house was getting chilly.

"Obviously the furnace can't work without electricity, you dolt," she mumbled to herself.

Cussing a blue streak because the last couple of days had gone to hell in a handbasket, she got up, went to her bedroom, grabbed the comforter off the bed and then returned to her chair in the living room. Wrapping the comforter around herself, she sat and brooded and cried a little and positively wallowed in self-pity.

It felt good to just let go.

Chapter Five

The men conversed very little during the ride back to the compound. The rain was more mist than droplets, but days of bad weather were getting them down. Again Chuck and Matt rode side by side, and occasionally one of them would remark about something. But they, too, were mostly silent. Physically weary and emotionally sapped, the group rode huddled in their ponchos, with the brims of their hats low on their foreheads and their heads down in attempts to keep rain off their faces. They were tired of mud, flooding creeks, the added bulk to their ordinary clothing of rain gear, and standing water that was dangerously deep in spots and not to be taken lightly.

Their work today had been successful; all the cattle on the ranch were munching wet grass on high ground. Ordinarily, moving small herds was a simple job, but the horses and cattle had slipped and slid so much in the mud that work that should have taken only a few hours had kept Matt and his crew out until late in the day. In fact, night began falling before they reached the ranch compound.

They were still about a mile away, when Matt narrowed his eyes and squinted in an effort to see the ranch more clearly through the dreary, drizzly twilight. There weren't any yard lights on, he realized after a few moments, which meant the electricity was out again.

He muttered a frustrated curse, then said to Chuck, "The damned power is off again."

Chuck looked ahead then nodded his agreement. "Looks like it. Phone's probably not working yet, either."

"It's days like these that I wonder why I followed in my father's footsteps and kept his ranch from being sold after his death," Matt said grimly.

"Yeah," Chuck said, putting total understanding in that one drawled word.

"I wonder how long Hope has been without electricity," Matt said.

"Do you think it would scare her?"

"I think anything scares her, Chuck. Her grasp on reality is pretty thin. Have you ever known an amnesiac?"

"Once, way back, there was a guy who'd lost his memory in a car accident. He'd gotten broken up pretty bad, and after he came home from the hospital I remember us kids going past his house and seeing him sitting on the porch just staring at nothing."

Matt felt a deep chill shoot through his system. "Did he get over it?"

Chuck shrugged. "Truthfully, Matt, I don't remember. Is Hope your first experience with amnesia?"

"Yes, and it scares the living daylights out of me. I don't know if I should hand her that newspaper article, let her read it and then tell her what I know about the Stockwells, or if I should just keep my mouth shut about the little I know of her background until a doctor sees her. Is my ignorance making matters worse for her, or is silence the best therapy until she gets medical attention?''

Chuck drew a long breath. ''That's a quandary, all right.''

The two men fell silent, listened to the squishy clip-clopping of their horses' hooves on the soggy earth and watched the ranch buildings gradually getting closer.

Finally Matt said quietly, tensely, ''The family has put up a $50,000 reward for information about her.''

''It said that in that article?''

''Yeah, it did.''

''That's a fine sum of money. You could sure use a nice sum like that right about now, Matt. Fifty thousand would pay a lot of bills.''

''Sure would,'' Matt agreed, ''but how does a man take money just for helping a fellow human being? I don't think I could, Chuck.''

Chuck pondered awhile, then said, ''Right now you probably couldn't, Matt. But if it's offered when Hope's back with her family and getting better, I think you should consider it. I probably shouldn't stick my nose into your business like this but you haven't tried too hard to keep your financial problems a secret.''

''Hard to keep that kind of thing a secret when I can't pay the men a steady wage and I have to keep selling off hay and cattle just to cover the utility bills.'' After a minute he added grimly, ''I'm three months behind on the mortgage payments, Chuck. Maybe you should start looking for another job.''

''Not yet,'' Chuck said calmly. ''Never can tell what might happen tomorrow or next week, and I like this job just fine.''

''Well, I'd hate to lose you, that's certain.''

Finally they reached the compound, and they dismounted and unsaddled their horses. "I'll take care of Dex," Chuck offered. "You'd better go to the house." He didn't say "to check on Hope," because none of the other men knew about her yet. Chuck figured that if and when Matt wanted them to know, he'd tell them himself.

Matt nodded. "Thanks. See y'all later."

One of the men called out, "Are you coming to the bunkhouse for supper, Matt? We're gonna heat up some leftover stew on the propane stove."

Matt kept walking. "Probably not. I'm beat and I'll just grab a sandwich at the house. G'night."

He could hear himself walking as he strode to the house, and his footsteps sounded loud to his ears. His poncho had its own creaks and swishes, and some change in his pants pocket clinked together just enough to become part of the misty, eerie scene. The house was too dark, Matt thought uneasily. Hadn't Hope lit the lanterns?

He stamped his feet on the back porch mat to rid his boots of the mud they'd gathered that afternoon, then opened the door and walked in. The house was not only too dark, it was too quiet.

Matt's system went into alert mode, which meant he moved more deliberately and thought through every possible scenario. Hope was ill. No, she'd lost touch with where she was and had numbly walked away, in which case she could be wandering helplessly in any given direction.

Matt's stomach sank, and he realized that Ms. Hope LeClaire had become more than just another "fellow human being," as he'd described her to Chuck. It was a surprise revelation for Matt, because he'd been so positive for years now that he would never care enough for another woman to matter, especially a wealthy woman.

"Revelation, my left foot! That was the most stupid thought ever to enter your head," he mumbled under his breath. "Hope LeClaire is *not* any more important to you than anyone else, and don't you forget it."

He shed and hung his poncho and hat, then sat down in the kitchen just long enough to take off his boots, because they were still muddy. It was too dark inside to see much, so he went to the laundry room for a lantern. His veins got a little icier when he saw that they were all there. Hope hadn't lit one, which made no sense at all.

Hurrying then, he turned on the fuel valve of one of the lanterns, quickly lit it with a match, picked it up by its handle and went to look for Hope, actually praying that she was somewhere in the house. The bedroom she'd been using seemed to be the most logical place for her to be, and that was where he went.

The room was empty. Swirling, Matt shouted, "Hope? Hope? Where are you?"

She opened her eyes, but was groggy from sleeping so soundly and wasn't sure she hadn't dreamed a voice calling her name.

"Hope?" Matt walked into the living room, holding the lantern high to get maximum light from it. His legs got weak when he saw her lying on the sofa with the comforter from her bed tucked snugly around her.

She blinked at him. "Matt?"

"Yeah. Are you okay?"

The anger she'd battled on and off all afternoon because she was so helpless in the dark and cold in this strange place suddenly exploded.

"No, I am *not* okay! There's no electricity, no heat, no lights and I've been alone for hours. What took you so long?"

"I told you I'd be gone most of the afternoon."

"I'd say the afternoon is long gone, wouldn't you? It happens to be night now!"

"It took us longer than I thought. Why didn't you light

one of the lanterns, for God's sake. Or all of them, if you were afraid of the dark?''

"I tried, but I didn't and still don't know how to light those—those prehistoric contraptions," she shrieked.

"Don't yell at me," Matt said through clenched teeth. What in hell had made him think this nasty little woman was even slightly important to him? She'd been trouble since he'd first spotted her out there in the mud, and she was going to be trouble until the day he got rid of her.

"I'll yell if I want to," Hope shouted. "You're not the one stuck in a foreign land without a memory, you big jerk!"

"Good Lord, you're not in a foreign land, you're in Texas!"

"It *feels* foreign, and so do you!" Hope's anger suddenly dissolved and she began crying. "Everything feels foreign," she sobbed. "And yes, I'm scared. I don't want to be, but I can't seem to do anything about it."

She sounded forlorn, a woman without a link or a lifeline to anything that made life worth living. Matt's lifeline was the ranch. Since his downhill financial slide began, he'd wondered many times what he would do if he actually hit bottom and lost his home. The imagery wasn't at all pleasant, and the worst thing to face was that it could happen.

His and Hope's situations were not even close in nature, but trouble was trouble, whatever form it took on. His heart softened toward her, along with his expression.

"Let's get you more comfortable," he said gently. "Stay under that blanket, and I'll start a fire in the fireplace. It won't heat the whole house, but it will make this room nice and warm."

He'd become an impatient, frequently cynical man, he thought while quickly and easily building a roaring fire in the huge fireplace. But he shouldn't take out his frustrations with the human race and the unforgiving world of finance on anyone else, least of all a woman who certainly wasn't under his roof by choice.

"There, all set," he said as he closed the metal mesh curtains to keep sparks from flying out of the fireplace. He thought of something else and held up his forefinger. "I'll be right back." Leaving the lantern for her, which along with the dancing flames provided plenty of light, he walked from the room.

Hope wiped her eyes with the back of her hand. She felt terribly remorseful for screeching at Matt. He'd probably saved her life, and how could she be anything but grateful with him? It was just that she'd become so frightened when it started getting dark and Matt and his crew still hadn't returned. And this place did feel foreign to her. In her mind's eye she saw the ranch as a house and some barns plunked down in the middle of a vast wasteland. Actually, when she'd looked out the windows today, hoping to see Matt and the men coming back, the word *wasteland* had occurred to her more than once. Everything was so dark and dreary looking. Surely Texas didn't look that way when it was dry and the sun was shining, but she'd never seen it that way. Or if she had, she couldn't remember it.

She'd wept off and on all afternoon, suffering stupefying self-pity one minute and trying desperately to stretch her memory the next. It had been a dreadful day, mostly because the damned electricity had gone off. Even though she couldn't recite specific recipes, there was a peculiar confidence inside her that had to do with cooking, and if the power had remained constant, she knew that she would have passed the time in the kitchen.

Matt came in, loaded down with bedding and another lantern. "I'm going to fix you a nice bed by the fire," he told her.

"That's not necessary. Matt, I—I'm sorry I yelled at you."

Matt was spreading thick, soft, down-filled sleeping bags on the rug in front of the fireplace, and he stopped to look at her. She certainly wasn't a raving beauty at the moment, but he saw past her sorrowful red and swollen eyes to the beautiful, unconscious woman he'd undressed and gently washed mud from. The memory made him uncomfortable, and he dropped his eyes.

"Forget it," he said gruffly, and spread out another sleeping bag on top of the first two he'd laid down.

"Forget it?" she repeated. "I should forget being unforgivably rude to the man who saved my life? Why, Matt? Why do you want me to forget it?"

"Because you're upset and worried, and who in hell wouldn't be in your shoes?" Matt shook out a clean sheet over the sleeping bags. "I'll get some pillows and blankets," he said, and left while Hope was contemplating what kind of reply a person in "her shoes" could possibly make to his inarguable but still very difficult to accept observation.

Truth was, she couldn't read between the lines with Matt, she thought with a ponderous sigh. Maybe that was the way she was with all men. Maybe she was that way even with women. God forbid, but what if she was a tongue-tied, giggly bubble brain around attractive men, and a complete moron with intelligent women?

Watching the dancing reflections of firelight on the otherwise dark ceiling, she again felt the pressure of painful questions. Was she educated? Did she work? If so, was her work a career or simply a job? Other than her mother, did she have any family? Was anyone worried about her? Anyone at all?

Dear God, how did I end up on a ranch where no one knows me? There must be a reason for my being in Texas

in the first place. I realize that reason could be any num-
ber of things, but what on earth brought me to this par-
ticular piece of Texas?

Matt returned with pillows and blankets and finished
making the bed. "Come on over here by the fire," he
said, "and I'll scare us up some supper. You'll be much
warmer and a lot more comfortable stretched out on this
nice soft bed than you are on that sofa. It'll only take me
a few minutes to put together some eats. Come on, Hope,
cooperate. I'm just trying to help."

In her heart she believed him, but she had so much
misery to deal with that she had no desire at all to cooperate with him or anyone else. If there was anyone else,
that is.

Tight-lipped, she forced herself to get off the couch and
walk to the makeshift bed. Matt didn't wait to see if she
actually lay down, figuring that he'd done what he could
and the rest was up to her. He went to the kitchen instead.

Hope was surprised by the comfort of the bed, and the
fire was warming and pleasant. She felt the strain of the
lonely, frightening day diminishing until she actually began feeling relaxed. If her brain was working even a little,
wouldn't she have been able to figure out how to build a
fire and to light those damned lanterns? What if she never
recovered and remained a helpless, pitiable creature for
the rest of her days?

It was a horrifying thought that brought tears to her
eyes, but she didn't want to be all weepy and self-pitying
when Matt returned, so she dried her face and finger-
combed her hair back from her face in an effort to look
halfway presentable. Her fingertips encountered the heal-
ing cut on the back of her head and she wondered if that
small injury had actually been the cause of her amnesia.
It really didn't seem very likely, and her mind then struggled to come up with other reasons why a person would

lose her memory. Nothing sensible or logical occurred to her, but she suddenly felt icy fingers walk up her spine and instinct told her that whatever had brought her to the McCarlson ranch and caused her amnesia was neither sensible nor logical. Which left what? Something on the wrong side of the law?

Seized by sudden panic, she thought frantically, I'm not a criminal, am I? "Oh, my God," she whispered.

Matt walked in with a large tray and saw Hope staring into the fire with an expression on her face that looked to be no more than one small step away from severe hysteria.

His pulse leapt in alarm. Setting the tray down on the floor between Hope and the fireplace, he sat next to her on the sleeping bags and blankets.

"I can't begin to guess what caused this," he said quietly while laying what he hoped she would view as a comforting hand on her upper arm, "but you can't let the situation get you down. Amnesia isn't a permanent condition. Your memory could return in a flash at any moment."

She turned her head to look at him. "Do you know that for a fact?"

"I've never had any medical training, but I've read and heard things. Probably everybody has. Amnesia isn't one of those rare diseases that no one's ever heard of, you know."

"Disease? Amnesia is considered a disease?"

She was still on the brink of hysteria, Matt realized. "No—no. I said it wrong. Amnesia is not a disease, it—it's caused by some sort of trauma to the head. That cut you have—"

Hope broke in. "Did not cause it. I'm positive of that, but what other kind of trauma did I experience that night?" Turning even more so that she was flat on her back, except for her head on two stacked pillows, she dug her hands into the front of Matt's shirt. "Matt, what happened to me?"

Her eyes pleaded, and Matt felt so much empathy that he nearly choked up. Clasping his own hands around hers, he spoke a bit raggedly.

"Hope, can't you stop thinking about it?"

"Can't you give me a better answer than that?"

He knew she was a Stockwell. He knew what the newspaper article said about her being missing. But did he know anything that would relieve her anxiety at this moment? No, he did not.

"If I had a better answer, you'd have heard it before this," he said gently. "Now, let's have some supper. It's nothing fancy, but I'm hungry enough to eat just about anything. How about you?"

Hope sighed. "I guess so."

Hours later, Matt awoke with a start. He'd been sleeping on the sofa, so he could keep the fire going. He had suggested that Hope spend the night in front of the fireplace and it hadn't taken much persuasion to convince her.

But he hadn't slept nearly as well as he would have in his own bed. For one thing, he kept setting his watch alarm to wake him every hour so he could add wood to the fire. Second, he heard each movement and sound Hope made, and he doubted if she slept more than ten minutes through without thrashing about in bed or crying out over some damned dream.

What woke him this time, though, wasn't tortured whimpers from Hope but an out-and-out bloodcurdling scream. Matt jumped from the sofa and rushed to the sleeping bag bed to gather Hope into his arms. She quieted almost at once, and he simply gave up and stayed where he was. At first he realized that he was back where he'd been last night, in bed with Hope and holding her close. But he was so dog tired that after a while he drifted off to sleep.

Before long the fire died to embers, and Matt was so out of it he didn't hear his watch alarm when it beeped. Thus, when he felt the chill seeping into the room, he groggily crawled under the blankets and snuggled even more intimately with Hope's warm body. Somehow, even in his sleep, Hope's bare legs tangled with his became vaguely and sensuously apparent. She was wearing a long shirt of his, he knew that much, but it had crept up during the night and other than the lacy little panties he'd taken off her that first morning, she was all silky, hot skin and curving femininity.

His arousal was sudden and hot as Hades. Still groggy, he rubbed against Hope's naked thigh and without direction from his brain his right hand began exploring the incredibly luscious contours of her body. Erotic images formed behind his closed eyelids; he desperately needed to make love, to put out the fire searing his loins.

Hope came awake slowly. Matt's hand was gliding over her skin in a most delicious way, and she could feel his hard manhood against her thigh and the rest of his long body all but surrounding hers. She felt no alarm. In fact, the heat developing in the pit of her belly was much too pleasurable and demanding for her to do anything but enjoy it.

She blamed her amnesia on the fact that this felt like the first time that a man had ever caressed her so intimately. It couldn't possibly be true, of course. Her driver's license indicated that she was twenty-eight years old. Even without a bank of knowledge to draw upon, a twenty-eight-year-old virgin simply wasn't logical.

Still, as fantastic as Matt's obviously very experienced hand made her feel—it was definitely getting bolder, now slipping into her panties and between her legs—Hope's confusion grew over whether she'd done this before. He was sliding down her panties when she began realizing where so much heat and mind-boggling pleasure was heading.

"Matt," she whispered, and reached down and stopped his hand from attaining its goal.

Her voice, wispy as it was, brought him fully awake. He became very still, his hand in hers, his arousal against her thigh.

"Guess I was sleeping," he said thickly.

"So was I."

"Are you angry with me?"

"Not about this," she whispered. "How could I be when it...felt so good? But, Matt, is it right for us? What if I'm married, or engaged?"

"I don't think you're either." The article had said nothing about a husband or fiancé.

"But you don't know for sure," she said softly. "And you know I don't." She knew one thing, though. She should move away from him, or ask him to move away from her. But his lean male body pressing against hers was such a fabulous sensation that she didn't want to put space between them. In fact, she would like to let go of his hand and let him do anything he wanted. What would *anything* be? she wondered as she battled a feverish desire to find out.

Matt discovered an internal battle of his own. He'd read only one newspaper report about Hope—obviously the first to be published—and he couldn't doubt that there'd been a new article in that paper every day since. There was no telling what the media had learned by its own methods, let alone what information her family might have given out to aid in Hope's recovery. If he'd been receiving his newspaper regularly he would know for certain if she'd been involved with someone at the time of her disappearance. As it was, he shouldn't assume anything, nor should he press her into an intimate relationship.

And not for just her benefit, he thought with a ponderous sigh. His own peace of mind was at stake here, maybe even more so than hers. One spoiled-beyond-belief, rich woman was enough for any man, plus the tragic ending to a tragic marriage that he'd lived through really put a damper on any desire he might otherwise have had to become seriously involved with even a woman of little means.

Hope was right, he thought grimly. They should not be doing this. He withdrew his hand from hers but kept his other arm under her head. "Let's just sleep," he said softly. "Would you prefer that I return to the sofa?"

She hesitated, then said, "I'm concerned about expressing my feelings without giving you the wrong impression, but let me try. I feel safe with you next to me. Please stay."

"I'll stay." It took a while, but Matt finally fell asleep again.

Hope, on the other hand, could only pretend to sleep. The feelings Matt had stirred within her would not die down. What kind of woman was she, that all a man had to do was lay next to her and touch her to make her all hot and longing for...for... What was she longing for, a middle-of-the-night affair? Was that something she frequently did? Her aching body told her yes, but there was something in her mind that said no, don't even think it!

Tears filled her eyes. She was so confused that she felt like screaming, and it was all she could do to restrain herself. How much longer could she maintain her sanity? Completely losing what little mind any amnesiac had left must be his or her greatest threat. Something had to give somewhere—the weather, the phone service, something.

If it didn't, would she fall apart so badly that she could never be put back together again?

Hope's thoughts turned to the man beside her. Her entire world consisted of Matt McCarlson. Was it any wonder that she would physically respond to his touch when he was her only emotional connection to any kind of reality? And even though the word *reality* meant very little to her, she knew deep in her soul that it was crucial to her mental health—pathetic as that was—to grab hold of whatever reality she did recognize and hang on to it with every ounce of strength in her body.

She lay pondering that principle until something rather stunning seeped through her thoughts: it was no longer raining.

Getting up cautiously so she wouldn't disturb Matt's slumber, she went to a window and looked out. Not only had the rain ceased, the sky was clear and a bright moon hung over the ranch.

Her knees suddenly felt weak. The electricity and phone lines would be repaired as quickly as possible. She was going to have to face the world very soon. Could she do it?

Visualizing herself phoning Madelyn LeClaire, the person named as her mother in her wallet, scared Hope nearly to death. What would she say to a mother she couldn't remember? And who else couldn't she remember—sisters, brothers, friends? Would she have to call other people besides Madelyn? Others she had absolutely no memory of?

And then would she have to leave this ranch and go out into a huge, unfamiliar world? She'd told Matt the truth. With him she felt safe. Instinct told her she would not feel safe anywhere else, or with anyone else, at least not until she regained her memory. It would happen, wouldn't it?

"God, help me," she whispered, and then turned it into a prayer. "*Please* help me."

Chapter Six

Dawn was just beginning to break when Matt got up noiselessly, took his clothes and tiptoed from the room, leaving Hope in a deep sleep. He went directly to the bathroom he always used, automatically flipped the light switch and then blinked in surprise when the lights came on. Since the storm had obviously died out, maybe the electricity would stay on this time, he thought with a satisfied nod of his head.

It immediately occurred to him that the phone might be working as well, and he hurried to try the one in his bedroom. The dial tone in his ear was just about the sweetest music he'd ever heard. Now, at last, he could do something about Hope. She was a dangerous woman, and the sooner she was transferred to the Stockwells and out of his hair, the better off he'd be. Look what had almost happened last night. He accepted full blame for their nearly making love, but blame and responsibility weren't the point. What he viewed as just plain scary was Hope's fervent physical response and then her talking about the possibility of already being romantically involved with some guy she couldn't remember. So much logic didn't seem to be in tune with amnesia to Matt's way of thinking, and besides, his advances last night hadn't been made with romance in mind. Being in bed with a sexy woman had caused a perfectly natural reaction, and there'd been nothing romantic about it.

"Women," Matt mumbled, thinking that he was darned glad this morning that Hope had gotten logical instead of cooperative last night, because she thought of sex as romantic and he thought of it as simply the most pleasurable function of the human body. Damnation, she'd probably be talking about the magic of falling in love this morning if they'd actually done the deed. Good thing one of them had put on the brakes.

After shaving, brushing his teeth and getting dressed, Matt returned to the telephone and checked the dial tone again. With enormous relief he wondered if he dared call Doc Pickett at this unholy hour. But what if this is my only opportunity to phone anyone? he mused with genuine concern. After all, the electricity had come on and then gone off again; the phone could do the same damned thing.

Before he could completely argue himself out of waking up the doctor, he dialed Adam Pickett's home number. Matt could hear the Pickett phone ringing, but before it was picked up Matt heard something else—Hope's voice. She was crying loudly, almost hysterically, and it startled Matt so much that he slammed down the phone and ran to the living room. She was not in bed, but rather rushing around the room as though the devil himself were on her heels.

"Hey, hey, take it easy." Matt caught her by the shoulders, and she spun on him with crazed eyes and clawing fingernails. For his own protection, he grabbed her hands and hung on tightly. "Good Lord, woman, what's the matter with you?"

"Leave me alone. Let go of me!"

"Hope, for crying out loud, calm down." The terror in her glassy eyes scared him, and then it dawned on him that she wasn't really seeing *him*. Was she seeing someone who'd maybe hurt her? The person who had caused the trauma that had resulted in her amnesia?

Matt gentled his voice. "Hope, what's my name? Who am I? Look closely at my face. You know me. Say my name."

She had stopped struggling to free her hands because he was so much stronger than she was, and the soothing sound of his voice began penetrating her terror. Blinking her wet eyelashes, she finally looked at Matt's face and into his eyes.

"Matt," she whispered, and her legs collapsed completely.

He stopped her from falling, then picked her up and brought her to the sofa, where he sat down and cradled her on his lap. "What happened?" he asked softly. "Was it another dream?"

Weeping quietly, she buried her face in his shoulder. "It was awful. A man was trying to—to—you know."

"To rape you?"

"Maybe. I was terrified, but then I—I seemed to be trying to—to seduce him."

"That's a mighty strange dream, Hope?"

"I know it is."

"Hope, was he the same man you've been having other nightmares about? Did it feel as though you knew him? Do you remember his face?"

"I don't know," she moaned. "But I'm sure we were in a hotel or…something."

"A room in a motel or hotel?"

"Yes, I think so." Hope brought her right wrist up and looked at the red marks on it. "Something horrible happened to me, Matt. I was tied up, these marks are proof of that."

"Were you tied up in this dream?"

She thought a moment, then sighed. "Not that I can remember. Matt, what if it wasn't all a dream? What if I'm reliving the same horrible experience over and over in these nightmares?"

"It's possible, I suppose," Matt said slowly. "But thinking logically, the nearest motel is about a mile this side of Hawthorne, and how did you get from there to here?"

"Maybe that dreadful man brought me here."

"For what reason? If there's any truth to your dreams, you were already in his clutches in a motel room. It doesn't make sense that he would take you way out here."

"No, it doesn't," she said in a shaky whisper. "But I got here somehow. Did—did I walk?"

Matt frowned thoughtfully. Why were her clothes so torn and snagged. She'd done *some* walking, that was certain, and through some very thorny bushes, to boot. But all the way from Hawthorne?

"Not likely," he said introspectively, as though speaking only to himself. A chill suddenly went up his spine. Was it possible that some pervert had abducted her and then she'd somehow managed to get away from him? And what if the guy wasn't a sex offender but someone after the Stockwell money? *My God, he could still be after her, watching the house from a distance with binoculars and just waiting for another chance to snatch her!*

In all that rain?

He was probably warm and dry in a comfortable vehicle.

Aren't you getting just a bit melodramatic over some dreams, for God's sake?

Could be, but it's also possible that Hope is starting to remember her past, and why wouldn't she recall the last events first? Especially if they were as terrifying in reality as they were in her dreams.

He realized all of a sudden that his hand was cupping her sweetly curved behind and her breasts were pressing into his chest. Instantly he became aroused, and he seriously considered just throwing caution to the winds and doing what he wanted and suspected what she wanted as well, because it kept happening every time they touched each other.

Dammit! Why was this happening to him? Abruptly he moved her from his lap to the sofa, then got to his feet. "I'm going to make some phone calls."

"The phone is working this morning?"

Matt was startled by the fear in her voice and eyes again. "The storm's over, Hope," he said firmly but quietly. "It's time this ranch got back to normal."

"And me?" she said in a shaky little voice. "What's normal for me, Matt?"

She looked so lost and forlorn that he nearly caved in and took her in his arms again. Instead, he kept his emotions under control and his hands to himself.

"That's what we have to find out," he said. "I'm going to call Doc Pickett, and maybe you should think about phoning your mother." Hope cowered back against the sofa cushions as though she were hoping to hide herself in them. Matt frowned. "Are you afraid to talk to your mother?"

"I don't know her," Hope whispered. "Please don't make me talk to anyone yet. I'll get stronger, I know I will, but I—I'm not ready to…talk…to…strangers.'' Her wispy voice trailed off to nothing.

Unnerved by the shaky insecurity of her demeanor, Matt raked his hair with both hands. All right, fine, he thought. I'll lay that one on Doc along with everything else and let him deal with it.

"Forget I mentioned it," he said gruffly. "I'll be in my office for a while. Rap on the door if you need anything."

"Yes…all right." Hope watched him leave and then suffered a deluge of painful emotions. She was not Matt McCarlson's responsibility and she was behaving as though it were his duty to shield her from her own fears. "Oh, Lord," she whispered, and despairingly put her forehead in the heel of her hand and shut her eyes. *I can't go on like this for much longer. Matt's going to phone his doctor friend about my condition. Will Dr. Pickett come out here and see me? Will he be able to help? I feel like my brain is in a thick, dark fog, and what could anyone, even a doctor, do to clear my head so I can remember?*

But what if the doctor does drive out here and then, after an examination, decides that I need to be…what's the word? Institutionalized?

Stunned by the thought, she clenched her hands into fists. *No matter what the doctor says, I will not leave here, I won't!*

But she didn't need a memory to know that she was in one very precarious situation. Sitting around weeping, feeling sorry for herself and acting like a wimp over bad dreams would never convince anyone that she was an emotionally sound person.

It was time that she woke up and smelled the coffee. She could function without a memory, and she would start proving it immediately.

* * *

Matt had Dr. Adam Pickett on the line. "You say she can't remember anything?" Doc asked.

"That's her story, Doc, and I have no choice but to believe her. She didn't even know her name until she saw her driver's license."

"And you found her outside lying in the mud?"

"In the mud and unconscious. I have no idea how she got here and neither does she."

"Strange...damned strange business. Matt, have you ever seen her before? I realize you don't know the woman, but have you ever seen her around town or anywhere else?"

"No, never." Matt was withholding the information that Hope was a Stockwell. Not that Doc wasn't trustworthy, but Matt was getting very protective of Hope and it just seemed best to him that no one knew where she was. The more he pondered the kidnapping theory, the more sense it made. It also made sense that if the kidnapper was lurking around the ranch, as Matt had initially contemplated, he could have made another attempt to grab Hope yesterday when all the men were out on the range.

So, if there really was a kidnapper and if he hadn't given up on cashing in on his nefarious scheme...? Hell, was it possible the kidnapper had no idea in which direction Hope had gone after she'd escaped his clutches?

Realizing that even though his theory contained an awful lot of assumptions it could be more true than not, Matt frowned, decided again to keep Hope's Stockwell relationship on a had-to-know basis, just in case someone should innocently let her location slip around the wrong person, and asked Doc Pickett, "Can you come out here and check her over, Doc? I think you could make it in your four-wheeler."

"Tell me how she is physically."

"She seems fine. I thought the cut on her head was

worse than it was, and at first I was concerned about other injuries. She has a few bruises, of course.'' *And chafing on both wrists, which look to me like rope burns.*

"Then I'm not even going to try to go out there, Matt. Some people were seriously injured during the storm, and I can't leave them to check the degree of a woman's amnesia, who is apparently sound otherwise.''

"But what should I do? I mean, is there anything I should be doing to help her regain her memory?''

"Well, one thing you should probably do, now that you have phone service again, is to call the sheriff's office and find out if anyone has filed a missing person report on her.''

"Yes…yes,'' Matt said rather impatiently. "But is there anything *I* should be doing for her?''

"Treat her like you would anyone else. Listen, Matt, amnesia is a peculiar condition. Odds are she'll regain her full memory in a reasonable span of time without any treatment whatsoever, and here's the most peculiar part of it. No one can predict how it will occur. It could come back in bits and pieces, or her whole life could suddenly open up to her without rhyme or reason. Then, of course, there's the chance that some small event, or a smell, or the sound of someone's voice, or any one of any number of things, could trigger some memory that in turn triggers another and so on and so on. If that should happen, you could be sitting in the same room with her and be completely unaware of her metamorphosis.''

"Great,'' Matt mumbled. The only thing he'd learned from this conversation was that he was on his own with Hope until Doc got freed up in town, unless Matt turned her over to her family, and that option wasn't nearly as appealing as it once was. Truth was, talking to his doctor friend had confused more than aided him.

But there was one more question he had to ask. "Doc,

is there any chance of my doing something to cause her amnesia to become a permanent condition?''

"It's very unlikely, Matt, and not something you should be worrying about. As I said before, treat her as you would anyone else. Let me ask you this. Is she emotionally depressed?''

"Wouldn't you be?'' Matt returned dryly.

Doc Pickett heaved a sympathetic sigh. "Yes, anyone would be. Matt, just do the best you can, and you might think about this. If my four-wheeler can make it across muddy open country to your ranch, one of yours can make it to town. Bring the lady to Hawthorne and I promise that I'll squeeze out a few minutes to see her.''

Matt froze. Take Hope to town where just anyone could get a look at her? Give whomever it was that had caused her to lose her memory in the first place another chance at her? He wouldn't even know which pair of eyes to mistrust.

"Thanks,'' he said a bit thickly, simply because he felt so numb. "I might do that.'' It was a lie; he had no intention of putting Hope in further danger by taking her anywhere. Here, on his ranch, he felt she was relatively safe. No, she hadn't been safe yesterday when he and all the men had been off working, but she'd definitely be safe now that he'd started figuring things out. At least he *thought* he was starting to figure things out. He could be miles from the truth, he knew, but there could only be so many explanations for her being way out here without a vehicle during a fierce storm. And if he really wanted to be generous and give her the benefit of the doubt, what about that nightmare she'd suffered again only this morning? There could very easily be a connection between her situation and her dreams of a motel room and a man who scared her half to death.

Matt said goodbye to Doc Pickett and hung up the

phone. Then he sat back in his chair and brooded. Hope was afraid to talk to "strangers," but he certainly wasn't. Should he take it upon himself to phone the Stockwells and let them know that Hope was all right?

Maybe he shouldn't go that far, but what about letting Sheriff Cliff Braeburn know the score? Cliff was a good friend and as honest as the day was long. Besides, Cliff was a stand-up guy who never tried to feather his own nest by speaking out of turn. Whatever he did or didn't do in Hope's behalf would never cause her a moment of discomfort or concern.

And, Matt added in his own mind, neither would anything Cliff did about Hope cause *him* a problem. He picked up the phone again and dialed the sheriff's office in Hawthorne. "This is Matt McCarlson. Is Cliff around?" he said to the person who'd answered the call.

"Hold on and let me check."

In a minute, Cliff's voice was in Matt's ear. "Hey, Matt. Are you treading water out there?"

"Damned near, Cliff. At least we were for a while. Listen, there's something I need to talk over with you, and I don't want anyone hearing any part of our conversation. Would you call me back on your private line?"

"Sounds serious."

"It is."

"I'll call you back right away."

The line went dead and Matt set down his phone. It rang in seconds, and he grabbed it and put it to his ear again.

"Okay, what's wrong?" Cliff asked.

Matt wasted no time on small talk. "Hope LeClaire is at my place."

"The Stockwell heiress?"

"One and the same."

"Well, what in the devil is she doing with you? Everyone in Texas is looking for her."

"I don't doubt it, but until this morning I had no way of letting anyone know about her sudden appearance. Short of smoke signals," Matt added wryly.

"No phone service, huh?"

"No electricity, either. We haven't exactly been living the life of Riley out here, but the topper was finding a half-drowned, mud-soaked, unconscious woman lying near my mailbox the second morning of the storm. I swear to God I thought she was dead, Cliff. I was on horseback and from a distance she looked dead. Anyhow, to make this story short, she was very much alive and not even hurt very badly, except for one thing. She had absolutely no memory. Still doesn't."

"Then how do you know who she is?"

"Because of the article in the newspaper that day—my last delivery, incidentally—and because she had a purse with a wallet in it with items that identified her. Okay, here's the situation. She knows her name because of the things in the wallet, although she remembers nothing of herself. But I didn't tell her about the newspaper article. Truth is, Cliff, I'm scared of doing or saying the wrong thing with her. I called Doc a few minutes ago, hoping that he could drive out here with some sort of miracle cure for amnesia, but he said he had too many seriously injured patients to leave town. Sounds like we weren't the only one treading water during that storm."

"You've got that right, Matt. It was a son of a gun of a storm, and there was some pretty bad flooding in several areas. We got everyone evacuated in time, but not before a lot of folks got hurt trying to save their livestock and other possessions. There were some vehicle accidents, too, so I'd have to say that Doc is probably running in circles trying to keep up."

"I guess we all have our problems," Matt said. "What do you want me to do about Hope?"

"Well, now, that's one problem I'm not trained to solve, Matt."

"Neither am I," Matt said flatly. "But you're the law, and there's something else you should think about. I don't know how she got way out here in the storm, Cliff. And she's having really weird nightmares about a motel or hotel room and a very scary guy. I think she was kidnapped, held in some strange room, and she somehow managed to escape. Incidentally, her wrists have rope burns, so I believe she was tied up."

"She was tied up in a motel room and then she escaped and did what? Walked to your ranch?"

"Walking that far is not impossible, Cliff. But maybe she stole the guy's car and it conked out before she got here. Maybe she got lost and disoriented and just wandered onto my land. Hell, Cliff, I can't fill in the details, but something damned unpleasant sure caused her to lose her memory." After a long silence, Matt said, "Cliff?"

"I'm here. Just doing some thinking. Okay, assume the lady was kidnapped and got away from her captor. Doesn't it make sense that he'd hightail it out of the area before she could bring in the law? And considering her medical situation, she wouldn't even be able to give us a creditable description of the guy."

"That's true, Cliff, but what if the jerk is persistent and still hanging out somewhere, waiting for another opportunity to pick up a load of Stockwell money?"

"You mean, kidnap her again?"

"Cliff, I know this whole scenario is nothing more than speculation, but do we dare take the chance that it's not?"

"Ignoring a possible criminal activity is not an option, Matt. Your theory is feasible, even if it is merely speculative at this point. While I'm trying to sort it out, though,

I think I should call the Stockwells, tell them where Hope is and relieve their worry.''

"I agree. Would you also call Hope's mother in Massachusetts? Hope doesn't want to talk to anyone, and I really don't think she should be forced into anything. The woman's name is Madelyn LeClaire and I have a phone number from a card in the wallet where she can be reached in case of an emergency concerning her daughter.''

"Yes, I'll call her. She should be reassured, as well as the Stockwells.''

Matt recited the phone number. "Anyhow, Cliff, I believe there's a kidnapper out there, and probably not very far away from either of us, so I think you should impress on both the Stockwells and Mrs. LeClaire to keep Hope's whereabouts to themselves. What do you think?''

"Until we know more about what happened to Hope, I fully agree. You realize, of course, that without proof of criminal behavior that all I can do is suggest that no one hold any press conferences to celebrate Hope's safe haven.''

"Cliff, I've seen you in action. Your suggestions are usually followed to the letter.''

"We'll see," Cliff said. "I'll do what I can. That's all I can guarantee, Matt.''

"Thanks, Cliff." Matt put down the phone and realized that he felt much better. At least Hope's family would no longer be worried sick over her absence.

Of course, he hadn't helped his own case any. Hope was still under his roof, still in his hair, still underfoot and *under his skin!*

"Damn," he muttered, and got up from his desk chair to start the day's work, of which there was more than enough to go around, considering all the cleanup from flooding and then the repairs needed to the roads on ranch property. The county would take care of road damage beyond McCarlson land, but the roads on Matt's property were his responsibility.

The thing that put a knot in his stomach was that the damage repair might require money as well as hard work.

Cursing under his breath, he left the office and headed for the kitchen. The aroma of perking coffee and cooking food startled him. He stopped in the doorway and gaped at Hope, who was busy at the stove.

She felt his presence and glanced over her shoulder to see him. "I'm making French toast and bacon for breakfast. The coffee's done, so grab a cup and sit down. I couldn't find any syrup but I'm making some. Everything will be ready in just a few minutes."

Matt didn't move fast. Rather, he walked slowly to a cupboard for a mug and then, almost in slow motion, filled it with coffee. Apparently Hope had stopped shivering over that nightmare, and her transformation was amazing and hard to understand. Unless, as Doc had told him might happen, she'd gone through the metamorphosis from amnesiac to normal.

Clearing his throat, Matt leaned against a counter and watched her. "Uh, how do you make syrup?" he asked, thinking that was a safe enough question to begin a conversation that might tell him she had remembered everything about her past.

"With brown sugar, butter and a little water. If I had some heavy cream I could create an incredible sauce for the toast, but what's simmering in that little pan will do."

"You're quite the little chef, aren't you?"

Hope took her eyes from the pans on the stove to give him a quizzical look. "I wonder if that's true."

Matt's hopes faded. She hadn't remembered anything important. Apparently cooking was as natural as breathing for her, and... Wait a damned minute! Wasn't there something in that article about Hope LeClaire and some cooking school?

Setting his mug on the counter, Matt said, "I'll be right back."

"Don't be long. Everything's almost ready."

Matt went to the laundry room and opened the drawer in which he'd secreted the newspaper containing the article about Hope. Keeping an ear cocked in case she should decide to see what he was doing, he quickly scanned the article. Sure enough, there was the reference to Hope's education he'd just recalled. Hope LeClaire recently graduated from the distinguished London cooking school, Le Cordon Bleu. Stuffing the paper back into the drawer, Matt returned to the kitchen.

"You look…odd," Hope said when she saw him. "Is something wrong?"

Matt's expression grew wry. "Other than the obvious?"

"Sorry," she answered. "I know I'm a terrible burden. But I'm trying very hard not to be such a…uh, burden. Matt, did you phone Madelyn LeClaire?"

He could see the idea terrified her. "No," he said, and retrieved his mug of coffee and sat at the table. "That food smells terrific and I'm famished."

"Good," Hope said quietly, and began dishing it up.

Once Sheriff Braeburn phoned U.S. Marshal Rafe Stockwell, a marathon of telephone calls ensued. Rafe passed on the news that Hope was safe and physically well to his brothers Jack and Cord, and to his sister Kate. Hope's amnesia was a shock to all and extremely confusing. What should they do? they wondered to each other. And was Matt McCarlson as trustworthy as Cliff Braeburn indicated? Of course, they had to discuss this with their mother, Madelyn, and they decided to make it a conference call so they could all reassure her that Hope truly was safe and sound.

The thing was, the Stockwell siblings weren't as positive of that as they sounded when they talked to Madelyn, who had already been told the news but was very pleased that her other children were as concerned about Hope as she was. After a few minutes of conversation she said, "Do you think I should come to Texas?"

"Come if you wish, Mother," Rafe told her. "You are always welcome. But there's something else you should know. Hope has amnesia."

"Amnesia! How? Why?" Madelyn asked in obvious horror. "The sheriff didn't tell me that."

"No one knows what caused it," Rafe said quietly.

"There's foul play afoot," Madelyn declared then. "I suspected as much. Rafe, are you sure we all shouldn't go to the McCarlson ranch en masse and—and just haul our darling Hope out of there?"

"Hope is terribly frightened, according to Matt McCarlson, Mother," Kate said gently. "I don't think any of us should try forcing her into anything. For the time being, I believe we should content ourselves with the fact that she's physically well and safe in the McCarlson home."

"Rafe, can you vouch for Mr. McCarlson's integrity?" Madelyn inquired.

"Sheriff Braeburn can," Rafe said. "And I trust Cliff implicitly. But there is one other thing to consider, Mother. Hawthorne and the surrounding area have suffered a hell of a storm. According to the sheriff, anyone trying to get to the McCarlson ranch at present just might find himself stuck hubcap deep in mud. In a few days the area should be pretty much dried out, and let's all keep in mind that a lot can happen in two or three days. Maybe by then Hope's amnesia will have disappeared and she'll remember her family and want to see us. That would be so much better than everyone descending on her when she has no idea who we are.''

''I suppose you're right,'' Madelyn concurred, though there was a definitive note of concern in her voice.

The conference call ended with everyone promising to stay in close contact. Hope was safe, at least, and while they all wanted to see her with their own eyes, they agreed not to aggravate her medical condition by barging in on her. Also, they agreed to tell no one where Hope was, which further reinforced Madelyn's belief that her youngest daughter had met with foul play and could still be in danger.

But she agreed with her other children not to notify the media.

From now on, they all knew it would be a waiting game, and each member of the Stockwell clan was on pins and needles.

Some burning questions were, regardless of Sheriff Braeburn's stamp of approval, just who in the devil was Matt McCarlson, and how had Hope ended up at his ranch?

Chapter Seven

Hope stood at a window, cautiously moved aside a curtain just a little and looked outside. The sun was shining and steam was actually rising from the dark, dank earth in places. She would have loved to take a walk and feel the warm sunshine on her face and arms, but Matt had warned her adamantly to stay inside and out of sight.

The strange thing was that she hadn't argued with him about it. Now she questioned her blind obedience, her acquiescence to something of which she had no understanding. *Why* should she stay inside and out of sight on such a beautiful day? Frowning, she pondered Matt's making sure the front door was locked before he left, then telling her to keep the back door locked as well. And he'd said, "I have keys. Don't open either door for anyone, under any circumstances."

Again she'd agreed without debate or objection, and now she wondered about Matt's peculiar concern and her own acceptance of it. Even though she had no basis for second-guessing her reactions to anything he might do or say, she couldn't quite see herself as being a person who meekly accepted orders.

But behind all attempts to understand herself—and her benefactor—lay something dark and sinister, and when she let it develop within her, fear overwhelmed her and she dropped the curtain and moved away from the window. There was safety within the walls of this house, and she felt in her soul that until she regained her memory she would not feel safe anywhere else.

"Nor *with* anyone else," she whispered tremulously. Matt had saved her life. Any doubt she might have once entertained on that score had vanished completely. But he'd also taken care of her since, and she felt bonded with him, connected in a way that was so precious to her troubled mind that she treasured it as her one and only possession.

She realized, however, that she was not a precious treasure to Matt. How could he think of her as anything but a burden he didn't need? And hadn't he let her know that first day that nothing about her moved him?

But haven't there been moments when you lay in his arms and sensed something from him?

Hope contemplated that question for a while and decided that what she occasionally sensed in Matt was a streak of tenderness in an otherwise tough-as-rawhide man who probably was so accustomed to hiding his personal feelings from the world that no one ever saw beneath his granite exterior.

It was odd that he lived alone in this big house. Had he never been married? Was there no one important in his life at the present? Surely he had female friends.

The storm, you dolt. He couldn't even phone a woman

*friend, let alone drive someplace and see her, and neither
could she come to the ranch.*

Feeling oddly deflated over a mental image of Matt
with another woman, Hope sank into an overstuffed chair
in the living room and put her head back. For some reason
she began thinking of herself, and how she must look to
Matt. How she would look to any man, for that matter.
Almost immediately the most awful embarrassment began
burning within her. She was wearing Matt's clothes,
which were umpteen sizes too big and cut off at the arms
and legs so she could at least use her hands and not trip
over her own feet.

On top of that her hair—although clean—was a bird's
nest, and her face was completely devoid of makeup.
Could any woman look worse? My God, she thought with
an audible groan. How could Matt stand the sight of her?
Even without a memory and decent clothes, she could still
fix her hair and add some color to her face with cosmetics.
She couldn't possibly be one of those careless women
who didn't give two hoots about her appearance.

And, doggone it, why weren't there any women's
clothes in this house? Some miscellaneous blouse or
sweater, anything at all left behind by a female guest?
There had to be. Matt McCarlson was not a monk, after
all, and he must have women visitors once in a while.

Hope bounded up from the chair. She was not going to
sit and do nothing all day, not when she had a big house
to search for feminine garb, a burning desire to fix her
hair and look nice, and a knowledge of cooking that offered no explanation but she gratefully accepted.

At least she could stay busy until Matt returned later in
the day.

The sun was so bright and the sky such a brilliant blue
that Matt wore dark glasses to protect his eyes. On a day

such as this, one could easily believe that a storm had not occurred in years. That is, one could believe if he kept his eyes heavenward and paid no mind to the flood-carried debris littering much of the ground. The creek and pond waters were receding rapidly, but the storm had caused an enormous mess.

Matt and Chuck were following the ranch's main road—the one that led to the county road—on horseback, inspecting the washed-out spots and determining just what was needed to repair it. Matt's expression was grim as worry roiled in his gut. He didn't have the money to hire heavy equipment to come in and put the road in good order, which meant he and the men would have to do it with ranch equipment. Chuck knew Matt's financial situation so he didn't even hint that someone else could do the job faster and better than cowhands using a couple of field tractors with small blades. Actually, both men knew they'd all be wielding picks and shovels, and moving a lot of dirt in wheelbarrows. In truth, it was going to be backbreaking labor to get the road in shape again, but it must be done and the quicker the better.

"Wait a sec," Matt said, and got down from the saddle. Chuck sat by and watched his boss walk to the right and pick something off a thorny bush.

Matt then returned to his horse, staring down at a ragged piece of dark fabric in his gloved hand. "What'cha got there?" Chuck asked.

"This piece of cloth was torn from the dress Hope was wearing when I found her." Frowning speculatively, Matt continued to study the fabric. "How far are we from the county road, Chuck?"

"A little less than a mile, I'd say."

"And we're at least a mile from the house." Matt raised his eyes to his foreman. "I think this proves she walked from the county road that night." He then looked

off in that direction and added in a lethally quiet voice,
"Or ran."

"You think someone was chasing her?"

"Could be," Matt said after a brief hesitation. Slipping
the scrap of cloth into his shirt pocket, he mounted his
horse. "Let's finish this job and get back to the ranch,"
he said flatly, and nudged his horse to get moving. "Have
you heard any comments among the men about Hope?"

"Not a word. They've wondered once or twice about
you doing your own cooking, though," Chuck said wryly.

"That's not surprising. I don't know, Chuck. Maybe it
would be best if I told them about her. That way, everyone
on the place could keep an eye on her, should she decide
to leave the house, even though I told her to stay inside."

"Matt, you must've phoned her family by now.
What're you worried about?"

Matt's expression became even more tense than it had
been. "I think she's in very big trouble, Chuck. She didn't
run—or even walk—way out here during a bad storm
without a serious reason. Someone was after her then, and
he just might *still* be after her."

Hope got very caught up in exploring Matt's house. It
had four bedrooms, three baths and enough space to accommodate a good-size family. She wondered about other
homes as she opened cupboards, closets and drawers in
every room. Did she have a house in Massachusetts?
Surely she'd outgrown living with her mother.

She tensed at that progression of thoughts. One would
think that she would at least remember her mother and
where she, herself, lived. Frustrated anger suddenly as-
sailed her, and she slammed a drawer shut in the laundry
room that contained nothing but some old newspapers.
Her march to the living room was rather militant. She'd
searched every nook and cranny of every room, and she'd

not found one single garment that could be construed as feminine. If Matt had female guests, they were very conscientious about not leaving anything behind.

After ten, fifteen minutes of pondering a house that was pleasant, comfortable and convenient but also very impersonal, Hope sighed and put it all out of her mind. So what if Matt lived alone and liked it? Was it any of her business if he had women guests or not? She'd have her shower, fix her hair and makeup and then once again tie Matt's clothes on herself. What choice did she have? She should be grateful that he'd given her things she could cut off to fit better. At least she didn't have to tie a blanket around herself.

Heading down the hall to the bathroom, Hope stopped suddenly. In the ceiling at the end of the hall was a rectangular door with a short rope hanging from one end of it. Was she looking at the door to an attic? Excitement broiled within her. Attics could be wonderful places, full of old things that told a family's history, should one have the ability to read the signs.

Hope's jaw dropped as she wondered how on earth she knew anything about attics. Was that instinct based on memory? Did her house have an attic? Her mother's house? Somewhere, for whatever reason, she had spent time in an attic, or maybe more than one. She knew it for a fact, which was an incredibly satisfying sensation when she knew so few facts about anything.

Well, she must see Matt's attic, she decided, she simply must. Hurrying to get something to stand on to reach the short rope, she returned with a sturdy wood chair. Situating it just so, she climbed up on it. Stretching herself, she reached for the rope and pulled. Hope's eyes gleamed when she saw that further pulling would bring down a set of stairs.

But the chair had to be moved. Keeping a solid hold

on the rope, she stepped down from the chair and then pushed it out of the way. The stairs came down quite smoothly, although some dust came down on Hope's head, as well.

She sneezed and then laughed, and the sound of her own laughter startled her, making her realize that she had not laughed once since she'd awakened in this house. Matt must think she was an awful sourpuss, she thought, and eagerly climbed the stairs to peer into the room at the top. It was a large room, but only one end of it was used—and whatever it contained was covered with white sheets!

"What have we here?" Hope said softly, and then scrambled to the top of the stairs and walked directly to the sheets, that up close she could see were also dusty. Obviously this was not a place that Matt—or anyone else—visited often enough to keep the dust from settling.

Hope gingerly lifted the edge of one of the sheets and saw a gorgeous gold-and-ivory lacquered dresser. "It's bedroom furniture," she exclaimed, startled that the best furniture in the house would be secreted in the attic. Well, she had to see it all, that was all there was to it, and she carefully removed the rest of the sheets so the dust would not transfer itself to the furniture.

There were also a number of boxes, she discovered, sturdy cardboard cartons that just begged to be opened. But how nosy dared she be?

And then it hit her. This furniture was *definitely* feminine! She narrowed her eyes thoughtfully. There might not be an important woman in Matt McCarlson's life right now, but there had been, and he'd kept every possible memento of her, including the bed she'd slept in.

"Oh, God," Hope whispered as she moved among the pieces of furniture and gently touched one here and another there. Matt's keeping these things touched Hope deeply. He must have been very much in love with the woman who had used these things, so in love, in fact that he had not been able to part with one of her possessions.

Which raised the question as to what had happened to her. Where was she now? Why had she not taken her things with her? For some reason Hope felt that a great romance had once dwelled in this house, and then it had dwindled away for the woman. Matt had still adored her, but she'd no longer loved him and so she'd left him to live out his life alone, unloved and unwanted.

"How sad," Hope whispered, feeling very emotional over the scenario she'd devised and seemed so reasonable. Poor Matt, she thought. He had loved and lost, and he really was a very nice man and didn't deserve to live alone for the rest of his days.

Still, it was completely obvious from the layer of dust on the sheets that he hadn't climbed those stairs in a very long time, so he certainly wasn't crying himself to sleep every night. "He's definitely not obsessed with the past," Hope said under her breath. "Nor with the lady who used these things. I doubt that he'd care if I took a look at what's in those boxes, and what might be in the dresser drawers and such."

An hour later, Hope was breathless with excitement. The dressers and boxes were packed full of women's clothing—fabulous things of every description and type. She would not get carried away, but surely Matt wouldn't object if she took a few of these things to wear.

Hope picked out some washable pants, blouses, a cotton jacket—also washable—and some nightgowns and a robe. There were shoes, as well, and Hope added to her pile a pair of house slippers and some black loafers that looked as though they'd never been worn. Actually, everything looked as though it had been worn very little, but Hope decided that was probably because it was such an extensive wardrobe.

Carrying her load, she cautiously descended the steep stairs, then set down the clothes to raise the stairs again. She strained and tugged and tried every way she could think of to get those stairs back in place, but nothing worked. She simply wasn't strong enough to lift that much weight, and while her own lack of strength upset her, a bigger concern was how Matt would react to seeing those stairs and knowing what a sneaky little snoop she'd been that day.

Still, that was a ridiculous worry when she'd be wearing his ladylove's clothes, she thought, disgusted over the illogical way her mind worked these days. God forbid that logic and good sense wouldn't return with her memory!

Sighing heavily, wondering if memory, logic or anything else would *ever* be hers again, Hope took the clothes from the attic to the laundry room.

"Come on in and meet her," Matt said to Chuck when they got back that afternoon.

"Yes, okay. I'd like that. Thanks," Chuck replied, and after taking care of their horses, they walked to the house and went inside.

"Matt, something really smells good in here," Chuck said in an undertone.

"Sure does," Matt agreed. "She must be cooking again."

They walked into the kitchen, and there was Hope, dressed in pale yellow cotton slacks and a yellow-and-white striped blouse. Her hair was curled around her face, and she was wearing makeup. She was, without a doubt, the prettiest woman Matt had ever seen, and from the way Chuck was nervously rocking back and forth from one foot to the other, he was thinking the same thing.

The second that Hope saw Chuck, her pulse went wild.

Cringing back against a counter, she held on to it for dear life.

"Hope LeClaire, meet Chuck Crawford, ranch foreman," Matt said clearly, although he'd registered Hope's instantaneous fear in the pit of his stomach and was sorry he'd brought Chuck in with him.

Chuck took off his hat and smiled warmly. He, too, had registered Hope's reaction to seeing a stranger walking in with Matt, and it bothered him to be the cause of any discomfort for this beautiful, frightened lady.

"Nice to meet you, ma'am," he said to her.

"Th-thank you," she whispered hoarsely.

"Hope, Chuck's as trustworthy as the tide," Matt said. "There's not a reason in the world to fear him." He decided to get away from that topic entirely and he changed the subject. "What're you cooking? It smells incredible."

"It does, ma'am," Chuck echoed.

"Uh, you're probably smelling the meat…a cut of pork and one of beef, roasting together in the oven."

Matt went over to the stove. "And what's in these pans?"

"Potatoes in one, steaming vegetables in the other," Hope said.

Looking at her again, Matt knitted his brow. The pants and blouse she was wearing were vaguely familiar. Not that there was anything unique in their style or color, but where on earth had she gotten them? A chill raced up his spine when he answered his own question. There was only one place she could have gotten those things. Anger rose within him and he glanced at Chuck. If he wasn't here, he'd lambaste the hell out of Hope for daring to even go near the attic.

Or would he? Good Lord, what difference did it make if Hope or the entire population of Texas wanted to traipse through his attic? Matt's anger disappeared as quickly as it had developed, and he said to Hope, "Is it all right if Chuck eats dinner with us?"

Hope gulped. "Uh, yes, of course," she stammered.

But Chuck had his own ideas about where he should be eating his evening meal, and it sure wasn't in this kitchen with a woman who was unquestionably scared to death of him, and with Matt, who wasn't even close to his normal self in her presence.

"Thanks, but I'm going to eat with the men so I can talk to them about the road repairs." He smiled at Hope. "Good night, ma'am." To Matt he said, "See you in the morning." Settling his hat on his head, Chuck left the house.

"I'm going to take a shower," Matt said gruffly, and walked out of the kitchen with a distant, sour expression on his face that shook Hope so badly she didn't even know if she should finish making dinner.

Plopping on a chair, she fretted and worried and didn't care in the least that she finally looked nice. After all, it was pretty damned obvious that Matt hadn't noticed.

Matt had pushed the stairs to the attic back in place and felt another strong urge to put Hope LeClaire in her place. She could have asked how he felt about her exploring his house before doing it, after all. Amnesia or not, she was apparently a spoiled-rotten woman who did any damned thing she pleased. She'd seen the rope, which had resulted in a discovery of the attic, and she probably hadn't hesitated for even a moment to invade his privacy. If nothing else, it was damned rude and presumptuous of her.

Not that he cared about the clothes she'd obviously helped herself to. Hell's bells, he'd truly forgotten they were up there with that fancy bedroom furniture of

Trisha's or he'd have given the whole darned wardrobe to Hope.

He returned to the kitchen thirty minutes later, freshly showered and shaved and wearing clean clothes—comfortable-looking old jeans, a red flannel shirt and a pair of sheepskin-lined house slippers without socks. His head of thick, chestnut hair was appealingly damp and disarrayed, as though all he'd done after his shampoo was run his fingers through it.

"Sit down," Hope told him. "It'll take only a minute to dish up."

"How about *you* sitting down and letting me dish up?" Matt stared into her eyes and dared her to disagree. He wasn't at all sure she should be doing so much cooking, or even if she should be on her feet all day long.

Hope swallowed nervously. He was royally ticked with her, and she was pretty sure that she knew why, too. She never should've so much as touched anything under those sheets. For that matter, she should not have snooped throughout his entire house and touched anything of his.

But her wearing the clothes she had on was really the definitive and most unforgivable sin of the many she'd committed that day. The yellow pants and striped blouse belonged to the woman he was probably still in love with, and seeing them on her—a stranger in his house, a troublesome, mindless burden that no man deserved to have descend upon him—undoubtedly turned his stomach.

"Fine," she said in a near whisper and sat at the table. She was sure he'd be all thumbs with the pans and serving dishes, but he dished up the food as efficiently as she could have. Then he took his chair, picked up the bowl of mashed potatoes and held them across the table to her with an unreadable look that sent icy fingers up her spine, even if she *couldn't* decipher it accurately.

"Thank you," she murmured and took a small helping.

And that was how the entire meal went with the two of them passing dishes and saying thank you and otherwise ignoring the existence of the other. Throughout, Hope could feel the tension mounting in her system. She could barely get a bite down her throat, and she finally decided that she would rather have him yell at her than to maintain this abominable silence. She could almost hear him telling her to stay out of his attic, to get herself out of his ladylove's clothes and to ask permission to use anything of his before taking it upon herself to step on his toes again, as she'd done today. In all fairness, she deserved every nasty remark he might think up.

When she could bear the tension no longer she said, "Would an apology help?"

Matt put down his fork. "You're a remarkable cook. Dinner was incredible and I enjoyed it, but let's get brutally honest here, okay? I've never thought apologies were much more than the means for certain self-centered types to have things their way." He gestured with a wave of his hand and said coolly, "They do what they want, apologize for it later, after they've had their fun or satisfied their curiosity, or whatever it was that struck their fancy, regardless of anyone else's rights or feelings." His expression became hard. "An apology is just words, Hope, just a few little words."

She stiffened. "Am I understanding you correctly? Are you refusing to let me apologize?"

"Why don't you tell me what you think it would accomplish?"

She was suddenly furious, and she got up and began carrying dishes from the table to the sink. "Forget the whole miserable subject," she snapped. "Obviously I gave you a lot more credit than you deserve, Mr. Mc-Carlson, but that's just fine. It's one mistake I won't make again.'' Back and forth she marched, and her final trip was to the table, which she wiped off with a damp cloth.

"Maybe not, but you'll make others. We all do. Take those nightmares, for instance.''

Hope threw the dishcloth on top of the dirty dishes in the sink and then shrieked, "Do you think I keep having nightmares because I enjoy being scared out of my wits?''

"You didn't let me finish.'' Matt slowly got to his feet and then towered over her. He dropped his gaze to look into her eyes. "You can't help having the nightmares, I know that. But yelling for me to come and comfort you every night is something you should try real hard to avoid.''

"That's the mistake you think I'm going to keep on making? Think again!'' After a frowning pause she added, "But I'm not sure I exactly get what you mean. Why is my calling out in the night such a terrible mistake to you?''

"Don't you know? Don't you *really* know?'' Matt took two steps toward her, putting himself mere inches from her. His voice softened considerably. "Don't you know what you're doing to me night after night with your soft, warm skin and womanly scent?''

Hope's jaw dropped. "Are you serious?'' she croaked.

"I'll never be serious about a woman again, which is why so much togetherness for you and I is a mistake. Do you get it now? Did I speak clearly enough, or would you like me to explain the facts of life in anatomical detail?''

"Why are you talking to me like this?'' She backed up a step and felt the edge of the table against the backs of her thighs.

He took another forward step, laid his hands on her shoulders, then dipped his head and placed his lips but a breath from hers. "Maybe a demonstration will be more effective than further explanation,'' he whispered, and covered her mouth with his. He felt her gasp at just about the same moment his heart started pounding unmercifully hard.

When is a kiss not just a kiss?

When it brings you to your knees, you moron. Now you've started something, haven't you?

Common sense be damned, he thought next. He was not going to push away a woman who was making sensuous little moaning noises deep in her throat and kissing him back as though she wanted to devour him.

Well, he wanted to devour her in the same passionate way, and he laid her back over the table and then followed her down. Her legs were apart and he nestled himself between them, creating a perfect fit, body to body, man to woman, and he kissed her mouth again and again, until they were both gasping for air.

Caressing her hair back from her feverish face, he stopped kissing her to look into her eyes. "Are we going for the next step?" he asked in a husky, ragged voice.

"Is it…entirely my decision?"

"Damned right it is. If you make it mine, I'll take you right here on this table."

She licked her lips. Her chest was heaving, and the racking desire in so many places of her body—strongest and most demanding between her legs—pleaded with her to leave *everything* to him. *Make it his decision. Be brave. Don't think about anything but the almost painful aches you're feeling and the knowledge that he can soothe them away with sublime pleasure.*

"Uh, exactly what is the next step?" she whispered.

He pulled the hem of her blouse from her pants and slid his hand up to her breast and under her bra. She saw him close his eyes when he cupped her naked breast, and then saw the raw pleasure on his handsome face when he toyed with her nipple and whispered, "Perfect…perfect."

She could not deny him this; she could not deny herself what she was feeling. "It's your decision," she whispered huskily. "I give it to you...freely...eagerly. I want what you want. I'm on fire, and I—I don't believe I've ever felt like this before."

Matt looked into her eyes again. "You have, baby, you just don't remember it."

"Probably," she whispered, and then closed her eyes so she could savor every delicious step of this incredible event to the fullest.

Matt studied her face for a few moments then put the few niggling doubts she'd just raised in him aside. She was not a kid, for crying out loud. Of course she'd made love before.

Chapter Eight

Matt possessed an almost forgotten hunger. He couldn't seem to kiss or touch Hope enough. Her scent addled his brain, and his thoughts—those that managed to develop at all—were focused strictly on making love. With trembling hands he began undressing her, and it was especially gratifying—and incredibly arousing—to feel her trying to rid him of his clothes, as well.

It came to him abruptly that the kitchen table really wasn't the best place for this very special event. He didn't just want a quickie, after all, he wanted it all, the kisses and foreplay that would drive them both wild.

Hope found herself being lifted off the table and up into his arms. "Wha—what're you doing?"

He strode from the kitchen and headed down the hall. "Taking you to bed," he said in a completely masculine voice, and he slowed his steps just enough to kiss her lips while he walked.

"Oh, Matt…Matt," she said thickly, and pressed her face into the curve of his neck.

He entered his own bedroom and let her feet slide to the floor. But immediately he put his arms around her, kissed her passionately and lifted her again so their mouths were on the same level. His pulse went crazy when she wound her legs around his waist and her arms around his neck. It was an extremely intimate thing for her to have done, and he knew that even though she couldn't recall her past love life, she was a woman who liked, maybe loved, sex, and she also knew what a man liked. That, too, was a gratifying realization for Matt. If a man was going to fall off the wagon with a woman, far better that she be an experienced adult about the affair.

And, as he'd already told her, he would never be serious about a woman again. All this could ever be—as hot as it was between them—was an affair.

"Let's get rid of these clothes," he mumbled raggedly. She nodded, whispered, "Yes."

Undressing her brought back the memory of the first time he'd removed her clothes. Even then, though she'd been muddy, wet and bedraggled, he'd registered the perfection of her body. Any man would've, he told himself, and he was convinced it was true.

But he also recalled that his admiration had bothered him later on. This time he would suffer no guilty feelings over admiring a beautiful female body. Hope wasn't merely going along with this, after all, she was eager, glassy-eyed and breathless with anticipation. Plus, she was anxiously tearing at his clothes, just as he was doing with hers.

In seconds their clothes were on the floor, and they stood there, naked and unashamed, looking at each other. Matt reached out his hand and slid his fingertips down from her shoulder to the rosy peak of one of her breasts.

"You're very beautiful," he said in a choked, husky voice.

An objection to that obviously untrue flattery flashed into her mind, but she let it rush on through and said instead, "You're the one who's beautiful, Matt." She laid her hand on his chest, and when she raised her eyes to his again, he saw a mist of tears in them. "Kiss me," she whispered.

The shackles of self-control were becoming very weak for Matt, and he growled deep in his throat, took her into an almost smothering embrace and brought them both down to the bed. His kisses covered her face, throat and breasts; hers fell willy-nilly on whatever part of him she could reach and still stay under him. She liked being under him, feeling every manly inch of his hard body against hers. Without even a hint from him that it was time she did so, she inched her legs apart, and he instantly began rubbing his hot, throbbing member against her most sensitive spot.

The shooting pleasure she felt from that particular delight was stunning, overwhelming, and it was becoming more difficult by the second to get enough air in her lungs. But that kind of pleasure, she quickly discovered, was also a demanding pleasure, because it wasn't quite enough to satisfy the yearning in her belly.

She rocked her head back and forth on the pillow and moaned. "Matt—I need—I need—"

The degree of her desire was a joy for Matt. It was quite possible that he'd never been with a more passionate lady, and it was also possible that tonight was going to be the sexual highlight of his life. Yes, he might have stumbled over his own oath to never again become involved with a wealthy woman, but he fully intended to enjoy tonight's sin, no matter how painful tomorrow's remorse might be. And who knew? Maybe he wouldn't have to suffer any remorse at all. From Hope's fervent response to his initial advance, and considering how fast things moved after that, she must be a woman who took her fun wherever she found it. Probably one night of steamy sex was all she wanted, too. Then they'd both be physically sated and probably never touch each other again. After all, she wasn't going to be here very much longer.

Without further ado, he positioned himself for the final thrill. Kissing her with his heart full of affection for the giver of such boundless delights as he was experiencing with her, and with his body almost to the bursting point, he slid into her.

Or rather, he *tried* to slide into her. So startled over his discovery that he could barely think straight, he raised his head and looked at her. Her eyes were closed and her face bore an unmistakably aroused expression. He swallowed hard, kept staring at her and finally her eyelids fluttered open and she stared back.

"Uh, is something wrong?" She wasn't positive of the actual mechanics of the act of lovemaking, but surely it didn't include long, idle lapses.

Matt honestly didn't know how to handle this. She was a virgin? Was that even possible? Well, there was nothing for him to do but to spit it out.

"You've never done this before," he said flatly.

Shock widened her eyes. "What do you mean by that?"

"I meant that you've never made love before."

"How would you know that?" she scoffed though her heart was beating fearfully fast. How *would* he know?

"Hope, this is making me feel pretty damned foolish. Don't you remember anything about your own body?"

"Like what?'

"Like the barrier that every female is born with, that's what!"

"Barrier?" she echoed weakly. "Where—where is this so-called barrier?"

"Use your imagination." He tried to move off her, but she became panicky and clung to him with all her might. "Hope, don't you realize the significance of what I just told you? Dammit, you're a virgin!"

She started crying, silently but with huge tears dripping from her eyes. "If you don't finish what you started, I'll die. I will, Matt, I know it. Why would I want to remain a virgin, for pity's sake? You kissed me, and touched me, and I felt something that I will never, ever forget. For heaven's sake, don't leave me in this incomplete state."

"You don't know what you're asking me to do," he muttered darkly. There was a terrible anger in the pit of his stomach, because he wanted her so much he hurt, and she was making it almost impossible for him to be honorable about something so unexpected that he was trembling internally over it. Nothing about her had ever suggested virginity. Not her looks, not her demeanor, certainly not the way she'd snuggled in his arms after her nightmares. As for tonight, she'd been as wanton and lustful as the most experienced temptress.

She was *still* lustful! He could see it in her eyes, and feel it in the way she kept rubbing her body against his.

He could bear no more. She was right. Why would she want to remain a virgin?

"You win," he said gruffly, and lowered his head to take her mouth in a devouring kiss. She moaned in thrilled delight and lifted her arms to encircle his neck. Then, without any warning so that she wouldn't tense up, he gave one mighty push and thrust his manhood deep inside her.

She tore her mouth from his and cried out. "You didn't say it was going to hurt!"

"It won't hurt for long. Just relax, let me do the work, and I guarantee you'll enjoy it."

Twenty minutes later she cried out again, but this time it was from a most glorious feeling that engulfed her completely, then seemed to carry her far, far away from earthly concerns, where she floated on a soft pink cloud that gradually delivered her back to reality. Matt had moved onto the bed next to her, and when she opened her eyes, she saw that his were closed.

She breathed a small sigh, then could not prevent herself from stretching like a contented cat. Looking at Matt again, she wondered if he was really sleeping. He did appear to be, she thought, but there were a lot of things she would have liked to talk to him about. One question in particular would have to be asked sooner or later. Did all women feel what she had at the peak of lovemaking? Was it normal and right and decent for her to have felt so much? Goodness, she had nearly passed out from the explosive pleasure that had swept her away.

Another question seemed to be most urgent. Could they do it again? Hope frowned then. Was her amnesia especially overpowering, or was it the norm for people with her condition to forget even the most basic facts of life? Not knowing that she'd been a virgin, or even what constituted virginity, was really very embarrassing. Not that Matt would ever fault her for it. He was so very special, wasn't he? Hope's frown changed to a smile over that thought.

Matt was only pretending to be asleep. He could hardly believe what he'd just done. She'd been a virgin, for hell's sake, a virgin! And he'd taken advantage of her ignorance of sex and her own body. He would never forgive himself and if he knew of a way to get her the hell out of his bed without having to face and actually talk to her, he'd do it in a New York minute.

Instead, cowardly jerk that he felt himself to be over this fiasco, he feigned sleep and hoped she would decide to leave his room and sleep in her own.

She didn't. She sat up to switch off the lamp, then lay on her side with her back to him, pulled up the blankets to cover them both and went to sleep.

It was hours before Matt finally drifted off, hours of self-reproach. Actually, *reproach* was too mild a word for what he put himself through. He was the lowest form of life—a lecherous man who had preyed on an innocent woman.

God help him, if he didn't get Hope safe in the bosom of her family very soon, he was going to go so far off the deep end he would never be the same.

Hope stirred sleepily. The room was black as pitch and Matt had wound himself around her backside and was exploring her front side with a slow, deliberate and extremely sensual hand. She smiled as he caressed her breasts. Not for just a second or two, but for long, deliciously tantalizing minutes. Her nipples were hard and erect, so sensitized to his touch that thrill after thrill raced from whichever one he was concentrating on to her central core, which she had only learned tonight lay somewhere between the pit of her stomach and that warm, secret spot between her legs.

It was so marvelous to be touched and gently rubbed the way he was doing that she wanted to do the same to him. But he was pressed tightly against her, and his manhood was huge and hard at the back of her thigh and she could not reach around herself to caress him. She could always turn over, of course, but would that break the almost magical spell of Matt's very romantic attentions?

His hand began dropping, very slowly making little circles on her tummy, rising again to her breasts and then going lower again. Hope's heart hammered and her mouth got dry. Her body was expectant again, on the edge, full of achy wants and desires. Was Matt an especially sexual man? she wondered. *Oh, he must be. To make you feel like this so easily, he must be very potent and knowledgeable. I wish I knew everything he does about making love.*

I wish I knew everything about myself. She heaved a sigh and berated herself for feeling sorry for herself at a time like this. *For heaven's sake, do what Matt told you to do, relax and enjoy it.*

Which she did, and when his hand slipped between her thighs, she willingly opened her legs so he could reach that part of her that seemed to be in flames.

He whispered in her ear then. "You're hot and wet."

Her heart skipped a beat, for it was the first thing he'd said since awakening her with his extremely intimate caress.

"Should I be?" she whispered back.

"Definitely." His forefinger found and gently stroked the small bud that held the key to her desire. "Do you like that?"

She nearly choked. "Yes...yes."

"Then I won't stop doing it."

"Good...please don't."

He turned her slightly so that her legs were spread farther apart and she was almost lying on top of him, then he entered her from behind and began moving in and out while he continued playing as before. She panted and gasped and moaned and whimpered. And finally she was able to croak out a few words. "I—I wondered if we could do this again."

"Again and again and again, as often as we want." *You dog, how can you do this to her?*

"Really? As often as we want?"

"With a little rest in between, that is." He was starting to move faster, and his voice was losing strength, becoming hoarse and gravelly. "Are you going to hate me for this when you regain your memory?"

"Don't talk," she gasped. "We'll talk...later."

He suddenly reared up, laid her on her back and thrust into her from the front again. He was so aroused and driven that he pounded, almost roughly, into her until she cried out with a powerful climax. Seconds later, he reached the same incredible plateau, then he collapsed on her and laid his head on the pillow next to hers.

Her breathing finally slowed, and she could hear Matt's returning to normal, as well. "Would you like to talk now?" she asked softly.

He rolled away from her, so disgusted with himself that he wanted her to hate him. "You do know what this is, don't you?" he said coldly.

"I don't think I understand." Where was the warmth she'd heard in his voice only minutes ago?

"Well, let me clarify it. You're in my house, a damned beautiful, sexy woman and probably the most willing I've ever run into. What we're doing tonight is what respectable people call an affair. Then there are those who call it a one-night stand, a roll in the hay, or a poke in the whiskers. Are you following what I'm saying?"

"But—but—" She was so shocked she couldn't speak. Then from nowhere came a coherent thought, one that made sense to her confused brain. "Are you saying you don't love me?"

"Good Lord, where'd you get the idea that I did?"

"Does—doesn't love and lovemaking go together?"

"Hell, no!"

She was completely befuddled. Why was there an inner voice insisting that love and lovemaking *did* go together?

And why was Matt being so mean now when he'd been so sweet and loving before?

Her blood turned to ice then. *Because you're the most willing woman he's ever run into, and he wanted a piece of the action. Wasn't that what he said? That you're beautiful and sexy and willing? Is this the way all men behave? No wonder I was a virgin!*

Without turning on the lamp, she jumped out of bed and ran from the room. Startled, Matt sat up and nearly called her name. Now he felt like a dog for hurting her feelings with pure hogwash, just to appease his own conscience.

Besides, it hadn't worked. His conscience wasn't even close to being appeased, and he doubted that he'd get another wink of sleep tonight. Damn, was he never going to learn that falling for the wrong woman only brought a man misery?

Hope moped around the house the next morning. Matt had left early—she'd heard him get up and go, but she was never going to speak a civil word to him again, even if she was stuck on his horrible ranch for the rest of her life.

And neither was she going to stay inside his horrible house, just because he'd told her to! The sun was shining, it was a warm, lovely day and she was going for a walk! To hell with what he might think about it, and he'd better not start preaching to her about it when he got home again, either, because she was in no mood to hear any more of his offensive remarks, the jerk.

Why, oh why had she succumbed to physical persuasion and let him...? She cringed every time she thought of the things she'd let him do to her, and worse, the things she'd done to him without him even asking. It was as though she'd known what to do instinctively, for as sure as the Texas sky was blue, Matt had liked every move she'd made.

"You're a terrible person," she said out loud to herself. "No wonder no one gives a damn about you."

But that probably wasn't a hundred percent true. What about her mother? Madelyn LeClaire must care about her or Madelyn's name would not be on that In Case of Emergency card in her wallet.

Hope knew she should use that telephone number and phone her mother, but she couldn't force herself to even consider it seriously. Regardless of Matt's ruthless seduction, he was still the only person she really knew and trusted. Not that she should trust him after last night, but she did. It wasn't something she could talk herself out of, either.

She left the house for the fist time, and the first thing she did was lift her face to the sun and inhale the clean, fresh air. There were still some puddles here and there, but the earth was drying rapidly, and it was easy enough to skirt the muddy areas. She started walking and noticed three men near a corral gawking at her. *Haven't they ever seen a woman before? I certainly doubt that, considering their boss's sexual appetite.* Smiling sweetly, she waved at them and called a hello. The trio then took off so fast they were tripping over each other's feet.

Hope laughed and continued her walk. It occurred to her that it was possible that those cowboys hadn't known of her presence on the ranch, and seeing her had really been a surprise they hadn't expected. There didn't seem to be any reason to her for Matt to keep a secret, but God only knew what went through his mind when he wasn't looking for "willing" women.

That description still smarted, and Hope vowed again to never forgive him. She had really come full circle on the subject of Matt McCarlson, she realized, because at

first she'd been positive he'd barely noticed she was female and now she was positive it was all he *had* noticed
about her. And to think he'd undressed and bathed her
while she was unconscious!

In the big horse barn, Matt looked up when three of his
men came roaring in, all of them talking at the same time.
He caught the gist of their gibberish and shook his head
in disgust that Hope was so furious with him that she
would deliberately badger him by leaving the house.

"Okay, so now you know," he told the men. "I have
a lady staying with me, which is the reason I've been
eating at the house. That's all I've got to say about it, but
the three of you feel free to spread the news to the other
men and to speculate and gossip to your heart's content."

"Aw, heck, Matt, we ain't gonna do any gossiping,"
one of them said with a teasing snicker.

"Yeah, right," Matt drawled. "Does Chuck have you
guys working on the road?"

"Yeah, he sent us back to make some sandwiches and
haul 'em back to the crew."

"And it takes three of you to make sandwiches?"

"Heck, no, Matt. Joe's gonna make the sandwiches
while Farley and I get another load of gravel. We got
Chuck's pickup."

"Okay, fine. Talk to you later." As soon as the men
had left him alone, Matt strode to the door of the barn
and had no trouble at all in spotting Hope, walking along
as though she didn't have a care in the world. "You little
fool," he mumbled, then realized that his groin was once
again aching for that "little fool."

"Aw, hell," he groaned. He'd never have another moment's peace until she was off his ranch and out of his
sight. Why in hell hadn't he left well enough alone last
night? He hadn't had to kiss her in the kitchen, or push
her down on the table, or lose every drop of self-control

just because she'd kissed him back like the hottest little number in all of Texas.

Life and its nasty little traps were really starting to get him down, he thought wearily. Turning his head, he watched Chuck's pickup heading for the small gravel pit that he was fortunate to have on his own land, because he sure as hell couldn't afford to buy any gravel or anything else for those road repairs. And until the roads were usable, he was stuck with Hope.

That wasn't entirely true, of course. He could load her into a four-wheeler, cut across fields, ford creeks, puddles and small rivers, and drop her off on Doc's doorstep or at the sheriff's office. Either of them would see that she was turned over to the Stockwells, which was exactly where she belonged.

But could he force himself to do that to her? She didn't even have the grit to phone her own mother, just because she couldn't remember Madelyn LeClaire for herself.

"What a damned mess," Matt muttered. And now he had to catch up with Hope and talk her into returning to the house without giving away his own fears for her safety.

Well, might as well get to it, he thought and started walking. He was a few steps behind Hope when she heard him. Spinning around, she glared at him.

"Before you say one single word to me, I am not going back to the house," she snapped.

"So, don't. Why would I care?"

Hope blinked in confusion. "You told me before—"

"Only because of the slipperiness of the ground." Matt made a big deal of glancing around. "Seems dry enough now that you shouldn't slip and take another fall, as you apparently did the night before I found you unconscious."

She almost fell for that, until she remembered something. "Which is an excellent reason for keeping the doors locked and not letting anyone come in when you're gone," she said with searing sarcasm. "What do you think I am, a moron? And if you say yes just because I temporarily lost my memory I swear that I'll brain you!"

"Hell, you don't need to go into volcanic eruption mode." Matt stared off into the distance for a moment, then took off his sunglasses and looked into her eyes. "I have the feeling that anything I said to you today would cause the same reaction. You left my room in a huff last night, and you're still ticked." He drew a breath. "You have a right to be. I never should have touched you."

"You did a hell of a lot more than touch me, sport."

"I know I did, and I'm trying to apologize for it."

"I thought you didn't believe in apologies."

"There are exceptions to every rule."

"Only because people like you make them up as you go along. And let me add this. You're hiding something from me, and don't insult my intelligence by continuing whatever charade it is you're playing. Why order me to stay in the house with the doors locked one day and then lie about your reasons the next? For God's sake, if you know something you haven't told me, please spit it out!"

"All right! I'm concerned that the nightmares you've been having are about a real person."

Hope narrowed her eyes. "And...?"

"Maybe you ran here to get away from him, and maybe he's watching and waiting for another chance to...to, uh, hurt you."

A chill went up Hope's spine, and she took a quick, suddenly nervous, look around. "Watching from where?"

"Hope, with strong binoculars he could be a mile away. Up on that forested hill to the left, for one example."

"What?" She spun around to see the hill, which was covered with trees and brush that could conceal a small army of terrorists. Was there someone up there right now, peering at her through powerful binoculars? Strangely, instead of fear she felt anger, and it was an angry face that she turned back to Matt. "If you really believe that, shouldn't you be calling the police?"

Despite her anger, she was still not ready to take responsibility for herself, Matt realized. She was all bluff and bluster.

"I have called the police," he said quietly. "I've talked to Sheriff Cliff Braeburn."

Hope sucked in a startled breath. "And what's he going to do, come out here and get me?"

"Would you like him to?"

"No!" Whirling, Hope started running toward the house. Matt took off after her, and they both reached the door at about the same time.

Inside, he saw the panic on her face, the near hysteria, and he put his arms around her and held her tightly, until the trembling in her body subsided.

Then, leaning his head back slightly so he could see her face, he said softly, "You don't have to go anywhere until you are ready to leave here."

The tears swimming in her eyes blurred her vision, but she looked into his eyes and still managed to see kindness. What had last night been all about? she sadly asked herself. He'd been crude and cruel after making love to her, and why had he done that when his natural tendency was kindness?

"I don't understand everything that's happening," she said huskily.

"I know you don't, but let's keep you as safe as possible until things get straightened out and the dust settles, okay?"

"Okay," she whispered, and laid her head on his chest.

Matt caressed her hair and felt her wrap her arms around his waist and snuggle closer to him. A feeling of resignation weakened his resolve to never again lay a personal hand on her. She smelled so good and felt so perfect against him, and he was only human, after all.

He kissed the top of her head and whispered, "You're making me want you again."

She knew that and more. She was also making herself want him again, and she'd vowed to be cold and acerbic with him. Had she no willpower whatsoever? Apparently she was not a promiscuous woman—not when she'd been a virgin until last night—but Matt did something to her that she couldn't seem to control. Hadn't she met any men with that provocative charm before?

Still, however feverish Matt made her feel, she couldn't quite forget the things he'd said last night. Without preamble, she disengaged herself from him and crossed the room to put plenty of space between them.

"There will be no more one-night stands between us," she said quietly but firmly.

Matt felt stabbed, but he'd brought this on himself and he couldn't start telling her now that an affair wasn't an affair, or that he'd been really stupid in labeling their truly glorious lovemaking as a one-night stand.

He cleared his throat and also tried to clear away the sexual energy vibrating through his body with a few nonchalant gestures—lifting his hat and resettling it on his head, and putting on the sunglasses that he'd stuck in his shirt pocket outside.

"I'll be getting back to work now," he said with what he hoped was a semblance of dignity. All she did was nod, and he left the house cursing himself, her situation, his situation, his behavior last night and just about everything else that wasn't right in his world.

The toughest nut to swallow was that he didn't know how to *make* things right.

Chapter Nine

Hope listlessly wandered the house after Matt left. Was what he'd told her true? Was some nut watching and waiting for an opportunity to get to her? Were her nightmares more real than not? Some awful event had brought her to this isolated ranch in the middle of a stormy night, of that she had no doubt.

But neither did she have any memories of that night—unless they were taking the form of terrifying dreams. If only she could put a face on the man that haunted those dreams, or would even that clarify what had caused pure disaster to nearly kill her? If the man was a stranger, for instance, if she hadn't met him prior to that night, would recalling his face do her any good?

Of course, she hadn't really been that close to death. Matt had rushed to the rescue, or something like that. All she'd lost was her memory, after all, not her life. *Bet he wishes he'd never gone riding that morning.*

It was a mean, small-minded thought. He'd done everything a man could do for a damsel in distress, hadn't he?

Yes, and then he seduced you! You, a virgin. Is that the act of an honorable man?

And you loved every minute of it. You'd like it to happen again, and you know it.

Oh, shut up!

With a grim set to her lips, Hope went to the kitchen and began checking the grocery supply. She no longer doubted her ability to turn out a delicious meal from simple ingredients. What's more she was beginning to know what ingredients would have added greatly to the rather mundane dishes—though tasty—that her limited larder permitted. Fresh greens, for instance. Specialty vinegars and oils. Almost any kind of seafood or fish. And milk and cream and wine and...

She stopped short, thinking that she'd seen some bottles of wine when she'd searched the house for women's clothing. But where?

She started going through cupboards once again, and on the bottom shelf of the dining room hutch she found three bottles of wine. They were sealed and corked and dusty. If Matt was a wine drinker then he'd forgotten about this supply, Hope thought as she carried the bottles to the kitchen. Reading the labels told her brand names and the type of wine—two were white, one was red—in each bottle. None of the information meant a whole lot to her, and sighing over how little she really knew about anything—other than cooking, which seemed to be a natural-born talent—she located a corkscrew and opened a bottle of the white wine. Pouring an ounce or so in a glass, she tasted it, smacked her lips and took another swallow. She had no idea if this was a good vintage, but it sure did taste as though it was. Finishing what was in the glass, she poured some more and drank that, too.

Humming then, she took a chicken from the freezer, removed its wrapper and placed it in cold water for a quick thaw. She was going to make coq au vin, and she had to laugh because she had no knowledge of the meaning of the term and yet knew exactly how to prepare the dish.

"And how about some dessert tonight?" she murmured. After a few minutes of contemplation she took out the ingredients to make vanilla-flavored custard, making substitutions where she had to. Then, extremely pleased with her planned menu for tonight's meal she poured more wine into her glass. Sipping as she worked it was quite a surprise to her that when it came time to cook the chicken in the wine there wasn't a whole lot left in the bottle. She opened the second bottle of white and poured it in the pot with the chicken.

Then she eyed the bottle of red wine and decided that she really should taste it, too. Giggling over nothing at all, she got out the corkscrew again.

By late afternoon all the wine was gone and Hope was seeing everything through a most delightful rosy-hued haze. Staggering to the stove, she turned off the burner under the coq au vin, took the custard from the oven and turned that off, as well, then wondered just when Matt would be coming in for the day.

Thinking of Matt and last night's escapades made her feel warm and tingly all over. He was quite the man, wasn't he? After all, he'd accomplished what no other man she'd ever known had done. Not that she could remember any others, but good grief, it was only reasonable to presume that she'd known lots of men in her previous life. Obviously none of them had moved her the way Matt did, or she would not have still been a virgin.

She recalled then how Mat had held her that morning and told her that she was making him want her again. "One-night stand, my left foot," she scoffed. He would have followed her to the bedroom in the blink of an eye, if she'd been inclined to do any blinking.

"But I would like to do some blinking," she said with another tipsy giggle. "A whole *lot* of blinking. There must be a way to let him know it without coming right out and saying it. I really couldn't just blurt out, 'Matt, I'd just love to blink you again.'"

Her own wit struck her as so hilarious that she fell on a chair and laughed until she cried. Wiping her eyes some minutes later, she thought of how good it felt to laugh over something silly.

But there was nothing silly about the heat building in all the erotic places of her body that Matt had so easily brought to life, and she remained on the kitchen chair and fantasized ways to get Matt to repeat last night's adventures—minus the nasty remarks afterward, of course.

A most delightful fantasy took shape in her mind, and she knew that she was just tipsy enough to go through with it. Laughing again, this time low and seductively, she got up and hurried away to take a shower. Her plan would work only if everything was ready when Matt came in for the day. She had no time to waste.

"Chuck, would you like to come in and say hello to Hope?" Their day of hard work was over and they were talking in the yard, not far from the house.

Chuck considered the invitation. "I don't know if I should, Matt. She's scared of me."

"She's scared of everything, and it's understandable. But I'm positive she'd like you if you gave her the chance to know you better."

"Yeah, probably," Chuck admitted. "But not tonight, okay? I'm pretty beat. You must be done in, too. Damn, that road work is sure a lot harder than herding cattle around, or even cutting hay and I ain't never been particularly fond of haying time."

Matt grinned. "Okay, go on to the bunkhouse and put your feet up. See you in the morning." They started to walk away from each other when Matt called, "Chuck, the men are bound to have some fun over a woman staying with me, now that they've seen Hope. Just let 'em think or say anything they want to, okay?"

"If you say so. Good night, Matt."

Matt was one step into the kitchen and sniffing the delicious aroma in the air when he saw some fabric on the floor. He picked it up and frowned curiously. It was the blouse Hope had been wearing that morning. Odd that she'd thrown it on the floor, but maybe she'd merely dropped it on her way to the laundry room.

Carrying the blouse, he peered into the laundry room, saw nothing unusual then left that area of the house to go down the hall to his bedroom. He stopped in his tracks. There on the floor right in front of his boots was another piece of clothing—a pair of slacks. He looked ahead and saw two more things on the floor, only they were much smaller piles and a pretty peach color.

"What in hell?" he muttered, recognizing Hope's underwear. It was as though she'd raced from the kitchen to his bedroom, throwing off her clothes as she ran. Why in hell would she have done that?

In the next heartbeat he knew why, and his body responded so quickly to an image of her naked in his bed that he nearly choked on his own breath. Good Lord, what if Chuck had taken him up on his invitation and come in with him?

And what was going on in Hope's mind? After what he'd told her last night about how dead set he was against a serious relationship, did she really want to continue what he'd made plain enough could only be an affair between them? Not that he wouldn't cooperate to some extent. Hell's bells, he was hard just thinking about making love to her again. But did *she* think she could change his attitude with sex?

"It's not going to happen, Hope," he said softly, and went on to the door of his bedroom, picking up her personal garments on his way.

And there she was, in a striking, provocative pose of bare legs and arms, with the corner of a sheet just barely covering her torso and her hair tousled and arranged in an intriguing manner on the pillow under her head. Her eyes were closed, as though she were sound asleep and totally unaware of how seductive she looked.

"You little fake," Matt said under his breath, and walking into the room he tossed her clothes on the end of the bed. He stared at her, positive that she would at least peek at him from partially opened eyes and maybe even laugh a little. After all, she'd devised this sexy scenario and must see some humor in it.

But she never moved. Neither did he, except for the deeply furrowed frown that gradually formed on his forehead. She *was* sleeping! On his bed, stark naked and in a pose that would make any man hot.

Matt was suddenly angry. What was this cat-and-mouse game that neither of them seemed to be able to elude? Not that he could speak for Hope—hell, how could she disconnect adult games from meaningful feeling when she had nothing to go on but the present? But he couldn't say that about himself, or make excuses for his behavior when he knew the score. Obviously he was thinking with something other than his brain. No matter how frequently or seriously he told himself to stay away from Hope, he was there every single time she beckoned.

Granted, most of those weak moments were caused by

genuine concern for her fears. It had to be unspeakably painful not to remember anything at all about oneself, and his compassion for her plight knew no bounds. Then, too, his worry for her safety was something he couldn't rid himself of with any amount of commonsense arguments. Regardless, wasn't he getting in just a bit too deep with a woman from one of the wealthiest families in Texas who would be throwing her financial weight in every direction if she knew the true facts of her life?

The telephones in the house rang, including the extension on his bedside stand, and Matt grabbed it before it could ring a second time and wake up Hope. He hoped that she'd stay asleep for the time being, because he knew in his soul that if she moved that sheet only a few inches to her right he'd be a gone goose again. In fact, there was a picture in his mind's eye of himself and Hope that kept getting more erotic by the moment.

Turning his back to her, he said a gruff "Hello" into the phone.

"Is this Matthew McCarlson?" a female voice asked.

"Yes, I'm Matt. What can I do for you?"

"We've never met, but I'm sure you'll recognize my name. I'm Kate Stockwell Larson. I've debated about making this call ever since learning of Hope's whereabouts. Would you mind giving me what information you have about her? As you might imagine, we're all very concerned about her medical condition. Does she really have amnesia?"

"Unfortunately I can't talk now." Matt was speaking so quietly he could barely hear himself, but if Hope woke up now and started asking questions, he wouldn't know what to tell her. "Could I call you back in an hour or so?"

"Certainly." Kate Larson recited her phone number and said goodbye.

Matt noiselessly set down the phone and glanced at Hope. Her eyes were wide-open and staring at him.

"Your girlfriend, I presume?" she said coldly. God, she felt like the worst fool alive, naked in his bed with her pose and body language all but begging him to make love to her. And had he been on the verge of doing it when his girlfriend called? Was he still planning on an "hour or so" of fun before returning the lady's call?

Matt heard something foreign in Hope's voice, a slight slurring of syllables that rang a bell in his head. She was tipsy! On what?

On wine, of course. She'd found those old bottles of wine in the hutch.

Matt rarely drank alcoholic beverages, even wine. He simply did not have a taste for it, and those bottles had been in the hutch for years, purchased by Trisha and forgotten by him.

"You're drunk," he said bluntly. "I wondered about this imaginative little scene, but the minute you spoke I knew what had brought it on."

Hope was genuinely shocked. She jerked herself up to a sitting position, holding the sheet to her bosom. "I most certainly am not drunk!" she said forcefully.

"You most certainly are. It's as obvious as the nose on your face, baby."

"I would appreciate your not using that insulting term with me," she said haughtily, totally unaware that she'd really said, "I would aperchate your not ushing that asulting term with me."

Matt shook his head. "Go get in your own bed and sleep it off, *baby.*"

"You did it again!" Forgetting the sheet altogether, Hope clumsily got to her knees. Swaying back and forth on her unsteady perch, she said, "How come you're so mad at me?"

When that sheet dropped, so did Matt's willpower. She was so lushly beautiful, so sensually ripe and female, and his head was already full of last night's ardent lovemaking. How could he resist both her and the seemingly indestructible desire in his own body? He could calm the savage beast she'd given life to within him with fiery lovemaking, but it reared again every time they were together.

"Dammit!" he muttered, and moved closer to the bed. "You're going to fall over if you don't sit down," he said raggedly.

"Better yet," she purred, "why don't I lie down?"

"Yeah, that's a whole lot better," Matt said grimly when she was on her back. Especially when she slowly spread her legs apart in blatant invitation. "Even without a memory you know how to make a man crazy, don't you?" he said, and began taking off his shirt.

"You make me crazy, too, you know," she replied throatily.

She was tipsy and he knew that he should get the hell out of that room. A scrupulous man would never take advantage of an inebriated woman, and he'd always taken pride in his high moral standards.

But instead of leaving, he finished removing his clothes and then got on the bed with her.

"Don't lay on the bed, silly." She giggled. "Lay on me. And do it. I've thought of us doing it again all afternoon."

He moved on top of her, guided his arousal into her and began moving. Her laughter died a sudden death. "You own me," she whispered feverishly. "You've made me yours, and there's something way down deep inside of me that knows nothing is going to change for us. Not ever."

Matt's mouth went dry, but he couldn't stop making

love to her. If she was right, heaven help him. At the moment he was in no position to debate the point, so he didn't even try and instead concentrated on the mind-blowing pleasure of being where no man had gone before—inside her hot, clinging body.

It didn't last for long. When she began writhing under him, clawing at his back and shouting his name, he brought them both to climax with fast, hard thrusts.

Afterward, sated and too drained to even talk, they both fell asleep, with Matt once again curled around her backside.

The second that Matt awoke in the middle of the night he remembered Kate Stockwell Larson's phone call and his promise to call her back in "an hour or so." *She probably thinks I'm some kind of lying jerk. Dammit, why didn't I remember it in time?*

Yeah, right. You were so busy nailing Hope again that nothing short of an atomic blast would've brought you to your senses.

Disgruntled and more than a little irritated with himself, Matt moved away from Hope so he could at least turn off the lights. Since there was no reason to even try to act as though he were still an honorable man—he'd totally destroyed that dignity—he crawled back in bed with her.

The inevitable happened. She awoke just enough to snuggle against him, which was all it took to bring on another bout of the hottest lovemaking that he'd ever experienced. Afterward, when Hope was sleeping again, Matt stared into the darkness and finally admitted that he was sunk.

The knowledge that he could only blame himself for his slide from grace made his misery even worse. There'd been a dozen opportunities for him to push Hope away and to explain to her that nothing personal was ever going to happen between them. Instead, he'd let his libido do the talking and the decision making, and in the process he'd lost sight of the man he'd been before all of this began.

If only she didn't have that damned amnesia! Did he dare have a much needed talk with her about the various types of sex? Yes, people in love desired each other, but desire also came wrapped in other packages, and that was what he wished he could impress on her. *Hope, you and I are not going to spend the rest of our lives in bed together, however convincingly your inner voice spoke to you. I do not own you, nor do I want to own you. Good Lord, I don't want to own anyone! Please, please get that idea out of your head.*

Then, for some unknown reason, his entire train of thought went in another direction. A picture developed in his brain, a picture of his house as it had been before he'd carried Hope into it—colorless and stagnant. That image was followed by one of himself, and his lifestyle, which had consisted of work and worry and very little else. Day after day, nothing had ever changed, except to get a little worse, a little duller, a little more boring. And obviously he'd gotten dull, too—at least dull-witted—along with everything else, because he hadn't done so much as considered that instead of being proudly independent and private, he was lonely and miserably unhappy.

He thought of Trisha, and how unhappy she'd been living there. When the passion of their love had been in full bloom, the seclusion hadn't mattered. But gradually the lack of a social life had made her hate the ranch, and because Matt loved every foot of ground he owned, they had grown farther and farther apart. He recalled taking Trisha to Hawthorne for an occasional night out, but her distaste for local color had ruined every attempt he'd made to lift her spirits. Truth was, she'd been in high society before their marriage, and it was what she'd started longing for again.

Matt frowned. Why in heaven's name was he going over that old ground again?

But he knew why. Deep in his gut he knew *exactly* why. It was because the same damned thing would happen if he gave in to his seemingly insatiable hunger for Hope and sweet-talked her into believing that she owned him, as well.

He set his lips into a thin, grim line. They connected in bed, yes, but it was the only place they functioned on the same wavelength. It was something he'd be wise to remember, and anytime he got foolish ideas about a long-term relationship, he should remind himself of what lay ahead for Hope. Once she found out who she really was, and then when she remembered everything for herself, well, hell, she'd forget him so fast it would be like the whole thing had never happened.

Knowing all that, wasn't he a total bastard for making love to her at every opportunity? Especially since he'd taken the one thing a woman could only give once—her virginity?

Groaning, Matt forced his eyes to close. He had to stop thinking about it. He had to get some more sleep. He and the crew would be working on the road again tomorrow, and he needed his rest.

But he also had to return Kate Larson's phone call in the morning. With their money the Stockwells could engage the best doctors in the world for Hope. Matt had a feeling that Kate was working toward that very conclusion. After all, now that the Stockwells knew where their sister was, why would they leave her alone with her amnesia and a strange man?

* * *

Matt left the house early the next morning, but he returned around nine. Hope smiled when he walked in, and her thoughts about last night were written all over her face.

"Hi," she said, sounding breathless.

She looked good enough to eat, in a pink flowered skirt and pink tank top. Matt was thankful that he didn't remember seeing those same clothes on Trisha, but he still wasn't overly thrilled with Hope wearing them, only because he was tired of reminders of the past and what a damned mess he was making of the present. Hell, if the downward trend of his life continued, he'd be homeless, friendless and looking for free handouts so he could eat in the future.

"I came to use the phone," he told her in a flat, emotionless monotone that did not invite conversation.

Hope's smile faded. "Oh."

Matt passed through the kitchen and went to his office. Shutting the door behind him, he sat at the desk and dialed Kate Stockwell Larson's number. She answered on the second ring.

"Mrs. Larson, this is Matt McCarlson. I'm sorry I didn't get back to you last night, but something came up and when I remembered your call, it was too late to return it."

"That's all right, Matt. Is it all right if I call you Matt?"

"Of course."

"And you must call me Kate. Matt, how is she?"

"She still doesn't remember anything, Kate. I talked to a doctor I know in Hawthorne, and he told me that amnesia is not ordinarily a permanent condition. Actually, his opinion was that Hope's memory could return at any time."

"Did he examine her?"

"He was too busy in town. Apparently a lot of people

were injured in the storm. Then there were the road wash-outs to contend with, which made it darned near impos-sible for anyone to get out here.''

"Are you still stranded?"

"We've only got a little more work to do on the road from the highway. Actually, it's passable now, though there are still some pretty rough spots to traverse.''

"I see. Well, that's good news, at least. Matt, I want to see her. Do you have any idea how she would react to a visit from me?''

"Kate, she doesn't have the slightest idea of who she is, let alone you or her brothers. She won't even phone her mother...I mean, your mother. When I suggested it, Hope nearly fell apart. She's terrified of strangers.''

"We're hardly strangers to her, Matt.''

"You and I know that, but Hope doesn't.''

"She should be under a doctor's care, Matt. You cer-tainly must agree with me about that.''

"Kate, the only thing I know for sure is that Hope is getting by on very little information and not unhappy about it.''

"Matt, you couldn't possibly be aware of our suspi-cions, but we've discussed the possibility of Hope having been abducted and then somehow escaping her kidnapper. I wasn't going to tell you that since we have no proof to substantiate the theory, but something unforeseen hap-pened to her. The plan was that she would deplane and then wait for our driver to pick her up and deliver her to our deceased father's home. I doubt very much that she simply forgot a much discussed plan and walked away from the Grandview Airport of her own volition. At any rate, just how safe is she at your ranch? Do you use night patrols as a matter of course? Some ranchers do, I know.''

Matt's blood suddenly ran colder. He wasn't the only person who'd come up with that kidnapping theory and other people—especially Hope's family—thinking the same thing made it seem even more probable.

He cleared his throat. "I'm keeping very close tabs on her, Kate, that's about all I can say."

"You don't believe she's out of danger, either, do you?" Kate exclaimed. "Let me put it another way. You decided for yourself that she's *been* in grave danger and it could happen again! Oh, Matt, I'm so frightened for her. I have to do something, I simply have to. What's the name of the doctor you spoke to?"

"Dr. Adam Pickett." Matt gave her Doc's phone numbers in Hawthorne, then added, "Kate, as long as I draw breath, Hope is safe. Count on it." A long silence ensued, until Matt said, "Kate, are you still there?"

"I'm here. She's come to mean something to you, hasn't she?" Kate said softly. "Oh, Matt, I've been told you're a widower and a very nice man. I very much hope you don't end up hurt over this. The doctors I've been talking to said that the person she is with amnesia could disappear completely when her memory returns."

Matt felt jolted, but he didn't let on. "Don't worry about me. I only want what's best for Hope."

After a short hesitation, Kate agreed. "That's what we all want, Matt. Goodbye for now, and thank you for talking to me."

Feeling like a pricked balloon, Matt put his head in his hands and sat there numbly for a long, long time. Finally, he heaved a sigh and got to his feet. He had to get back to work, but he wanted a few words with Hope before he went. While he was not going to risk her mental health with more information than she could possibly digest, there were a few things she had to know about him—the most urgent being some personal history about himself that he should have told her before this.

After all, he didn't want to be hurt any more than he

wanted her hurt. He could deal with almost anything except heartache over a woman he couldn't have, and hadn't he already admitted last night that he was getting in way too deep with Hope?

It was time to destroy her romantic notions, and to pray that if he managed to turn her off him, he'd be strong enough to keep his hands to himself.

As for last night's ludicrous thoughts about loneliness and unhappiness once Hope was gone, everyone knew that middle-of-the-night blues were the worst kind.

He was becoming a damned wimp, that's what was happening, and it was time he put an end to that destructive process, as well. After all, Hope *was* going to get better, and she *was* going to leave the ranch. And with Kate Larson's determination in play, that day was just around the corner.

"Get used to it," he muttered to himself as he left the office and headed for the kitchen.

Chapter Ten

Hope turned from the counter to look at Matt when he came in. The expression on his face made her uneasy, although she wouldn't let herself think it had something to do with her.

"Is anything wrong?" she asked.

"Good guess," he said brusquely. "We need to talk. Would you please sit down?"

At least he'd said *please,* Hope thought, although her uneasiness had become a sense of impending doom. Sending worried little glances his way she walked to the table and pulled out a chair. "Aren't you going to sit, too?"

"Maybe, maybe not." Matt filled a glass with water at the sink and drank it down. Then he began walking around the room. "I'm going to tell you about my wife."

Hope thought her heart might stop beating. "Your... wife?"

"Whose clothes do you think you've been wearing? Whose things do you think are stored in the attic?"

Hope's shoulders slumped in abject misery. He had a wife and he'd repeatedly made love to *her!* Would he have been such a disgusting opportunist if she hadn't had amnesia? Surely that was the cause of her own irresponsible behavior, wasn't it?

Matt could almost read her mind. "Don't jump to conclusions," he said gruffly. "My wife is dead."

Hope's eyes widened in horror. "And you let me wear her clothes? My God, what kind of man are you?"

"Not nearly as revolting as you're thinking right now." Matt pulled out the chair across from her and sat on it. "My marriage started great and ended badly. Trisha couldn't or wouldn't adjust to ranch life. Her family is very wealthy and she'd been raised with the best that money could buy. But it wasn't my much smaller bank account that did the real damage to our relationship. It was living here, too far out of the loop, so to speak. She was accustomed to parties, parties and more parties, and trips to fancy resorts all over the world with her rich friends. They traveled in droves, or maybe a better word is *herds*. I knew that I never fit in, and to be honest about it I didn't try all that hard. I also knew we were as different from each other as night and day, but apparently love just swept us away."

His last sentence had been cynically drawled, and Hope realized that he didn't have much respect for either love or marriage.

"And then she died?" she asked in a weak little voice.

"She died on the very day she was leaving me. It was a crazy, freakish thing." Doing his best to speak without emotion, Matt related the events of that awful day.

Hope covered her mouth with her fingertips and listened in horror. When he was finished, or seemed to be, she said, "And that's why her clothes are still here."

"No, her clothes and that furniture in the attic are still

here because I had Chuck get them out of sight while I was in Dallas for the funeral, and that was where he put them. I never go up there, and I forgot about my intention of donating it all to charity. I tried giving her things to her parents at the time, but all they wanted was a few personal mementos.''

''I—I'll go change clothes,'' Hope said tremulously, and started to get up. ''I had no idea...I mean...I'm so sorry.''

''Sit down. I'm not through talking yet.'' Hope slowly sank back to the chair. ''First of all, I don't care about your wearing anything you find in this house. There is something I do care about, though, and it's your misguided belief that you and I have a relationship.''

''Misguided?'' she echoed while her stomach started tying itself in knots. ''What does that mean, exactly? It sort of sounds like I was wrongly guided. If I was, who was guiding me, Matt?''

His face colored to a dark crimson. ''Go ahead and blame me. I've got broad shoulders.''

She studied him and sorted out the flush and the bluster. ''Poor Matt,'' she said quietly. ''Living alone and liking it, with just a few female skeletons in the attic that he conveniently forgot about, and then along came a woman and turned his safe little male kingdom upside down.'' Her voice hardened. ''Now you're worried that I might be falling in love with you and it scares the living daylights out of you. Why? Are you actually planning to live alone for the rest of your life?''

''I'm not planning anything. The days come and go all on their own, and so do the disasters, the pitfalls, the problems.''

''Is that all you've gotten out of life?''

''It wasn't a hell of a lot more,'' he replied, sounding bitter.

Hope had her fill of this depressing discussion and she got to her feet. "Whether you approve or not, I still feel safe with you. For the sake of your peace of mind, which you deserve as much as anyone else, I promise not to fall in love with you. Also, I'll stay in my own bed at night. If you stay in yours, as well, that should eliminate any more intimacy between us. I do have to ask one thing from you, and that's your permission for me to stay here until my mind clears at least a little. In return I would cook all the meals for your crew. I wasn't sure I could do it before, but I know now that I can."

Matt felt like he'd just beaten her over the head with something. "You don't have to do that. All I was trying to get across was that I don't want you getting hurt over something you're probably not understanding very well."

"Oh? Like what?"

He flushed again, but he had to tell her "what." "I took your virginity and I had no right."

She rolled her eyes. "Oh, for pity's sake, get over it!" Turning, she left him alone in the kitchen.

In her bedroom with the door closed, though, she fell across the bed and wept from sheer confusion. If Matt was worried about her falling in love with him, she must have shown signs of it happening. He certainly knew more about love than she did, after all.

Sitting up, Hope blew her nose. It was possible that she knew much more about love than Matt McCarlson, but the knowledge, or even the lack thereof, was concealed behind a locked door in her brain. It was strange, though, that if she'd ever been in love she hadn't *made* love. The virginity that Matt was so remorseful of taking from her seemed so puzzling, because obviously she was neither cold nor inhibited.

Unless, of course, the amnesia had altered her personality so drastically that she wasn't the same woman she'd been before the occurrence of her memory loss. Certainly the word *chastity* had very little impact in her present state and it just may have been her personal protocol at one time.

Pressing her fingertips to her temples, Hope shut her eyes, gritted her teeth and concentrated so hard on remembering something from her life—a face, a voice, a place, anything—that she soon had the seedlings of a headache. But along with tension pangs she felt a resurgence of fear, and for once she knew—without question—its source: her nightmares!

A chill permeated her body, and she dropped her hands from her temples to wrap her arms around herself in an attempt to melt the ice in her system. Swallowing dryly she forced herself to recall as much detail about those frightening dreams as she could dredge up.

Her conclusion after much deliberation was that the man threatening her in every single dream was a real person and not a figment of a terrified woman's imagination. What's more, she felt in her ice-cold bones that, as Matt had warned her, he was *still* a threat, even if she had no idea why anyone would want to harm her.

She couldn't leave here, she just couldn't! But during this morning's disturbing conversation Matt hadn't promised she could stay, had he?

Hope slid from the bed and stood on her feet with all the determination she could muster. She'd offered a trade, her cooking for his protection. When he came in for dinner this evening and realized that she'd also cooked for his crew, wouldn't he feel obligated to let her stay?

It was worth a try, she decided while battling a wave of panic she dared not let overcome her. Breathing deeply in an attempt to bolster her courage, she headed for the kitchen.

* * *

When Matt walked in that evening and saw the amount of food Hope had prepared, he felt like a complete jerk. Hope wasn't in the kitchen, but it was obvious she'd cooked for everyone on the place. Hurrying back to the outside door to catch Chuck before he reached the bunkhouse, Matt yelled, "Chuck, come and give me a hand, would you?"

Together they carried steaming pots and pans of delicious-smelling food to the bunkhouse for the men's dinner.

"This is sure gonna beat Harvey's warmed-up stew," Chuck said with a grin a yard wide. "That little gal sure can cook, can't she?"

"Yes, she sure can cook," Matt agreed grimly.

"Funny that she can remember recipes when she can't remember anything else."

"Yeah, it's a laugh a minute around here these days."

"I didn't mean ha-ha funny, Matt."

"I know what you meant, Chuck. Sorry for being such a grouch." Reaching the bunkhouse, they went inside and set the pots and pans on the stove. "Enjoy," Matt said brusquely, and left the hungry men to their own devices. The crew was excited about the unexpected meal, which by aroma alone promised to be something special, and Matt was glad for their sakes. But as for himself, the direction of his life, his unwanted, tormenting feelings for Hope and the stupid way he was dealing with them were all getting Matt down, and he slogged back to the house with a sour, down-in-the-dumps expression on his face.

Inside again, he saw that the kitchen was still vacant. Obviously Hope was avoiding him and could he blame her? Considering the way he'd talked to her that morning, it was a wonder she hadn't throttled him.

But he still didn't know a way to tell her they'd never be more to each other than they were right now than what he'd already said. He felt bad about hurting her, but she'd be hurt a whole lot worse if he let her go on thinking they were headed for some sort of fairy-tale romance when they weren't. At least, he wasn't. That was the problem, of course: her romantic notions versus his realistic attitude about sex between consenting adults.

His own dinner was in the oven, and he decided to shower before eating it. He had to pass Hope's bedroom door on the way to his own, and he was surprised to see it standing wide-open. He couldn't resist a quick glance into the room, and he saw her sitting on the bed with pillows behind her back, reading a book.

She spoke without looking at him. "Let me know when you're through with your dinner, and I'll go and finish doing the dishes."

"Uh, fine, okay, thanks." Matt continued down the hall to his room, confounded by her subservient demeanor. It was as if she'd changed from guest to servant, and he knew in his soul that he could never think of her as a servant.

"Damn her hide," he muttered. Why was it that females were born knowing how to get and keep the upper hand with men? She'd worked all day in his kitchen so he'd feel like a dog over their talk this morning. And it had worked. He felt exactly like a mangy old dog that had deliberately taken a bite out of baseball, apple pie, motherhood and the American way.

Cussing a blue streak, he gathered some clean clothes and went to take a shower.

He hoped that he would accidentally drown under the shower spray and be put out of his misery.

Hope awoke again in the middle of that night, sweating and terrified, but she hadn't screamed, and she fought the smothering fear all by herself instead of running to Matt.

This nightmare was different from the others she realized when her pulse finally slowed to a more normal rhythm. She'd been running...running so hard...winded and gasping for air and running in a pouring, blinding rainfall, slipping and sliding in mud. And the man from her previous nightmares had been behind her, chasing her, reaching out for her with clawing fingers, but before she'd escaped his clutches in that motel room she had struck him with something, and she'd seen his face.

He had red hair!

"Oh, my Lord," she whispered. Just as she'd suspected, her troubled mind had been remembering instead of dreaming!

But who was the red-haired man, and why in heaven's name had she been in a motel room with him in the first place? Did she know him? If so, why had she struck him with...*with a whiskey bottle?* Hope's eyes became big and startled. A whiskey bottle? Could that possibly be true?

Burying her face in her pillow, she moaned miserably and managed to keep it quiet, which was pretty remarkable when screaming was what she felt like doing. But if her past consisted of whiskey bottles, men and motel rooms, did she want to remember any more of it?

The next morning Hope got out of bed when she heard Matt moving around. She was dressed and leaving her room when he came out of his and saw her.

"Go back to bed," he said gruffly. "We're all used to making our own breakfast, and there's no reason for you to be up at this hour."

Hope lifted her chin, a defiant gesture. "We have a deal."

"No, Hope, we don't."

Her defiance disintegrated, and her lower lip began quivering. "Are you kicking me out?"

He looked at her morning-fresh face and felt her vulnerability in his own body. "No, I'm not kicking you out," he said gently, and he couldn't stop himself from touching her. He laid his hand on her cheek, and the sensation of her soft, dewy skin on his palm was almost enough to make him forget everything but the two of them.

But this was a mighty big world and they weren't the only two people in it, though there'd been times since her arrival that he'd felt as though they were. For the most fleeting of moments he savored that image—a man and a woman, loving each other so much that neither of them needed anyone else.

That's the craziest idea you've ever had!

Yep, it sure is.

Matt dropped his hand to his side. "Didn't I tell you days ago that you could stay here for as long as you wanted?"

"I guess you did. But then things, uh, happened between us, and—"

Matt broke in. "Maybe what happened between us should be forgotten. You know, one of these days whether you're here or someplace else, you're going to regain your memory. Hope, when that happens everything that took place on this ranch is going to be nothing but litter to you."

"Litter! Whatever are you talking about?"

"Litter. Trash. Garbage."

She sucked in a stunned breath. "Everything between us is garbage to you?"

"No, but it's going to be to you."

It was such a devastating idea that Hope nearly crumpled. She couldn't disagree with Matt about it because there were no arguments against that possibility in her befuddled brain.

Since she didn't want him to see the tears that burned her eyes and threatened to spill at any moment, she walked back into her bedroom and quietly closed the door.

Matt was startled by her sudden retreat. Also, she'd let him have the last word on a subject that had disturbed her, and that concession seemed sweetly feminine and affected him in an unaccustomed way. For one thing, he was getting damned good at disturbing Hope, and he didn't much care for the aftertaste.

In fact, all along he'd been lumping Hope and Trisha in precisely the same too wealthy, self-centered category, and the two women had very few traits in common. Actually, comparing them at all wasn't fair to Hope. She didn't even know she had money, and any self-centeredness she'd shown during her stay was merely worry about her own mental condition.

Feeling the pain that Hope must be living with in his own system, Matt rued every harsh thing he'd said to her since day one of their association. He almost rapped on her door to tell her so, but he was so wretchedly confused about what might be happening to him. His feelings for Hope had a unique quality, a newness he was positive he'd never experienced with anyone else.

That bit of honesty was enough to scare him away from her door, and to hurry his steps through the house to go outside. Heading for the bunkhouse, he saw Chuck coming out of the building. Chuck was carrying a load of pots and pans, obviously in the process of returning them to the house.

They stopped when they met up with each other. "We cleaned and washed these pots after we emptied them," Chuck said with a big grin. "We sure did have a fine meal." Matt continued to look pinched around the mouth, so Chuck stopped grinning. "Do you want to take 'em from here?"

"Nope." Matt walked away, leaving Chuck to stare after him and to wonder if he'd gotten another threat from the bank holding the mortgage on the ranch. Something had caused Matt's dark mood and Chuck couldn't imagine anything worse for a rancher than to lose his land.

Wishing he had the means to help his boss, Chuck continued on to the house. He was concerned about alarming Hope by just walking in, but it was very early and she might still be asleep.

He entered quietly and tiptoed to the longest counter. The utensils were stacked one in another for carrying, and he cautiously set the stack on the counter and then tried to separate it into several smaller piles that wouldn't fall over—without making any noise. He might as well have stomped in and then deliberately tossed the pans around the room, because the whole stack toppled and flew every which way, banging and clanging against the cupboards before they finally landed on the floor.

"Dagnab it!" Chuck scrambled to pick up the pans, knowing in his heart of heart that if Hope *had* been sleeping, she was awake now.

The initial racket reached Hope's ears. She stiffened and then panicked. Someone was in the kitchen—the red-haired man? Hope nearly dove headfirst under the bed, until common sense told her that Matt had left her alone only minutes ago and could still be in the house.

Soundlessly opening the door, she peered down the hall. A noise from the kitchen made her jump, but only Matt wouldn't care if she heard him.

Still, what was he doing? Hope suddenly saw red. If he dared to be making his own breakfast after their disagreement earlier about *her* making it, she was going to…to… Well, she didn't know what she would do, but she'd think of something!

Marching militantly down the hall, she entered the kitchen. "Chuck!" she exclaimed.

He straightened up with a pan in his hand and a look of self-disgust on his face. "I woke you up, didn't I?"

She realized that she wasn't completely comfortable with Chuck Crawford, but he really did look harmless. He was around fifty, with silver-blond hair and a bit of a paunch. *For God's sake, give it a break. He's Matt's right-hand man and look at the kindly concern in his eyes.*

"No, you didn't wake me. You brought back the cooking pots."

"Thought you might need 'em." Chuck smiled at her. "That was the best meal any of us have ever eaten, Hope. I'd like to say thanks for all your hard work."

Hope walked over to the coffeemaker and began preparing the pot. "Cooking isn't hard work for me, Chuck." She laughed briefly, a bit sharply. "Not that I know why it isn't, you understand."

"Yeah, Matt told me about your having amnesia," Chuck said sympathetically. "I'm real sorry about that. I can't even imagine what it must be like."

"Nor could I explain it so you'd know what it's like."

"Maybe you feel like a bundle of loose ends."

She smiled. "That's as sensible an explanation as any that I could come up with."

Chuck was pleased that she no longer seemed scared of him, and, in fact, was actually talking to him. "We scrubbed the pans real good, Hope."

"Yes, I can see that. They're shiny clean. Thank you."

"Well, guess I should be going," Chuck said, and made a reluctant move toward the door.

Hope suddenly trusted him implicitly and didn't want him to go. She would be alone for the rest of the day, alone and thinking about the red-haired man.

"Must you?" she said with a warm smile. "I was hoping you'd have a cup of coffee with me."

"Really?" Amazed at her friendliness this morning, Chuck turned away from the door. "Well, heck yes, I'd like that a lot."

"So would I." Hope began setting the table, and it flashed through her mind that Chuck probably knew everything there was to know about Matt. Chuck had known Trisha and had been at the ranch when she'd been killed. He'd lived here ever since and he could be the closest thing to a friend that Matt had. Chuck was undoubtedly a fount of information where Matt was concerned, and Hope didn't feel an iota of guilt over her impulse to charm Chuck into telling all, either. Matt was an almost unbelievably on-again, off-again type of man, and why shouldn't she use every possible avenue to learn more about him after what they'd been doing when no one was looking?

Perhaps her justification was because of Matt's completely groundless—to her way of thinking—regret over making love to her. What seemed strange, though, was that even though he wanted her to believe his remorse was for her sake, she knew in her soul it was to preserve his own conscience.

And maybe, just maybe, Chuck had some understanding of why Matt McCarlson was such a complex human being.

When Chuck left an hour later, Hope was upset and sorry she'd led poor, unsuspecting Chuck down the garden path. Matt wasn't a womanizer at all, he was a man in serious financial trouble, which explained the tension she sensed in him most of the time. Also, Chuck hadn't been at all reticent about the ranch being in bad shape, and she'd heard a long list of expenditures needed to put it right. "That storm might have been the final straw,"

Chuck had told her solemnly. "Hope not, but I know Matt's sure worried about it."

Then he'd lightened up and done some joking around about Matt needing to find himself a rich wife, which had totally caught Hope off guard, because why would Chuck, who she'd assumed knew Matt so well, even joke about something that serious to Matt? Trisha had been rich, and that union certainly hadn't worked, so why would Chuck think another rich wife would turn Matt into a happy man?

What it boiled down to, Hope realized, was that Chuck didn't understand Matt much better than she did, which could be blamed on their being men and never really opening up with each other.

But she suspected that Matt never opened up to anyone, not even a friend.

So what chance did an intrusive, pathetically mindless person such as herself have with a man who never let normal people get close enough to know him?

"None," Hope said with a forlorn sigh. "Absolutely none."

Later on Hope realized that she was running out of food to cook. She kept going to the kitchen window and looking yearningly across the compound at the bunkhouse. Matt had said it contained a lot of groceries, and she would very much like to do some picking and choosing on her own.

But she'd have to show herself and now that she'd remembered the red-haired man, she couldn't shake the feeling that he was much closer than even Matt suspected. Would it have helped any if she'd told Matt about this morning's dream? Would Matt have said, "He has red hair? Hells bells, Hope, I know exactly who you're talking about. Let's call the sheriff and have the bastard arrested."

It was a silly fantasy and Hope knew it. The doors of

the house were locked, and those locks were her only protection whenever Matt and the crew were off working somewhere. If she dared fate by going to the bunkhouse for more food, it might be the last thing she ever did.

On the other hand, could she live without courage? Having no memory was an indescribable cruelty, but pile cowardice on top of that and she would be a total zero. She was sure that she was getting braver, anyway, because look how she'd shaped up and welcomed Chuck this morning.

She made up her mind. Without ingredients she couldn't cook, and if she couldn't stay busy in the kitchen, she just might lose the thin little hold she still had on reality.

Unlocking the back door, she took a big breath and then dashed across the compound to the bunkhouse. Twenty minutes later she was back and so proud of herself and thrilled with the marvelous array of groceries she'd gathered that she was practically bursting at the seams.

She was going to prepare a feast, and Chuck and the other men would be grateful, even if Matt's reaction to her sumptuous meal was to give her hell for going outside.

What difference did Matt's reactions make to her anyhow? Regardless of the feelings he aroused in her—feelings she couldn't even name, except for the erotic ones— Matt was pure heartache waiting to happen.

"Or to get worse," Hope mumbled after admitting that she was already suffering from heartache.

Chapter Eleven

The men had been fed, the kitchen was back in good order, and Matt was working in his office. Hope and he had hardly spoken that evening, and she hated the foolish, unnecessary animosity between them. In truth she really didn't understand it, no more than she understood Matt himself, although her chat with Chuck that morning about Matt's financial plight had given her something to ponder for the rest of the day...and to stress over.

If she had the wherewithal to help him over this rough spot, she'd do it in a heartbeat, she thought repeatedly. After all, at the very least he'd rescued her from the elements, and quite possibly he'd arrived on the scene just in time to save her from the red-haired man.

Thinking in that vein, Hope realized there were things about that day that weren't clear to her. If Matt had explained it all, then she must have been too woozy at the time to digest the information. Maybe she shouldn't interrupt Matt while he was engrossed in paperwork, but she felt that she really must talk to him.

She rapped on the office door and heard a gruff, "Come in."

Opening the door, she shaped a smile and tried not to look guilty for bothering him. "Could I have a few minutes of your time?"

He wanted to say no. He wanted to say, "Keep away from me, Hope," but what came out of his mouth was an almost cordial, "Sure. Come on in and sit down."

Matt toyed with his pen while she took the chair directly in front of his desk. She made him nervous. He couldn't look at her without burning-hot memories searing his conscience, which didn't relieve the yearning for more of the same that attacked his system whenever they were together. He inhaled slowly and quietly and tried to ignore all the signs of arousal he was feeling and dared not act upon. His inner warfare caused his face to harden, and when he turned his eyes on Hope, she saw in them glints of resentment. Unnerved because he so didn't want her in there with him, she drew a breath and rushed into her reasons for asking for a few minutes of his time.

"It occurred to me that I hardly know what took place the day you found me, and I also believe I recall the face of the man I was running from."

Was she speaking of a genuine recollection? Her first? Was this the start of a chain reaction that would perhaps start slowly but then gain momentum until she was flooded with memory? Why did that idea unnerve him so much? God knew he'd be better off without a sensual woman underfoot constantly causing him lustful urges.

He cleared his throat. "That's, uh, good. I guess."

Hope was disappointed in his lukewarm response. "He has red hair," she said.

Matt frowned. She had managed to pique his curiosity

with that definitive but incomplete description. "Are you talking about the man in your nightmares?"

Hope leaned forward. "Yes, but this wasn't a nightmare, this was an honest-to-goodness memory. I hit him on the head with a whiskey bottle, then I ran from the motel room. I kept running and it was pouring rain and my chest hurt, but I kept running because I knew he was behind me."

Matt's pulse went wild. Wouldn't he just love to get his hands on the bastard that had caused her—and him—such distress?

"Do you recall the location of the motel?" he asked anxiously.

Hope sighed. "I wish I did, but no."

"How about how long a time you ran? Or how far?"

"Not exactly, but I'm positive I ran for a long time." Hope's eyes glazed over as she recalled again the awful burning in her chest that night, the fear of stopping and the pounding rainfall. Her eyes cleared. "You're doubting me, aren't you?"

He'd been thinking again about "life after Hope," and how a man could know what was best for him and still dive headfirst into the deep end of a shark-infested pool.

"No, I'm not doubting you," he said with a grim twist to his lips. After a few moments, he added quietly, "I could never doubt you. You said the man has red hair?"

Hope's heart skipped a beat, because he'd sounded so loving and kind, showing once again that side of him that had made her trust and possibly even love him.

"Very red hair," she replied, hearing a huskiness in her own voice that was a result of her considering the possibility of having fallen in love with Matt. She couldn't think about it now, but she knew she would, later on when she was by herself.

"And you also remember his face?"

"His features aren't as clear in my mind as his hair is, but I think I would recognize him if I saw him again." A shudder suddenly shook her. "Not that I want to see him again, God forbid. The mere thought of it chills my blood."

"He really did terrify you, didn't he?" Matt clenched his hands into fists. Picturing himself smashing his fist into that terrorist's face was a gratifying fantasy. *It won't be fantasy if he ever shows himself to me!*

"Yes, and I have to wonder why. I don't mean why was I terrified. I mean, why was I with him in the first place? Did I know him? Did I willingly meet him in that motel room?"

Matt was convinced now that his kidnapping theory was a lot more fact than fiction. But Hope's questions warranted some exploration. *Had* she known her kidnapper, willingly gone to the motel with him and *then* realized she was in danger? That scenario indicated a personal relationship with the guy, like maybe they'd advanced beyond the kissing stage and had rented a room to be alone.

Matt narrowed his eyes on Hope. Had she been afraid of sex before the amnesia? Had she been a frigid woman who had tried to get over it with a man she liked, or possibly loved, but once things got steamy in that motel room she had panicked and ran? Of course, hitting a would-be lover over the head with a whiskey bottle was rather extreme…unless the guy wouldn't accept her change of heart and tried to force her. Hadn't she rambled after one of her nightmares about the man trying to seduce her—or her trying to seduce him—and unsure of which it had been?

Damn, he thought with disheartening frustration. He'd been so positive a minute ago that she'd been kidnapped, but the whole thing could have been a simple case of romance gone awry. Not every guy took rejection like a gentleman, especially if the woman teased, flirted and promised, and then didn't deliver.

"What?" Hope asked sharply as she grew uncomfortable under Matt's invasive scrutiny.

"I'm just trying to unscramble what really took place in that motel room," he said.

Something in his voice disturbed Hope. He'd been staring a hole through her, as though fixing blame. *Was* she to blame? Certainly she couldn't get all huffy because he might think so when what she did remember of that night was so sketchy.

She decided to leave that segment of her past in the twilight zone for the time being and move on to another.

"I've been wondering what you thought when you saw me lying in the mud," she said.

Matt met her gaze head-on. "I thought you were dead," he said flatly.

She sucked in a startled breath. "So I looked pretty bad?"

"You looked like a pile of wet rags. Then I realized there was a person in the pile, and it wasn't until I got down from my horse that I could tell you were a woman."

Hope looked away from him and became very still. "I—I'm remembering something else. A light." After a moment she added, "Yes, a distant light...not clear, not bright but there all the same. A wavering, unsteady beacon in the rain and dark."

Matt's eyes widened. "It could have been one of the yard lights." He became more emphatic. "It *must've* been a yard light! There aren't any other lights for miles in any direction."

"Isn't it strange?" Hope murmured thoughtfully. "There's so much nothingness out there, and I was led to this house by a light. Just think of how easily I could have missed seeing it."

An eerie sensation gripped Matt. It *was* odd that she'd run or walked or even crawled toward that light. Was fate playing with him? With both of them? Had destiny decided they should meet? Had something beyond his comprehension become annoyed with his solitary lifestyle and hard-nosed attitude toward the opposite sex and done something about it?

Get a grip, man! When did you start believing in heavy-handed spirits playing chess with the human race, for God's sake?

His eyes met Hope's, and neither said a word for a long moment. Everything that had happened between them lay on the path of their gazes. Regardless of what had caused them to meet, their lives were now intertwined. Maybe the comfort they'd found in each other would last beyond her recovery, maybe it wouldn't, but Matt couldn't deny its potency.

Nor could he convince himself that she wasn't beautiful and sexy and looking at him with beseeching eyes, because she *was* beautiful, she *was* sexy, and if the softly glowing light he saw in her gorgeous blue eyes was any measure, she wanted him in that same earthy, unpretentious way that he wanted her.

And after she's gone, then what?

It wasn't a completely new concern, but this time it packed a wallop that had Matt's head spinning. He hadn't fallen in love with Hope, had he?

Money problems and that, too? No! I'm not getting hooked into another relationship that was doomed to fail from its onset. It would be the same with Hope. They were from different worlds, her living on big bucks and him scrambling for loose change.

Hope saw a transformation take place on his face. For a time there she'd felt a connection with him that had set her heart to pounding, but something had abruptly severed it. She sighed sadly, because without that special link to Matt, she had nothing.

Besides, deep down and without any basis of fact, she knew that something had gone through his mind to break the spell that had held them both speechless only moments ago. What topic had intruded on those lovely few moments of intimate eye contact, his deceased wife, his financial situation, her amnesia, or something she wasn't even aware of?

She got to her feet. "I've kept you from your work long enough," she said quietly, holding back tears through sheer determination. "Good night."

Matt got up. "Good night. Sleep well." When she'd left the room, he groaned, put his hands on his desk and let his head fall forward. Just sitting and talking to her could sap his strength. He'd be the biggest fool alive to make love to her again.

But it's what you both want, so maybe you're the biggest fool alive whatever you do!

Hope was almost asleep several hours later when her eyes suddenly popped open. Matt was keeping something from her! He knew more about her than he'd told her, and that was what he'd been thinking of in his office when his mood had changed so drastically.

That's crazy. Why would he keep anything from me?

As troubling as the concept was, Hope couldn't argue it away. She suspected that Matt had phoned Madelyn LeClaire, the woman listed as her mother on that wallet card, but he hadn't talked about it. Not that Hope had encouraged discussion on that subject, probably because she didn't want Matt making her feel guilty for being too cowardly to speak to her own mother.

But she was so afraid. Just thinking of the immense world beyond this ranch was torture and caused her head to pound. She couldn't define what was out there that frightened her so; her fear was simply an irreversible part of the woman she was now.

And if Matt truly was keeping something from her, then perhaps it was because he understood her fears and didn't want to add to them.

It was a comforting thought to fall asleep with.

The major repairs to the road were finished. While the crew filled miscellaneous potholes they joked and laughed. Things were back to normal. They could go to town when they felt like it, and tonight seemed like a "darned good time to drive to Hawthorne and have a beer or two." They all knew better than to come back to the ranch drunk; drunkenness was something Matt wouldn't tolerate. But even he occasionally drank an ice-cold bottle of beer on a hot day.

Matt was surveying his men's work when he heard an approaching vehicle. Turning to watch it coming closer, Matt recognized the sheriff's car. Already the dirt road had dried enough so that the car was kicking up dust.

Chuck walked over to his boss. "Looks like we got company."

"The sheriff."

Chuck squinted at the oncoming vehicle. "And someone else, too."

That someone was Dr. Adam Pickett, Matt realized after another minute or so. When the car stopped, the two men got out and Matt shook hands with them, the sheriff first.

"I see you got your road back in pretty good shape," Sheriff Cliff Braeburn said.

Matt nodded and grinned. "Gotta have a road, Cliff. My men were about to take off walking to get to town."

The sheriff chuckled. "Don't blame 'em a bit."

Doc chuckled, as well, then asked, "How's your un-invited guest doing, Matt?"

Matt shot the sheriff a questioning look and realized that Cliff hadn't passed any information about Hope on to Doc.

"She's doing okay, considering," Matt replied.

"Still doesn't remember anything?"

"She might be starting to remember a few things, but it's hard for me to tell."

"Of course it is," Doc agreed. "Not having known her before the mishap, you're in no position to judge anything she might say. Well, I hitched a free ride out here with Cliff to meet this mystery lady...and to examine her, if she permits, so shall we get to it?"

The three of them piled into the sheriff's car and arrived at the compound a few minutes later. Hope heard the car and watched out the window with horrified eyes as two strangers—one in uniform, the other one carrying a black bag—got out with Matt and started walking to the house.

Even without memory Hope knew that the sheriff emblems on the car indicated that the law had arrived. For what reason? To bodily remove her from the McCarlson ranch and send her back to Massachusetts? And who was the other man? Another relative she knew nothing about?

Hope suddenly couldn't catch her breath. Fear was choking her, and she dropped the curtain and ran from the window. Getting away from whatever awful fate they had planned for her was all she could think of, and while the three men came into the house via the back door, Hope made an escape through the front door.

Matt brought Doc and Cliff to the living room. "Make yourselves comfortable. I'll be right back."

In the relentless grip of panic, Hope ran from the house. Her eyes darted frantically, searching for a place of concealment. *One of the buildings! Which one?* Some were small, and she bypassed those to rush headlong into the largest barn. There were horse stalls and various types of equipment here and there, and she ran the length of the building and realized with tears streaming down her face that she would be easily found if she hid in there.

But then she spotted the ladder, and it went up, up, obviously to another floor. "Yes," she whispered, and using the bottom of her skirt to dry her eyes, she scampered up the ladder without once looking down.

Inside the house, Matt was having a hard time believing that he couldn't find Hope. He'd looked first in her bedroom—where he'd fully expected her to be when she wasn't in the kitchen—then in the other rooms in the bedroom wing. He took a quick look into the office, then in the laundry room. Stymied, it hit him suddenly that the red-haired man she'd talked about had found her!

Something crashed within him, freezing his feet to the floor for a few shocked moments, then releasing abruptly. His mind cleared and he walked calmly into the living room. Until he'd searched the outbuildings and knew for a certainty that Hope was no longer on the ranch, he wasn't going to get everyone worked up by pronouncing her missing again.

"She apparently went for a walk. There's coffee in the pot in the kitchen. Help yourself. I know where she walks and I'll go and get her. I shouldn't be long, but don't get alarmed if I'm more than a few minutes. I've suggested she not take long walks and go too far from the house, but she pretty much does as she pleases."

"Really," Doc mused. "Then, even with amnesia she's a strong-minded woman. That makes me even more anxious to meet her."

Matt smiled weakly. "As I said, make yourselves at home. If you're hungry, raid the refrigerator. I'll hurry."

"Hurry" was exactly what he did as he left the room

and then the house. Quickly he scanned the yard and out-buildings. Nothing looked amiss. Nothing, that is, except for the sheriff's car.

Matt's stomach sank as he realized what had really happened. The red-haired man didn't have her; she'd run away at first sight of that car. Since she wasn't in the house, then she was hiding out here, and she couldn't be far considering that only about ten minutes had passed since he, the sheriff and Doc had driven up.

She could be in any one of the buildings, but for some reason Matt's gaze rose to the upper story of the barn. Functioning on gut instinct, Matt crossed the yard, walked into the big barn and headed straight for the ladder. He climbed it as quietly as he could, and when his boots were on the straw-covered floor, he stood there, looked around and wondered which haystack she had burrowed into for concealment.

Actually it took him about two minutes to figure it out, because there was a very interesting bump in the loose pile of hay near the back wall. He strolled over to it and said, "I know you're in there, so you might as well give it up."

Gasping because he'd found her so easily, she threw the hay off her face and tried to crawl away from him.

"Hope, for God's sake, cut it out!" Matt made a grab for her. She eluded his grasp and kept on clawing her way through hay, although she had no idea where she would end up. All she knew was that she had to get away.

Matt slogged into the haystack for a few hurried steps, then threw himself on top of her. She fought him like a tiger, but he finally nailed down her flailing hands with his. Then he glared into her face.

"What in hell's wrong with you?" he snarled.

"You bastard!" she sobbed. "You brought him here."

"Brought who, the sheriff? The doctor? Hope, you

need to see a doctor, and what do you think the sheriff's going to do, haul your butt to jail? Good Lord, woman, you're not a criminal. All anyone wants to do is help you.'' Looking at her teary face he felt her pain again, and he repeated in a softer, gentler voice, ''All we want to do is help you, Hope.''

It was true and it wasn't. All the sheriff and Doc wanted to do was help her, but his wants weren't all in her best interest. Right now, for instance, his interior was hot mush because of being on top of her again and remembering what making love to her had felt like to him.

Hope was having similar feelings, and her sobbing stopped. She gazed into his eyes and saw desire, hot and strong, in their depths.

''Kiss me,'' she whispered.

He swallowed. ''They're waiting for us. I lied and told them you'd taken a walk but I knew where you usually went and I'd get you and bring you back.''

''Then we have a few minutes. Kiss me, Matt.'' She slid her hands around him to his backside and pressed down so that he would more closely fit between her opened thighs.

''Hope, don't do this,'' he pleaded in a thick, unnatural voice. ''There isn't time.''

''You're wasting what time we do have, and I'm so ready, Matt.''

He couldn't resist a second longer. His mouth descended to hers in a devouring kiss, and while they kissed hotly, passionately, he unzipped his jeans, shoved them down and then went under her skirt. Within two minutes they were intimately joined and nearly frenzied in their need of each other. She met his every thrust with one of her own, and somewhere in the back of Matt's mind was the incredibly gratifying knowledge that she'd never done this with another man, that whatever she knew of lovemaking and sex, she'd learned from him. He was her lover, her teacher, her protector, and as long as she had amnesia he could be her constant companion because what she'd run away from was the fear of being separated from him.

He rode her fiercely, possessively, and she reveled in his physical strength and his emotional power over her senses.

As mind-blowing as this unexpected encounter was, Matt knew he couldn't prolong it, not with Doc and the sheriff waiting in the house for them. Worried that he might be going too fast for Hope, he nevertheless held nothing back and reached completion in mere minutes. When she cried out over her own release at almost the same moment that he did, he became very emotional and actually felt tears in his eyes.

Taking a minute to pull himself together, he finally lifted his head and looked into her eyes. "You are one very special lady."

The hoarseness of his voice and ardent light in his eyes were lovely for Hope. "You already know you're special to me," she said softly. "Matt, don't let the doctor or the sheriff take me anywhere."

"That's not why they're here."

"Promise me, Matt. Swear it."

"All right, I promise. Does that make you feel better about seeing them?"

"Do I really have to?"

"You have to see a doctor, Hope, and Doc's the only one in the area. He's sixty years old and one of the nicest people you'll ever meet. He's a friend, Hope, believe me."

"Well, why is the sheriff here?"

Matt tried to make light of that question. "Because he's nosy as hell and often goes on Doc's calls just to keep abreast of what's going on in his county. Come on, we'd better get ourselves back together and go to the house. They're probably on the verge of sending out a search party for both of us.''

Before he could move away, Hope pulled down his head, kissed his lips, and then asked, ''Will you sleep in my bed tonight?''

He hesitated. ''Can we talk about that later on, after Doc and Cliff are gone?''

''You're always sorry after we make love. Would you please tell me why?''

''I can tell you what I'm feeling right now, okay? If we keep this up, one or both of us is going to get hurt very badly when you regain your memory.''

''What makes you think that? I could never hurt you.''

''Hope, you have no idea what you used to be capable of doing, and will be again once you're back to normal. Now, let's get a move on, all right?'' Matt pushed himself up and away from her, then got to his feet and yanked up his jeans.

Hope got up and started plucking hay from her clothes and hair. ''You're wrong, you know,'' she said. ''I don't care what I remember about myself someday, I know in my heart that I could never hurt you.''

''Guess we'll just have to wait and see about that,'' Matt said. ''Let me take a look at you and see if you're carrying any clues that would tell them what we've been doing. You check me out, too.''

Hope withstood his scrutiny in silence. There was a piece of hay sticking out from his shirt collar, but she would bite off her tongue before letting him know it.

They went down the ladder, Matt first so he could catch her if she slipped, and then walked to the house. Just before they went in, she said again, ''You're wrong about me, and someday you're going to know it. I only hope it won't be too late.''

Puzzling over her final remark, Matt followed her into the house.

Chapter Twelve

Sheriff Braeburn decided it was time that Doc learned the true identity of the lady staying with Matt. He made his explanation brief but as accurate as he knew it.

Doc was predictably surprised, but his primary concern was for Hope. "Has the Stockwell family been informed of her amnesia?"

"I talked to Rafe myself," Cliff replied.

"And Rafe agreed to leave her here?"

"For the time being, yes. According to Matt, Doc, she remembers nothing about herself or anyone else. That's why he hasn't told her who she really is or anything about her relatives. He doesn't want to bog her down with information she probably can't assimilate. And we've all got to realize that however big and powerful the Stockwells are in Texas, they're strangers to Hope and she's especially afraid of strangers. So, please don't say anything about...well, anything, when you examine her."

"I won't, because you're right. In Hope's condition, everyone's a stranger," Doc murmured.

"Everyone except Matt."

Doc frowned slightly. "Which makes her extremely dependent on him."

"Is that a problem?"

"Not as long as Matt is willing to be there for her. Is he? Has he mentioned that aspect of the situation?"

Cliff shook his head. "No, we haven't discussed anything like that. What if he's not? Doc, you know Matt as well as I do. Since Trisha's death he's hardly left this ranch. He can't be very thrilled with having an ill woman on his hands."

"From what Matt told me, she's not ill, Cliff. Amnesia can affect a person physically if it's caused from actual damage to the brain. Of course, I can't make an accurate diagnosis until I examine Hope, but it's my impression at this point that her only medical problem is memory loss. Which can be serious, don't misunderstand. In most cases, however, amnesia is a temporary condition." Doc walked to a window and looked out. "What do you suppose is keeping them?"

"Couldn't say, but Hope going out for long walks seems like a good sign to me."

"If she's deathly afraid of strangers, Cliff, then she shouldn't wander too far from the house."

"I doubt there are very many strangers out here, Doc."

"It doesn't take 'very many' when a woman is already scared out of her wits," Doc said dryly. "One's enough." He cocked his head to listen. "Sounds like Matt and Hope are coming in now."

About an hour later the three men were seated in Matt's office. Doc was doing the talking. "Without sophisticated equipment and testing, which I doubt is needed, my opinion is that Hope is physically sound. The cut on her head has healed nicely and her vital signs are those of a healthy young woman. I checked her reflexes and found no retardation of response. She *is* living with fear, however, which we already knew and is to be expected in any amnesiac. But Hope's fear is such a large and deeply established part of her that I suspect she will not be separated from it until she regains her memory.''

Matt and Cliff exchanged glances. After a few moments of ponderous thought, Matt said, ''She's afraid of a red-haired man, Doc.''

''She said that?''

''At first she had terrifying nightmares, but gradually she realized that she was doing more remembering than dreaming.''

''Then she *has* experienced segments of memory? She didn't tell me that.'' Doc sat silently thinking, then said quietly, ''She obviously underwent some sort of emotionally traumatic experience before you found her.''

''And it was caused by a guy with red hair,'' Matt said grimly. ''Doc, everyone involved has agreed to keep Hope's whereabouts a secret, and I'm asking you to do the same. We all believe she was kidnapped and somehow escaped her captor. I don't know how she ended up here, but she has memories of running in the dark, through the rain, and she believes with all her heart that the red-haired man was behind her, chasing her. That might be true, it might not, but I'm not willing to risk her safety by announcing to one and all where she's staying.''

Matt sat back in his chair. ''Besides, I'm the only person she *feels* safe with.''

Doc met Matt's gaze. ''I know that. In fact, Hope told me just how welcome you've made her feel. It appears that with nothing more than instinct to assist you, you did everything right for a woman with a problem that can baffle physicians, even in this day and age. What you must understand, however, is how dependent upon you she is now. After talking to her, I'm quite certain that she is thoroughly convinced that she could not exist without you. She was almost fiercely adamant against anyone trying to force her to leave here, Matt, but no one would blame you for worrying about the enormous responsibility Hope represents. Along with the state of her mental health—even though you've done a fine job dealing with that so far—if she really was kidnapped and you think there's a chance the thug might try again, is she really safe here? Cliff, how do you feel about that?''

''Well, during the storm my deputies had their hands full, but if you'd like some extra manpower out here, Matt, I could spare a couple of men for a while.''

Matt's stomach had begun tying itself into knots when Doc started talking about how welcome he'd made Hope feel. Could he even be considered a decent man after what he'd done? No, he hadn't forced Hope into anything. But the word *dependent* kept going around and around in his brain and it hit him that Hope probably believed he could do no wrong. Why wouldn't she make love with the only person she knew in the whole damn world? The man upon whom she was totally and completely dependent?

He cleared his clogged throat. He was ashamed of his behavior and grateful that Hope hadn't told Doc everything that had been going on between them. No more, he vowed ardently, and then remembered that he'd already taken the same oath several times, for all the good it had done. *This time I mean it, dammit, I really mean it!*

Strangely, belying the inner turmoil he was suffering, he sounded quite normal when he answered Cliff. ''I don't think that's necessary. Between Chuck, the other men and myself, we'll make sure Hope is well protected.''

He got away from that subject as quickly as he could,

turned his attention to Doc again and said the first thing that popped into his mind. "I guess my main concern right now is the way I've been keeping things from Hope. Do you think I should tell her what I know about her? I still have that first newspaper article, and if I gave that to her to read—"

Doc held up his hand. "Matt, just do whatever it is you've been doing. I like that old axiom. If it isn't broken, then don't fix it. My advice is to not change a thing, at least not yet. Hope is healthy but jumpy, and I frankly don't know how she would take so much information at this time."

Cliff spoke up. "That's well and good, Doc, but Rafe knows we were coming here to check on Hope today, and he's going to want to hear all about it. I'm going to have to make a pretty thorough report of today's visit, and is it your feeling that what's best for Hope might be in opposition to her family's wishes? One thing Rafe mentioned was that his sister Kate was champing at the bit to see Hope with her own eyes. He also said something about the family sending a head trauma specialist out here to examine Hope."

"I can't fault the Stockwells for worrying about her, and maybe a specialist *should* be brought in," Doc said solemnly. "What I'd like to do is to write a paragraph or so about Hope for you to include in your report, Cliff. Would that be too out of line for you to consider?"

"Not at all. You're a doctor and you examined her. I would think Rafe and the others would appreciate receiving your opinion."

"Actually, it's going to be a recommendation for them to leave Hope here a while longer. She's obviously starting to remember, and I firmly believe that taking her away from this environment, the only one with which she's familiar, could cause dire consequences."

Matt listened to the discussion between his friends and felt like a horse's ass. Doc thought he'd done a great job with Hope with nothing but instinct to guide him, and Cliff thought he was a courageous soul who would protect her with his life.

Well, he might do that—protect her with his own life— but he sure was a jerk in every other way!

But you've fallen in love, man. How could you not touch her? Matt gulped so loud that Doc's eyes flicked his way for a second.

Fallen in love? Have I suddenly gone nuts? His heart started pounding so hard it felt like it was making his shirt bounce. *I am not in love…I'm not!* His palms got sweaty, and he wiped them on the legs of his jeans.

"Matt, are you okay? You look a little clammy," Doc said.

"It's just warm in here. Doesn't it feel warm to you two?"

"Can't say it does," Doc said.

"Not to me," Cliff said.

"Okay, forget it. Probably just having a hot flash." Everyone laughed and Matt quickly steered the conversation away from him and his peculiar—to Doc and Cliff—pallor. "Cliff, when you told Rafe about Hope being here with me, what'd he say?"

"Well, he asked if I knew you, and I told him you were a hardworking rancher and a decent sort. When I vouched for you, he relaxed. Rafe's all right, you know. I've worked with him on a couple of different occasions, and he's a good lawman and a straight-up guy."

Cliff looked at Doc. "Anything else you need around here, Doc? I should be getting back to town."

Doc got to his feet. "So should I. My waiting room is probably overflowing with impatient patients." He offered his hand across the desk to Matt, who also had gotten up.

"Matt, call me if anything changes. Thanks for your time and hospitality."

After further goodbyes out in the yard, Matt watched the two men climb into the sheriff's car and drive off. Sick at heart and plagued by guilt and a genuine dread that the things he'd been thinking a few minutes ago might actually be true, Matt returned to the house.

Hope was sitting at the kitchen table with a cup of tea in front of her. "Have they gone?"

"Just now."

"They stayed quite a while. Did...the sheriff tell you anything about me?"

"Like what?" Matt went to the counter and poured himself a cup of coffee.

"Like what? Like anything. Did hc talk about me?"

Matt took a sip from his cup. "We all did."

"You *all* talked about me? What did Doc have to say?"

"He believes you're going to make a full recovery."

"That's what he told me, too. What about the sheriff? What did he say about me?"

A brilliant idea occurred to Matt. "He thinks you should go back to Massachusetts and be with your mother."

Hope gasped right out loud. "And what did you say to that?"

"Hope, she's your mother. What do you think she's going to do when you meet again, beat you over the head, mentally abuse you?"

Hope looked at him and tears started dribbling down her cheeks. "Would you really let the sheriff send me to a stranger in Massachusetts?"

Matt gave up. Setting his cup on the counter, he went through the kitchen door to the outside again. He took a big breath of air and was almost feeling better when he happened to glance at the second story of the barn. Making love with Hope in that pile of hay had been the most beautiful, fantastic sexual experience of his life.

He thinned his lips and walked off cursing under his breath. *Every* time with Hope was beautiful and fantastic. Was that fact finally sinking in?

Now what'll I do?

That evening Matt received a phone call from Sheriff Braeburn. "I wrote a full report...including Doc's professional opinion...and faxed the whole thing to Rafe Stockwell. He phoned a few minutes ago. Apparently he passed the report around the family, and his sister, Kate, is determined to see Hope no matter what he or anyone else thinks about it. You'll be seeing her day after tomorrow."

"Is she coming alone? You mentioned a trauma specialist when you were here today."

"I don't know about that, Matt. Rafe didn't say, but I think Hope should be told about it before Kate shows up."

"I agree. Thanks, Cliff, I'm not sure just how to break the news to Hope, but I'll figure something out."

Figuring it out wasn't easy, not when Hope had already shut herself in her room for the night and Matt was actually afraid of knocking on her door and possibly stepping foot in her bedroom. He and Hope couldn't seem to have a normal discussion about even the most impersonal of topics. On the other hand, he thought wryly, had they ever attempted an impersonal conversation? The very air around them seemed to vibrate when they were together, and now, dammit, he couldn't get rid of that ridiculous *love* notion that kept gnawing at his vitals.

"To hell with it!" he growled. Deciding to tell her in the morning, Matt retired early himself.

But then he lay in his bed and thought of Hope lying

in hers, and he worried about the possibility of his having fallen in love, and that maybe Hope thought she was in love with him, as well. Actually, wasn't Kate's determination to see her sister a good thing? Maybe Kate's presence would jar Hope's memory, Hope would experience instant recall and the two sisters would happily vanish with the sunset.

"Yeah, tell yourself another one," Matt mumbled disgustedly.

The sheriff paying her a visit kept bothering Hope. Doc was a darling and he'd been courteous, professional and sometimes funny during his examination. She had found herself relaxing with Doc, even laughing a few times Doc, she liked. Sheriff Braeburn worried her. Did a lawman have the authority to whisk a grown woman from Texas to Massachusetts against her will? Had Matt be hind her back—encouraged Braeburn to do exactly that?

Walking the floor the next day hours after Matt had left the house, Hope tried to figure out Matt's hot and cold attitudes toward her. One minute he was distant and guarded, and the next he was so hot to make love it was a wonder steam didn't pour out of his ears.

"Oh, don't get so melodramatic," she told herself. But exaggerated though her thoughts might be, they were rooted in fact. Matt *was* changeable. He *did* run hot and cold where she was concerned. How could she doubt the disruption of routine she'd caused him, or the probability of his wishing that she hadn't brought her troubles to his doorstep? According to what Chuck had told her, Matt had enough problems of his own to deal with; he certainly didn't need hers.

So, yes, it was indeed possible that he'd encouraged Sheriff Braeburn to send her to Massachusetts. It had been so uppermost in Matt's mind yesterday that he'd come right out and told her what the sheriff had suggested, after all. *And don't forget that Matt never gave you an answer when you asked him if he would let the sheriff send you to a stranger. His silence was darned meaningful, which you would have admitted before this if you weren't so head over heels for him!*

Wiping away a tear, Hope began gathering the ingredients to make cookies. Or trying to. The cupboards were getting bare. She'd done so much cooking and baking that the flour was almost gone and so were the vegetables and meat. In fact, how on earth would she put together this evening's meal with so little to draw upon?

She was still pondering the products she did have and what she might be able to do with them when the back door opened and Matt came in.

"Hello," he said coolly.

She answered in kind, a cool, snappish sort of hello. But she had to say more. If she didn't the men were going to have a very sparse supper. "There's nothing left to cook."

"What?" Matt was so engrossed in what he'd come in to tell her that what she'd said didn't immediately sink in.

"I said there's nothing left to cook, or very little. Someone has to do some grocery shopping."

"There's food at the bunkhouse," Matt growled.

"Not anymore."

Matt cocked an eyebrow at her. "You've used all that food?"

His accusing attitude angered Hope. "Ate every bite of it by myself," she said with scathing sarcasm.

Matt flushed. "Hope, I didn't mean—"

"You insinuated that I wasted your precious food! I cooked it and you and your men ate it!"

"You don't have to yell. I'm not deaf."

"I wasn't yelling. *This is yelling!*"

"Hope, calm down. You're upset over nothing. Make a grocery list and I'll drive to Hawthorne and fill it myself."

"Fine! It will only take me a few minutes, so please wait for it." She sat at the table and began writing her list.

The knot in Matt's stomach was getting painful. He had to tell her about Kate's visit tomorrow; he'd come to the house to get it over with and then got sidetracked over a grocery list. He seemed to have very little control over the events of his life anymore, and he didn't like the feeling.

He pulled out a chair and sat at the table. "There's something I have to tell you."

Hope's heart skipped a beat. He was sending her back to Massachusetts! The sheriff was going to return for her!

She laid the pen on the pad and spoke in clipped syllables that announced her fury more than any amount of shrieking would have, "I am not going to Massachusetts."

Matt's perplexed frown was so severe that his forehead looked like a road map. "What in hell are you talking about now?"

"You and the sheriff are *not* sending me to Massachusetts!"

"Who said we were?"

"You did. Yesterday."

Matt remembered what he'd said to her on that subject and groaned. "How can a woman with the memory of an elephant contract amnesia? Hope, I lied yesterday."

She stared. "You lied?"

"Cliff never even hinted that you should go back to Massachusetts. How could he? He doesn't have the authority to send you anywhere. That's up to your family, and speaking of family, your sister, Kate, is coming here tomorrow to see you.''

"My sister Kate? I don't have a sister! I only have a mother!''

"You have a large family, Hope. Three bothers and a sister.''

She covered her ears with her hands and whimpered, "Stop…stop! I can't bear to hear anymore.''

Rising, Matt walked around the table, took her hands in his own and gently pulled her to her feet. Holding her against his chest, he said, "I know this is hard for you, but you have to face it, Hope. Hiding your head in the sand isn't going to make the world beyond this ranch disappear. Your family is justifiably worried about you, and your sister, Kate, is going to come out here tomorrow to see that you're alive and well with her own eyes. She knows you have amnesia, so I'm sure she isn't expecting some gala welcome from you. But she loves you, Hope, and you have to meet her.''

Hope sobbed quietly into his shirt. "Hope,'' he said softly, "look at me.'' He took her chin and tipped up her face. Her tear-streaked face and terrified eyes reached deep inside him and wrung him out. "I'm sorry,'' he said, and brought her head to his chest again. "I'm so damned sorry about so many things.''

"Don't be,'' she whispered raggedly. "You've done nothing wrong.''

"Hope, things are beginning to happen for you. You're going to be your old self very soon now, and when you are, you're going to put all of this behind you and probably run like hell.''

She stiffened. "All of what? You? Everything you've done for me? No, Matt, I won't be running like hell from anything I've found here.''

"Well, neither of us really knows what you'll do, do

we? So let's not take sides and argue about it, okay?'' He let go of her to get a box of tissue from the counter. ''Now, dry your eyes and finish that grocery list.''

They sat down again. Hope's hand shook when she picked up the pen. *A sister...coming here tomorrow! What will she say, how will she look? What will I do? How will I look?*

''Matt, I hate asking for another favor, but could I write on this list a few things that just might lift my morale tomorrow?''

''Write down anything you need. I'll do my best to find it.''

''It's just a few cosmetics...things that weren't in my purse.''

Looking at her in her secondhand clothes, Matt got very emotional. Hope should have something new and pretty to wear tomorrow. He couldn't afford such generosity, but what the hell? He really couldn't afford the groceries on that list, either.

Finishing the list accomplished one positive thing for Hope; it took enough time that her terror diminished and her system calmed some.

''When all this began I asked if you knew any Le-Claires,'' she said, startling Matt because she had seemed so intent on her list. ''You said no.''

Matt didn't know how to respond. Doc felt that Hope shouldn't be overloaded with information, and yet Kate Stockwell was coming to see her tomorrow.

''Did you lie about that, too?'' Hope asked quietly. ''Do you know my sister and brothers?''

''No, I've never met any of them.'' *She's assuming Kate and her brothers are LeClaires!*

''But you had heard of them?''

''I didn't lie, Hope. I'd never heard the name *LeClaire* until we read it on the items in your wallet.''

"I see. In that case you knew nothing about my sister and brothers until yesterday. Apparently the sheriff told you about them."

Matt decided to exit this discussion before he found himself trapped in a corner. He rose and said as casually as he could manage, "The sheriff has met at least one of your brothers. Is that list finished?"

"Yes." Hope slid it across the table toward him.

Matt picked it up and without looking at it, folded it and slipped it into his shirt pocket. "I'll be gone for at least two hours. Stay inside."

Hope heaved a sigh of utter hopelessness. Did no one give a damn what *she* wanted? Her circle of acquaintances was growing without her permission or blessing, and after tomorrow a woman named Kate would be part of it, a woman who was supposedly her sister. Next, of course, would be the men claiming to be her brothers. Eventually she would have to meet Madelyn LeClaire, and how many other people were going to pop up, claim to be a relative and intrude on her safe harbor out here?

What hurt the worst was Matt's cooperation. She would have liked to keep everything exactly as it was during her and Matt's best moments together, and it didn't seem to bother him in the least that the world was gradually encroaching on their relationship, her life and his ranch.

Her disappointment was almost more than she could stand, and she went to her bedroom, lay on the bed and pulled a sheet over her head.

She would not think of any of it again today.

Outside, Matt was talking to Chuck. "I won't be a minute longer than I have to be. The house is locked, but stay close and keep an eye on it. If Hope should take a notion to come outdoors, talk her into going back inside. If you catch sight of anyone you don't recognize immediately, call the sheriff and guard Hope from inside the house. And when the men get back from moving those cattle, have them patrol the perimeter if you think it's necessary, although in all likelihood, I'll be back before they will. I'm leaving Hope in your hands, Chuck. Take care.''

''You can count on me, Matt.''

''I know I can. Catch you later.'' Matt climbed into his pickup and drove away with a tight crease between his eyes. He could have sent Chuck to town, but then he'd be alone again with Hope, and he didn't trust himself with her. Look what had happened yesterday in the barn, and he'd gone looking for her with only the best of intentions.

Gripping the steering wheel with white knuckles, Matt kept an eye peeled for anything out of the ordinary all the way to Hawthorne.

He drove directly to the town's only women's dress shop, parked the truck and went in. A lady with a pleasant smile approached him.

''Hello, Matt. Can I help you with something?''

''I'm looking for a gift for a…a friend. A dress, I think. Something in light blue. Size eight.'' That was the size of Trisha's things, and they seemed to fit Hope well enough.

Thirty minutes later he left with several packages. Next stop was his favorite grocery store, Cutler's Food Mart. It wasn't the biggest food store in Hawthorne, but Matt had done business with Bud Cutler for too many years to desert him when a large chain opened a supermarket.

But when he walked in Matt saw that Bud wasn't behind the counter today, which meant that he'd have to deal with his clerk, Harriet Meadows, who was also Hawthorne's most dedicated busybody. He said hello to Harriet, who gave him her usual suspicious look because she was one of the folks who still blamed him for Trisha's death, regardless of proof to the contrary, then took a basket and quickly began filling it. He paid no attention to other shoppers. He wanted to get back to the ranch as soon as possible, and he wasn't interested in making small talk with anyone, which could be the case if he ran into a friend.

He filled the basket in ten minutes and pushed it up to the counter. He didn't even notice the man in the baseball cap skulking around the magazine rack not five feet away. Harriet began ringing up the charges, and when she came to the feminine body lotion, scented shampoo and peachy-pink lipstick Matt was buying, she gave him a knowing look and said, "Well, isn't this a surprise? A bachelor buying cosmetics does raise one's curiosity, Matt. Now, which of the fair ladies of Hawthorne do you have holed up out at your ranch? Or could she be a newcomer to the area?"

Matt was in the proper frame of mind to snarl, "My life is none of your damned business, Harriet. Get your mind out of the gutter and finish ringing up my things. I happen to be in a hurry."

She shot him a venomous look, but she did as told. After he'd paid and hauled out his things, another customer appeared at her counter.

"Rude SOB, wasn't he?" the man said.

Harriet looked her customer over—a stranger to her but clean, neatly dressed and wearing a baseball cap that covered almost all of his red hair.

"Matt McCarlson is worse than that," she said maliciously. "I will believe to my dying day that he had something to do with his wife's death. He's lived alone ever since, that I know of, which makes his buying women's cosmetics darned suspicious, if you ask me."

"I fully agree. Where did you say his ranch is located?"

Chapter Thirteen

Hope pulled a pretty, blue dress from its sack and looked at Matt with shining eyes. "You bought this for me?"

"Figured you might like something new to wear tomorrow for your sister's visit."

"Oh. Well, thank you," Hope said listlessly, her delight over the gift overwhelmed by her dread of tomorrow.

Matt saw the result of her deflated spirit on her face and tried to buoy it up again with a smile and a question. "Do you think it will fit?"

"It'll fit well enough." Matt's thoughtfulness had been a thrill, and earlier Hope had worried about how she would look tomorrow. During Matt's absence, however, she had come to the conclusion that her appearance tomorrow was the last thing that should unnerve her. Kate was probably coming to the ranch with expectations of taking her away, possibly to Kate's own home, or maybe to an institution for mentally challenged people.

There was nothing wrong with her brain, Hope thought fiercely. She simply couldn't remember, which was awful in a way she, herself, didn't quite comprehend, but amnesia was not a contagious disease and she wasn't going anywhere with anyone!

After hanging the dress in the closet of her bedroom, Hope returned to the kitchen. Matt was taking groceries out of bags and setting the items on the table and counter.

"I thought you might want to put this stuff away so you'd know where it is," he said when she walked it.

"Makes sense to me. Thanks for thinking of it."

She'd spoken stiffly, and Matt knew she was still scared and troubled about tomorrow. People and events were starting to come at her from all directions, and it was only going to get worse. Her family was not going to forget about her, even if that was what she preferred. And sooner or later, one of two things was going to happen; either she would regain her memory and *want* to get on with her old life, or someone—a family member, a doctor—was going to convince her to go to some specialized clinic for treatment.

It could happen tomorrow!

Matt froze at the thought. Holding an empty bag, he stood there and looked at Hope. She was sorting groceries and arranging them in cupboards, the refrigerator and the freezer compartment.

She turned suddenly and looked at him. "You're staring."

"I know," he said softly. "Hope, you're so beautiful."

She recalled that he'd given her a much different impression during their initial time together. Had she completely misjudged him? "Do you really think so?" she asked in a startled voice.

"I know so."

She was silent for a long moment, digesting what to

her was the loveliest of compliments. But he'd never said anything that touched her in quite the same way before. She sensed that he truly meant it, and while it moved her emotionally it also caused her concern. He could just be in an on-again mood, she reminded herself, but there was sincerity in his voice and even in his stance that she wanted desperately to believe.

Still, an opposing point of view came to mind. Was he being especially nice because he knew something he hadn't told her, such as Kate's true purpose in coming here tomorrow?

"What's really on your mind?" she asked quietly, and lowering her eyes she began picking at the label on the bottle of rice vinegar in her hand.

Matt hesitated. He'd been worrying himself sick over the possibility of having fallen in love with her, but dared he tell her that? Once she got her memory back, she'd probably laugh herself silly over a hick Texas rancher thinking he was worthy of a Stockwell.

That prospect hurt really bad, which made the decision for Matt; he couldn't even get near the word *love* with Hope.

And, God help him, he shouldn't lay a hand on her ever again. But he wanted her so much he ached, and soon she'd be forever out of reach.

She wasn't out of reach right now, and she wouldn't be out of reach tonight. Kate's visit tomorrow could and probably would change everything.

He finally said in a raspy, unsteady voice, "What's on my mind is the same thing that's been there ever since I first laid eyes on you. I think you probably know what that is."

"The first time you laid eyes on me...or shortly there-after...you had undressed me and I was naked. When you

told me about it afterward when I had regained conscious-
ness you said my nudity hadn't meant a thing to you.''

"And you believed that a man could undress and bathe
a beautiful woman without feeling anything?''

"I wanted to believe it. What did you feel?''

"Hot, aroused and disgusted for having uncontrollable
desires. I swear that I did nothing wrong while bathing
you but I can't swear that I didn't *consider* doing a whole
lot of things. Do you hate me for that?''

"No," she whispered, and walked over to him. "I told
you before that I could never hate you. You want me now,
don't you?''

"Let's talk about what you want," he growled.

"This is the first time you've gotten angry *before* we
made love," she said, and seductively slid her hands up
his chest to lock together behind his neck. "I've come to
expect it afterward, but why are you angry now?''

He laid his hands on her buttocks and yanked her forward, where she felt exactly how aroused he was. "Chuck
knows I'm back. He'll be wondering what I'm doing in
here.''

She tipped her head back to see his face. "I just figured
it out. It's easier to talk yourself out of something if
you're angry. You don't want to want me, do you?
You've never *really* wanted what keeps happening between us, and right now you despise yourself because
you're hard and aching to make love. Matt, how do you
suppose that makes me feel? Between the two of us, have
I been the sole seducer?''

He was rapidly losing self-control, and when she snuggled even closer and rubbed her breasts against his chest
he simply gave up. Clasping the back of her head, he
kissed her hungrily, hotly, and when they came up for air,
he swept her off the floor and up into his arms. In seconds
they were in his bedroom and tearing off their clothes.

Naked, they fell on the bed and took up where they'd left off in the kitchen.

His lips and tongue ravished every inch of her body. By the time he was on the verge of bursting, she was writhing and begging. "Matt...darling...please...I can't wait any longer. Make love to me...please."

He thrust into her, locked her hands over her head with his own and watched her face while he pleasured them both. He almost said it. He almost said, "Hope, I'll love you till my dying day," but he didn't. Not out loud, he didn't. The words repeated in his feverish mind, though, over and over until every cell of his body recognized the irrevocable truth. Whether it was the smartest or the most stupid thing he'd ever done, he had fallen in love with this incredibly sensuous woman. What's more, she was nothing like Trisha. Comparing the two women was like weighing apples against oranges. Hope was down-to-earth and genuine, not walking ten feet above the commoners who dared to occupy her space. Hope was sweet and loving and...

Just as they both went over the edge Matt's brain finished that sentence. *Hope had no idea of what kind of person she really was, and neither did he!*

Groaning in utter anguish, Matt moved to the bed and crooked his arm over his eyes.

Hope raised to her elbow to see him. "Matt? What's wrong?"

He couldn't look at her. Jumping out of bed, he snatched up his clothes and strode from the room.

Tears trickled down Hope's face. She could tell he'd gone into his bathroom to dress, and it was all too obvious that he was angrily remorseful again. *Or remorsefully angry. What in God's name is wrong with that man? He wants me, he doesn't want me. Which one of us is really the crazy one?*

Matt walked up to Chuck. "I take it everything went okay while I was gone."

"Everything was fine. You sure were in the house a long time. I've been out here wondering if I should go in or what."

"You did the right thing by not going in," Matt said flatly.

"You and Hope got something going, don't you?"

Matt looked off across an open field. "Yeah, we do, but I don't intend to talk about it."

"Wouldn't expect you to, but I have to butt in a little. Hope's a mighty fine woman, and you'd be a darned lucky man to land a wife with a few bucks in her purse. Face it, Matt, you're on the verge of losing this ranch."

"Oh, I've faced it, Chuck, every damned minute of every damned hour of every damned day," Matt said bitterly. "But I haven't sunk so low that I'd marry a woman for her money. Come on, let's cut the chatter and go find something productive to do."

That night Matt ate with the men after a bunch of them transported the dinner Hope had cooked from the house to the bunkhouse dining room. Matt couldn't help laughing when the cowpokes licked the platters clean. They'd never even tasted food this good before, let alone eaten their fill of it, and one of Matt's thoughts while he enjoyed the meal himself was that even with amnesia and *his* misguided and undoubtedly selfish attentions, Hope was more than earning her keep.

He sighed heavily. She was the most unique, special woman he'd ever known, and years down the road, when he thought of this particularly eventful October, he would remember Hope with tears in his eyes and love in his heart.

Hope was in bed when Matt came in that night. Even with her bedroom door closed, she could tell that he had stopped just outside it, as though listening hard to hear if she was sleeping or awake. His moods were beginning to anger her, and if he thought for one moment that she was going to melt again just because he said something nice to her, he could think again! In fact, confronting him with that attitude was too appealing to ignore.

Slipping out of bed, she went to the door and abruptly opened it. "Is there something you want?" she asked bluntly.

The old white T-shirt of Matt's that she was wearing was practically threadbare from being laundered so many times, and the thin fabric left little to the imagination. He stared at her breasts, then at the shadow of dark hair he could see at the juncture of her thighs. Her head of thick hair was provocatively flyaway, and all in all she was so beautiful she took his breath. How would he survive when she was gone?

"How dare you look at me that way?" Hope asked with fire in her eyes.

Matt blinked, as though breaking free of a trance. "I can't look at you any other way, I guess."

"You guess. Well, isn't that great? You know something? I think *everything* is guesswork for you."

"Isn't everything pretty much guesswork for you, too?"

"I have an excuse. You don't! Why did you stop outside this door?"

"I really don't know."

"You damned coward!" She slammed the door in his face, and for good measure, snapped the lock in place.

The next morning Hope was already awake when she heard Matt getting up. She waited until he was dressed and gone before she got up herself, and the first thing she did was go and stand in the shower with her face turned up to the spray. Her eyes were pink and swollen from crying on and off all night, and she hoped a good long shower would make her look better.

She couldn't imagine anyone paying even a sister a visit at that early hour, so she put on a pair of Matt's too big, cutoff jeans and another T-shirt. She really couldn't wear Trisha's things again, not with all that was going on between her and Matt, she had decided at some point in the night, and she pulled down the stairs to the attic and put everything back where she'd found it. She would, of course, change into her very own, new blue dress later on.

Too nervous to eat much, she prepared a light breakfast for herself and had trouble choking that down. After cleaning the kitchen until it shone, she wandered the house, too on edge to sit still.

She kept going to various windows and looking out. It would have been kind of someone to find out exactly what time Kate planned to be there. Following that thought, Hope tried very hard to visualize her sister, and ended up so tense she felt brittle enough to break into a million pieces.

She tried then to get hold of herself. Obviously, intense concentration did nothing but threaten a breakdown; she'd tried it before with the same frustrating results. Besides, she would know today what her sister looked like and what sort of woman she was. Hope frowned. If only she could stop herself from thinking that Kate's visit had an ominous reason, such as forcing Hope to leave with her. Regardless of the problems intermingled with her and Matt's disturbing personal relationship, he was still her lifeline, her safeguard, and she was *not* going anywhere with anyone.

Matt came in around noon and saw what she was wearing. "I'm sure that Kate will be coming along at anytime. Maybe you should change clothes."

"Are you really sure or are you just guessing again?"

His face hardened. "You're not going to let me forget I said that, are you?"

"I won't forget it, why should you?"

"Well, I won't forget your calling me a coward, either."

"Good! Fine! Paint it on a sign and hang it over your bed!"

"I'm not a coward, Hope," he said with a dark scowl.

"You certainly couldn't prove it by me," she said with a toss of her head, immediately followed by a nose-in-the-air exit that made Matt laugh, much to his surprise.

He yelled down the hall, "You're a terrible actress, so forget that profession."

She yelled back, "And you're a terrible rancher!" Immediately she started giggling. It had been a totally inane comeback, which he had to know as well as she did. She wouldn't be saying such moronic things if she weren't nervous enough to fly.

Her urge to giggle vanished in the wink of an eye, and with her hands trembling and her insides feeling like a rocking boat, she changed into the blue dress. When she went to get her shoes, the only ones in the house that were really hers and fit her feet, she saw that they were gleaming like a new penny.

"Matt polished my shoes," she whispered, and sank weakly onto the edge of the bed. Was he the coward she'd called him last night because he kept shying from commitment, or was he the kindest, sweetest man alive?

With a pounding heart and a sensation of choking on her own breath, Hope watched from behind a window curtain as a woman and two men got out of a large, elegant sedan. Who are those men? She thought wildly. Doctors who were going to take her away from Matt and this ranch? If they'd come here with that in mind, they were in for a rude awakening. She would fight them tooth and nail, with every fiber of her being.

She looked at the woman again, who was walking with her two male companions and Matt toward the house, and gasped. It was like looking at herself! Kate had the same dark hair that she did, and from that distance, although Kate was getting closer, her eyes looked pale enough to be blue. Their figures were alike, and Kate appeared to be about her height.

Breathing hard, Hope all but fell onto the nearest chair. Kate really was her sister. She'd been hoping for some sort of miracle. A woman named Kate would arrive, they would have an impersonal discussion and she would leave again. *It's not going to happen that way! Kate's a busybody, maybe the family spokesperson, and she thinks her mission in life is to save you.*

Hope got to her feet when the foursome walked into the living room. She said nothing because she couldn't. Kate's eyes got teary—oh, yes, they were indeed blue— and she walked over to Hope.

"Don't be frightened," Kate said gently. "I'm so glad to see you, Hope. May I hug you?"

Hope backed up a step and whispered, "Please...no."

"Darling Hope, don't you remember me at all?"

"I'm sorry," Hope mumbled. "But no, I don't." Hope was keeping a wary eye on the two strange men. Matt had stayed in the room, although he'd distanced himself from the family group by leaning against a far wall.

"Hope," Kate said, "would you mind if I introduced my husband to you?"

"I guess not." Her husband? The younger man, of

course. And who was the distinguished-looking older man? Another relative, or was he the doctor she'd been fearing so much, the specialist who would claim to have a guaranteed cure for amnesia but it could only take place in some nightmarish clinic?

"Brett, please come over here," Kate said with a glance over her shoulder.

Hope took her eyes from the older man and watched Brett coming forward. He was tall and handsome, with dark hair and eyes, a man who struck Hope as being strong, intelligent and capable of doing anything he set his mind to. He had a nice smile, she saw, although she didn't trust him as far as she could have thrown him. After all, these relatives could be trying to put her off guard with phony pleasantries and smiles.

"Hello, Hope," Brett said. "It's good seeing you again."

"Hello," she said, giving him nothing but a meaningless word. She was too afraid to give him anything else. She was especially afraid of the older man; his polished demeanor seemed hugely suspicious to her.

"You're looking well," Brett said with another warm smile. "Pretty as ever."

"Yes, she is," Kate agreed with a smile of her own that quickly evolved into a more serious expression. "Hope, we brought along a friend, Dr. Glenn Heath, who's a trauma specialist. Glenn is a well-known authority on the subject of amnesia, and Brett and I would so very much appreciate it if you would talk to him for just a few minutes. May I bring him over?"

Oh, God, here it comes! Hope's frantic eyes darted to Matt. His slouch against the wall was overly casual and struck her as peculiar, since she'd not seen him so seemingly laid-back before. Always, no matter what he might be doing, she'd felt a coiled-spring aura emanating from him. It was one of the things she'd found so attractive about him right from the start, she realized now, but at this particular moment it scared the hell out of her. She'd constantly thought of him as her protector, but did guardians or champions go out of their way to appear loose and uninvolved in the face of the enemy?

But was Kate an enemy? Looking at her sister again, Hope felt a change come over herself. She could not be unkind or rude to Kate, and probably not to Brett, either. In fact, there was no call for rudeness to anyone, Hope decided, but there was nothing wrong with her speaking her mind in a polite and calm manner.

"Thank you for your consideration, Kate, but I already have a doctor," she said quietly. "I'm sure you've read his medical opinion of my condition, which I understand was included with Sheriff Braeburn's report."

"Yes, but Hope, Dr. Heath is a specialist. Dr. Pickett is a G.P., a general practitioner."

"Dr. Pickett is all the doctor I need right now," Hope said firmly.

Kate sent a helpless look to Matt, a silent plea for assistance. He frowned, because if he put in his two cents right now, he just might get shed of Hope forever. It still hurt that she'd called him a coward, but he was the only person in the whole damned world who understood the fears Hope had to live with. The worst one—simply because she couldn't remember what had caused such horrible fear in herself—was that someone would force her to leave the only place with which she felt connected. And leaving the ranch would also mean leaving him, and he was the only human being with whom she felt any connection at all.

Besides, if she left today the void in this house and in his life, for that matter, would forever remain deeper than the Grand Canyon. *Dear God, I do love her, I do.*

"Sorry, Kate," he said calmly, belying the increased speed of his pulse, "but I won't try to talk Hope into anything." Immediately he was at war with himself again. He'd believed ever since Trisha's defection, which had actually occurred long before her death, that he would never fall in love again, and now he was telling himself that he had? Maybe all he was doing was mixing up lust and love, because one thing required no debate: he definitely was in lust with Hope. A thousand erotic images hit his brain every time he looked at her, and even now, with everyone in the room so somber and serious, uppermost in *his* mind was the raw passion they had heaped on each other earlier in the day.

Hope had to forcibly stop herself from running across the room and throwing her arms around Matt. But perhaps later, after everyone had gone?

"Hope, please," Kate pleaded.

Hope shook her head. "No." She saw the good doctor heading her way, and she stopped him with a look. Then her eyes moved back to Kate. "Will you tell me the absolute truth about something?"

Kate nodded. "Of course I will. What would you like to know?"

"Did you come here today planning to talk me into leaving with you?"

"Hope, you need professional help. Should I be ashamed for worrying about my only sister?"

"No, but should I be ashamed for wanting to stay with the only person I really know?"

Kate turned a little to look more squarely at Matt. He knew then that she had figured out the status quo. Hope, herself, had given it away, although she probably didn't realize how revealing she'd just sounded. He flushed a bit, but returned Kate's disapproving look with what he hoped was an expression of denial that she would believe.

Clearly, much to Matt's relief, Kate was too much of a lady to pursue such a personal topic, because she turned back to Hope and asked, "Would you like to hear about Mother? Or any other member of the family?"

Hope was suddenly paler, Matt saw. He was the only one in the room that knew *why* she'd lost so much color: She *didn't* want to talk about people she should remember and couldn't. She's had all of this she can take, he thought, and pushing away from the wall he crossed the room to stand next to her.

"Maybe another time, Kate?" he said, putting his objection in question form and hoping she'd take the hint and cut this visit short. "I can tell Hope is getting very tired."

"You're hardly qualified to make that diagnosis," Dr. Heath said sharply.

Matt sent him a withering look. "Who in hell needs a medical degree to recognize exhaustion? And since you *are* so qualified, why didn't you recognize it sooner? Kate, I'm sorry, but I think Hope's had enough for today."

"Of course," Kate murmured. "Hope, may I come back...say sometime next week?"

"Yes," Hope whispered.

Smiling wistfully, Kate took her husband's arm. "Until next week, Hope. I'll call first."

"Goodbye, Hope," Brett said.

Dr. Heath grunted something unintelligible. He was obviously put out because Hope had refused his services, which made Matt think the physician was one egotistical SOB. After all, he was probably going to get paid plenty for just making the trip out here.

Matt walked them out and followed them to their car. While the doctor and Kate got in, Brett took Matt aside. "Matt, I think Kate and I better understand Hope's insistence on remaining here with you, but that kidnapping theory's got everyone in a tailspin. Do you have enough men to guarantee her safety?''

''She's safe, Brett. I'd give up my own life before I let anything happen to her.''

Brett nodded. ''Glad you feel that way, but we really would like to put some of our own men out here to help. I insist, Matt, and so do Rafe and the rest of the family. We've got four good men lined up, and they'll be here sometime tomorrow.''

Matt couldn't argue with logic. Hope's family was deeply concerned, and since she refused to go where they could closely guard her, then the guards would have to come to her.

''Fine,'' he said flatly.

''Incidentally,'' Brett continued, ''the reward the family put up is yours, you know. And I for one feel that you should also be reimbursed for any costs you might have incurred for Hope's care.''

At the first mention of money, Matt started getting stiff, and when Brett stopped talking, he said coldly, ''I did nothing to earn fifty thousand dollars, nor would I take one penny from you or anyone else for Hope's room and board.''

''Well…you should think about that, Matt.'' Brett offered his hand. ''I hope we meet again.''

''I'm sure we will. Goodbye.''

Brett was doing the driving, and when they were about a mile from the house Kate said, ''Look at the man over there! What's he doing, Brett?''

Brett took a quick look and saw only the dark pants of a man running into some brush. ''He's probably one of the guards, honey. Matt told me that he has plenty of manpower to ensure Hope's safety.''

"But you told him we were sending out some of our own, didn't you?"

"Yes, I did."

"Brett, do you know any cowpokes who wear baseball caps?"

"No, why?"

"That man I spotted was wearing one, that's all."

"Probably the only thing that means is that the man likes baseball caps," Dr. Heath said dryly from the back seat.

"No doubt," Kate murmured, although something was making her feel terribly uneasy. *Cowboys do not wear baseball caps, at least none that I've ever known did.*

When Matt returned to the house, Hope was waiting "Did you notice their clothes? Their car? Matt, I think my relatives have money."

"Could be," he hedged. "I've got a few phone calls to make."

"Go ahead," she murmured. "I'm going to change clothes and take a nap. I didn't sleep very much last night."

"I'll see you later then."

"Yes, later."

Matt went to his office and Hope to her bedroom. Seated at his desk, Matt dialed Dr. Pickett's number and convinced his receptionist that this was an emergency call. After a few minutes Doc came on the line, "Matt? What's this all about?"

"Kate Stockwell and her husband were just here. They brought a trauma specialist with them, and Hope refused to talk to him. She said she already had a doctor and gave them your name, but I think she wouldn't talk to Dr. Heath because she was afraid they'd come out here to take her away. Anyhow, I've got some questions. She still has no idea who she really is, but after Kate and Brett left Hope mentioned their expensive clothes and car. Doc, can I finally show her that article and tell her what I know of the Stockwells?''

''What specialist did she refuse to see?''

''Dr. Glenn Heath.''

''Matt, he's one of the best. Hope should have let him examine her.''

''Yeah, well, Hope does pretty much as Hope pleases. And she's scared, Doc, she's so damned scared that someone's going to haul her off against her will that she doesn't want to talk to anyone new. She did say that Kate could come back next week, so maybe that's some progress. Anyway, what's your opinion of telling her everything?''

''I wouldn't, Matt. Too much too soon could cause emotional damage that just might prove to be irreparable, and we don't want that. No, just let things happen on their own, Matt. If Kate continues to visit that could be the very best medicine anyone could give Hope.''

''Okay, thanks, Doc.''

''Anytime, Matt. Goodbye.''

Matt put down the phone, then laid his head against the back of his chair and sighed. He couldn't cure Hope's amnesia, but he sure could have added to the little knowledge she presently had about herself and her family.

But he would heed Doc's advice and keep his mouth shut. What choice did he have?

Chapter Fourteen

When Hope awoke her room was dark. Startled, she sat up, switched on the lamp and checked the time: 11:20 p.m. She could hardly believe her eyes. She'd slept away the day and half the night. What had the men eaten for dinner? She'd grown accustomed to planning and preparing good meals for Matt's crew, and with the cupboards and refrigerator full now from Matt's shopping trip, she could have made some very special dishes.

Feeling terribly guilty, Hope switched off the lamp and tried to get comfortable again. Then she heard the wind, a mournful howl with strong gusts battering the house. It made her jittery, and she pulled the covers up to her chin. She tried to clear her mind enough to relax, but the wind had an eerie effect on her and she felt haunted by ghosts of her forgotten past. Something was different tonight, she thought uneasily, something more than a spooky wind making her skin crawl.

She wasn't going to scare herself half to death with silly, adolescent ideas, she decided, and she sat up again to switch on the lamp. After getting up and pulling on one of Matt's big flannel shirts that she'd been using for a bathrobe, she turned off the lamp again and headed for the kitchen figuring that since she couldn't sleep, she might as well do something useful.

Baking was second nature for her, and she realized that she could have asked Kate all sorts of questions about herself, one of which could have been, "Kate, have I always enjoyed cooking?"

Assembling the ingredients for cookies, Hope sighed over the opportunity she'd let slip by today and told herself that if Kate came alone next week, she would be much more relaxed than she'd been with Dr. Heath watching every move she made. It was he, after all, who had made her so nervous, not Kate.

Well, Kate had unnerved her at first, she silently admitted while going to the refrigerator for eggs. Hope didn't realize how jumpy she still was—whether from her visitors today or because of that eerie wind—until a powerful gust shook the house and she dropped the eggs.

"Oh, damn," she mumbled, eyeing the mess on the floor. She went for some paper towels, then thought of a better way to clean up raw eggs. It was simple, really, just pour salt on the eggs and sweep them into a newspaper. "That's a memory," she said in utter amazement, the first one that didn't scare the breath out of her.

"It's starting to happen," she whispered emotionally. She was eventually going to remember everything and intuition told her that day wasn't far-off. Still jumpy over the wind but feeling a newfound joy because of a simple memory, Hope looked again at the soupy egg mess on the floor, then went to the laundry room.

The broom was stored in the closet next to the washer

and dryer, but what about a newspaper? It occurred to Hope that she hadn't seen a newspaper since she'd gotten there. How odd, she thought. Surely Matt received and read a newspaper, didn't he?

Then she remembered seeing some newspapers in a drawer in this room when she'd searched the house for something feminine to wear. That was the day she'd discovered the attic and what it contained. Her thoughts wandered for a moment. Matt had acted as though he'd forgotten Trisha's things were in the attic, which seemed a bit far-fetched. Would he deliberately lead her to believe that he had no fond memories of his ex-wife to influence her willingness to sleep with him?

But her willingness had needed no prodding, had it? She'd been willing right from the get-go, and her behavior was definitely not in keeping with her normal lifestyle, not when she'd been a virgin. That was one puzzle she would love to unravel, she thought with a frown as she began opening drawers.

The newspapers were easily found. Hope took them from the drawer—there weren't nearly as many as she'd thought there were—and then got the broom and returned to the kitchen. She leaned the broom against a counter and was about to set down the papers so she could get the box of salt when a headline caught her eye: Newest Stockwell Heiress Missing.

A cacophony of alarm bells went off in her system. The word *missing* caused her heart to race, and then she spotted her name in the first sentence of the front-page article. *My God, this has something to do with me!* On very weak legs, Hope went to the table and sank onto a chair. She began reading.

The youngest daughter of Caine Stockwell, Hope LeClaire, did not arrive in Texas as had been planned by she and her siblings during a family reunion at their mother's home in the town of Chatham on Cape Cod, Massachusetts, only a short time ago. Ms. LeClaire is presently listed as a missing person by law enforcement agencies, as she was scheduled to arrive by a commuter flight from Dallas to the Grandview Airport yesterday and seemingly vanished somewhere between Boston, Massachusetts, and Grandview. According to the Stockwell family, Hope was then going to rent a car and drive to her deceased father's home for yet another reunion. Unsubstantiated rumors are circulating about the reading of Caine Stockwell's will, which seems to coincide with the date of Ms. LeClaire's visit.

Hope LeClaire is twenty-eight years old, 5 feet 6 inches tall and weighs approximately 110 pounds. She has dark curly hair and blue eyes. Photos of Ms. LeClaire will be published when they become available. Her mother, Madelyn LeClaire, has told reporters that Hope was wearing a forest-green dress and matching coat. She left Boston with two suitcases, which, ironically, made it to Grandview in good condition and are presently in the hands of the police.

Ms. LeClaire was only recently brought into the Stockwell family fold. Madelyn and Caine divorced prior to Ms. LeClaire's birth, and it appears that her three brothers and one sister were told and grew up believing that their mother died in a boating accident, along with their father's twin brother, Brandon. The truth, which Caine related to his children in a deathbed confession, is that Madelyn and Brandon married and lived in Europe for many years before moving to Cape Cod. Madelyn is a well-known artist, whose paintings are becoming quite prized by collectors.

Brandon is a successful financier, and Hope Le-Claire, who was born in the U.S. but lived in Europe for most of her life, is a graduate of the famed London cooking school, Le Cordon Bleu. Ms. LeClaire worked as a master chef in London before breaking her two-year engagement to Mark Herriot, a man reputed to have connections with the royal family. Shortly thereafter Ms. LeClaire moved to Boston, where she was actively seeking employment in her chosen field when the family she'd known nothing about got in touch with her. Thus, the family reunion, and ultimately the plane trip to Texas during which she disappeared.

The Stockwells immediately posted a $50,000 reward to be given to anyone with information that would lead the law or themselves to Hope LeClaire's whereabouts. Readers who believe they may know something may contact this paper or any law enforcement agency.

Feeling numb from shock, Hope's vision blurred from the tears in her eyes. *They knew, they knew all along! Matt knew. The sheriff and Doc knew. Everyone knew and no one told me!*

Matt's deception hurt the worst. From the date on the newspaper he'd known who she was the day he'd found her. Had he delayed telling her with hope of pushing up the amount of the reward money? And he'd had the chance to suggest it, too, hadn't he? When he'd walked Kate and Brett out to their car.

She couldn't bear it. Laying her arms on the table, she buried her face in them and sobbed pitifully. Matt had made love to her, he'd taught her *how* to make love, in fact. She'd been so ignorant about making love, and he'd led her down the garden path as easily as if she'd been a total moron.

Which I am! She was still sobbing, telling herself that she hated Matt McCarlson more than she could ever hate anyone, when she heard a noise behind her. Thinking that Matt had been awakened by her middle-of-the-night need to cook herself sleepy, she raised her head to destroy him on the spot with a murderous look.

But it wasn't Matt she saw, it was Randy Biggers—*the man who had kidnapped her!*

In an instant she remembered everything...everything!

"Hope LeClaire?" She had just deplaned in Grandview, Texas. The airport was small but busy, and a red-haired man wearing a neatly pressed, nicely tailored black suit had just spoken to her.

"Yes?" she replied.

"I'm Randy Biggers, one of the Stockwells' chauffeurs. They sent me to pick you up and drive you to the mansion."

Hope frowned. "I was planning to rent a car. I'm sure they knew that."

"Kate mentioned it, but she thought you might have some trouble finding the place on your own. My instructions are to escort you to the car and then return for your luggage. Shall we go?"

Slightly befuddled but hesitant about questioning this unexpected change of plan, Hope kept stride with the chauffeur. It was raining, and once outside, they hurried. Hope barely had time to look around and certainly had no sense of direction. In minutes they had reached a parking lot, and Randy Biggers took her arm and rushed her over to a black car with darkly tinted windows.

Opening the front passenger door, he waited for her to get in, then quickly shut the door, ran around the front of the car, got in, started the engine and raced from the parking lot.

This isn't right! Whenever I've been driven by a chauffeur, he seated me in the back!

Suddenly dry-mouthed, Hope furtively studied the man from the corner of her eye. He was in his thirties, she estimated, tall and ordinary looking except for his flaming red hair. Was it possible she was frightened over nothing, that her imagination was running just a little bit wild?

She did her best to speak normally. "I thought you'd be driving a limousine."

"Not today," he said brusquely.

His tone was threatening; she knew then that she should be *very* afraid. Her hand crept to the door handle. "Don't bother," he snapped at her. "I've got the main lock on, and none of the doors will open until I release it."

"Wha-what are you going to do to me?" she asked, and the fear in her voice made her even more afraid. She had let this man talk her into leaving the airport with him, and she'd never done anything so stupid in her life. She was educated and inherently smart, and yet she'd gotten into a strange man's car.

"Shut the hell up," he snarled.

Too terrified to talk back, she sat without moving and stared unseeingly into the rainy, gray twilight. I can get out of this, I just have to use my head. Do as he says for now and keep alert for opportunity.

Though she had no knowledge of Grandview, it was obvious they were headed out of town. Icy fingers walked Hope's spine. Was he a rapist, a murderer or both? Tears filled her eyes, and she turned her face to the side window so he wouldn't see her almost paralyzing fear. Why hadn't she suspected his story and told him at the airport to get away from her before she called for security? He would have disappeared so fast he'd have been a blur.

Yes, but then he would have gone after some other unsuspecting woman, and—

Hey, wait a minute. He'd known the Stockwell name...and yours! You're the only unsuspecting woman he wanted, and you fell for his line so easily that he must feel incredibly superior. That could work in your favor...eventually. Or maybe not. Dear God in heaven, where is he taking me? And for what reason? Did he give me his real name—Randy Biggers—or is that an alias? Actually, with that noticeable red hair of his, he was taking quite a risk in approaching me at all. Surely someone in the airport saw him talking to me, and maybe someone even saw the two of us walking out together.

The drive seemed endless, though it was really less than two hours. They passed through several very small towns and then, finally, he turned into the driveway of a squatty, run-down little motel with a garish red sign. Bypassing the front units, he drove around back, parked directly in front of an end unit and turned off the engine.

Then he turned in the seat toward her and pulled a knife from under the seat. "Listen carefully," he said while laying the knife on her thigh. "I really have no desire to use this tonight, but I will if you force me into it. We're going inside. You are not to make a peep, understand? Not one sound, word, grunt or anything else is to come out of your mouth. I guarantee you'll be sorry if you try anything funny."

"Fine," she whispered, believing his every word.

"Good, I think we understand each other." Reaching into the back seat, he brought out two bottles of whiskey. "Carry these," he told her, and she took one in each of her hands. "Stay put until I open your door."

She followed his instructions to the letter, and when they were inside the seedy little motel room, he praised her.

"You're a smart woman. Stay smart and you won't get hurt. Do something dumb and you'll wish you hadn't."

Sinking to a chair, Hope's frantic brain was filled with images of him getting drunk and raping her repeatedly. Why else would he have brought her to a place like this with whiskey to drink?

She was so certain of his intent that she was startled when he took a rope out of his jacket pocket and ordered her to put her hands behind the chair.

"Why are you going to tie me up?" she asked fearfully.

"Maybe I'll tell you about it, maybe I won't. Just put your damned hands behind the chair and stop with the questions."

She obeyed, and felt how tightly he tied her wrists together. After he'd finished and walked over to the dresser for a glass for his whiskey, she tried moving her hands to no avail. There's not going to be an opportunity to get out of this, is there? Her spirit dropped to an all-time low. She was in the clutches of a madman. He might not be wild-eyed or ranting and raving, but he couldn't be anything but mad to do this to another human being.

She watched him warily as he threw back his first drink in one swallow and then refilled the glass. He went to a window, moved the soiled, scraggly drape just a little and peered outside. Apparently satisfied that no one had followed them, he picked up the bottle of whiskey, walked over to the bed, stacked the pillows against the headboard and then lay down, setting the bottle on the scarred stand next to the bed.

It was then that he began staring at her. Hope tried not to squirm under his scrutiny, and, in fact, tried to appear as though she couldn't care less if he stared at her all night. Deep down, though, that stare was worse than the knife he'd placed on the battered old dresser. He was sizing her up, and for what reason? If he'd brought her here to rape her, why hadn't he just thrown her on the bed and gotten to it?

She kept thinking about her virginity, and how she and Mark Herriot—the man she had loved so very much for so long and who'd turned out to be an unfaithful, cheating bastard—had talked about saving themselves for their wedding night. It had seemed so lovely and tenderly romantic to Hope that she had adored Mark for being so thoughtful, and all during their two-year engagement he'd played Hope for a fool while he'd slept with the woman he really loved. All he'd wanted from Hope was her money, which was a fortune because of her mother and the man she'd believed to be her father. Brandon had invested in her name since her childhood, and her net worth was now such a vast sum that she couldn't spend it in a dozen lifetimes. She'd been discovering a great deal of joy in researching charity foundations and then donating generously to the ones that really moved her.

Was money what Randy Biggers wanted from her? Heavens, if that was the case she'd give him any amount he wanted, if he'd just let her go!

She was working up her courage to bring up the subject when he said, "So, you're the baby sister that the Stockwell gang finally ran down."

Hope cleared her throat. "Apparently you know the Stockwells?"

"Course I know 'em. And they're gonna pay me a bundle for you, baby." Randy laughed uproariously, and Hope caught on that he was getting drunk very fast.

She stopped pitying herself and started thinking sensibly. If he got drunk enough, and if she played her cards right, he would never collect a dime from the Stockwells or anyone else for her ransom.

"Well, they can afford it," she said with a who-gives-a-damn twist of her lips.

"Are you putting me on?" he asked suspiciously.

"Look, I met them one time and once was enough. They're a bunch of snobs and someone should take them down a peg or two. How much are you going to ask for?"

Randy sat up and swung his feet to the floor. He narrowed his eyes on her. "How much are you worth, girlie?"

Another idea hit her, a chancy one to be sure, but one she dare not overlook. She could throw up afterward. Right now she was fighting for her life.

She put on her most seductive smile and crossed her legs in such a way that her skirt bunched above her knees. "Most men think I'm worth a whole lot," she purred. "Say, how about sharing that bottle with me?"

"You like whiskey?"

"I'm not a big drinker, but I enjoy a taste now and then."

"Well, sure," Randy said, and when he got up to go for another glass, Hope saw how unsteadily he walked. Why, he was already drunk! All she had to do was encourage him to keep on drinking.

When he stumbled his way across the room to deliver the glass of whiskey to her, she looked helpless and laughed. "Looks as though you'll have to hold it for me while I drink."

"Oh, your hands are tied. I forgot," Randy said, slurring his words so that they all ran together. Weaving back and forth he began staring at her again. "You're damned good-looking, you know. Didn't expect that."

"Why thank you, Randy. You're pretty good-looking yourself. I always did have a weakness for men with red hair."

Grinning, he ran his fingers through his hair. "Is that a fact?"

She moved in the chair, as though his nearness was

affecting her. "Let me have a swallow," she said, nodding her head at the glass.

"Okay. Hold on and I'll bring over a chair and the bottle."

With him holding the glass to her lips she took several sips of the ghastly stuff and pretended it was the most delicious drink she'd ever tasted.

"That's good stuff, Randy. You must really know your drinks."

"I do," he agreed. His drunken gaze probed her eyes. "I'm wondering about you, baby."

"Wondering what?"

"How far you'd go."

"Why don't you untie my hands and find out?" she said in that low, sexy tone of voice she'd adopted for his benefit. Her eyes went to the regular-size bed for a long moment, then returned to his face. "That small bed would accommodate two people well enough, if one of them was on top of the other," she said and saw him gulp.

"Uh, yeah, it would. Want to try it out?"

"I'm game. Are you?"

"You bet!" Staggering to his feet, he walked around Hope's chair and started fumbling with the knots in the ropes chafing her wrists.

She wanted to scream at him. She loathed him beyond words, and she was still frightened of that knife on the dresser and how quickly he might turn on her if she made the slightest mistake.

It took him at least five minutes to untie her, and by then she was ready to commit murder. Rubbing her wrists while he walked around her so that he could see her face, she weighed her options. Settling on one, she began her campaign.

"Would it be all right if I used the bathroom while you get undressed?" she asked.

"Can't stop nature," he quipped, and laughed so hard at his own stupid wit that he nearly lost his balance and fell over.

Smiling sweetly, Hope got up and walked into a horrible, smelly little bathroom. Shutting the door, she leaned her forehead against it. She felt weak enough to collapse, but her plan was working and she had to keep it rolling.

She rinsed her face and hands in cool water at the rusty little sink, which was a bit reviving, then examined the rope burns on her wrists. Listening, she could tell that it was raining harder than before. It didn't matter. If she managed to get to the door and unlock it before he grabbed her, she had a good chance of getting away from him. She was a good runner, and while running shoes would have helped her make better time, at least her pumps had low heels.

Finally she'd procrastinated as long as she dared, and she opened the bathroom door. She almost gasped out loud, because that jerk, that red-haired snake in the grass, that kidnapper, was actually in bed and waiting for her to join him. She saw at once that every stitch of clothes he'd had on had been tossed on a chair, so he wasn't just in bed, he was naked!

"Get undressed," he told her.

"Can we have a drink first? Say, how would you like to see a real sexy striptease? Is there a radio in here?"

"Nah, just that old TV. Probably doesn't even work. Go ahead and pour us both a drink, then let's see you strut your stuff, baby."

Hope's hands were shaking when she reached for the whiskey bottle. She knew what she had to do next, and her heart was in her throat and nearly choking her. But she managed to knock over the bottle, and the little remaining whiskey in it splashed on the floor.

"Oh, damn!" she cried. "If there's anything I hate, it's

wasting good whiskey. I'll have to open that other bottle you left on the dresser.''

''Well, get a move on, will ya? I'm thirsty.''

''Now, don't get all hot and bothered, sweetie,'' she said coyly. ''It'll only take me a sec to bring your drink, then I'll get one for myself.'' Stepping over to the dresser, she eyed the knife, but in that instant she knew she couldn't use it, not even to protect herself. She nearly doubled over from the agony in her midsection. Somehow she had to get out of here. How? How?

After that everything seemed to happen without direction from her brain. Carrying the full bottle of whiskey and Randy's glass over to the bed, she handed him the glass. The second he took it she slammed him over the head with the bottle.

Then she ran—frantically, breathing so hard she could hear herself. She struggled with the simple dead bolt on the door for what felt like an eternity and finally ran outside. The rain pelted her face, her clothes, her hair, but fear drove her on...and on...and on.

Oh, yes, she remembered everything now—her mother, Brandon, her family in Texas and Matt. She had so much to live for and this creep from another planet was not going to destroy her!

Jumping up from the table, she screamed loudly enough to wake the dead. Randy grabbed her then and clapped his hand over her mouth. Kicking and scratching, she fought him with every ounce of furious strength in her body.

''You little wildcat! Simmer down!'' Randy took a swing and hit her with a hard right to her chin.

The last thing Hope saw was Matt running into the kitchen in his underwear. The last thing she *heard* was the crunch of bone when Matt's huge fist flattened Randy's face.

She fell to the floor, out cold.

She awoke in her own bed, or what she'd come to think of as her bed. It wasn't hers at all, she thought sadly, it belonged to Matt. Her bed was in her house in Boston, and she'd come to Texas at the urging of her siblings to participate in the reading of their father's will.

The house was full of people. She could hear them moving around and talking. Doc stuck his head in, then called down the hall, "Cliff, she's awake now." Doc came in and sat on the bed next to her. "How are you feeling, young lady?"

"Is my jaw broken?"

"Just bruised. I've been keeping a close eye on your vitals, Hope, and you're doing fine. Do you remember my giving you a sedative?"

"Vaguely. Quite a few things about tonight are...vague," she murmured. But then her gaze sought Dr. Pickett's. "When I saw that man, I remembered everything."

"About your life prior to coming to Texas?"

"Everything, Doctor, my childhood, my parents, schools I attended, friends of all ages, the places in Europe I love...everything."

"And Randy Biggers?" Doc asked quietly.

"He kidnapped me," she said huskily.

"That's what we've all figured out. Here's the sheriff. Are you feeling up to having a little chat with him?"

"I think so. Yes, I'm sure of it." She looked up as the sheriff approached the bed and said, "Hello."

"Hello, Hope. You had quite an experience tonight. Or should I say last night? It's nearly dawn now. Doc, I'm going to bring that chair over to the bed. Would you mind moving so I can sit close enough to Hope to hear her better?''

Doc smiled at Hope and patted her hand. ''You've been speaking very softly, my dear. I'll leave you and the sheriff alone for now, but I won't be far. You just let someone know if you need me.''

She shaped a wan little smile for Doc, then watched the sheriff seat himself in the chair she'd brought over to the bed. ''You said it's almost dawn? What happened to the night?''

''Sort of slipped away on you, did it?'' The sheriff took a notebook and pen from his jacket pocket. ''Do you know the name of the man who attacked you tonight?''

''Randy Biggers. When I first arrived in Grandview weeks ago, he came up to me and told me he was a chauffeur for the Stockwells, and that they'd sent him to pick me up.'' Hope related the awful story she'd remembered earlier, omitting nothing.

''So you're saying you walked clear from the Roadside Motel that night? It was pouring rain, Hope.''

''Yes,'' she agreed with a weary sigh, ''it was. And I didn't walk, Sheriff, I ran. Before you doubt that statement, let me add that I do a lot of running. It's my favorite form of exercise, and I've entered a number of marathons. But I wasn't running for fun that night, I was scared out of my wits and positive that Biggers was only a short distance behind me. Never once did it occur to me that I might have outrun him, or that he'd gotten too late a start to catch up with me. Maybe I should have considered those options, but all I could think of was getting away from him.''

''You outsmarted him, Hope. Everyone's very proud of you.''

''Including Matt? Where is he, by the way? I can hear strange voices in the house, but I haven't heard his.''

"Matt and Biggers were both transported to Hawthorne Hospital. Matt wouldn't hear of anyone but Doc taking a look at you, so some other doctor must be stitching him and Biggers up in the emergency room."

Hope's eyes grew frightened. "Matt was hurt? How badly?"

"Broke his hand—or rather several bones in his hand—when he let Biggers have one. Biggers ended up with a broken nose and jaw, and Matt said his satisfaction in punching out Biggers's lights far outweighed the damage he did to his fist." The Sheriff shook his head. "Bet Biggers never knew what hit him. That bonehead came after you right in Matt's house. Never could figure out the criminal mind, but I'm sure Biggers will have a good long time in prison to ask himself why he wasn't a little more patient about waiting for another chance to grab you without witnesses." The sheriff grinned. "Or without a freight train like Matt on hand to bowl him over."

Sheriff Braeburn got up and returned the chair to its corner. "That's about it for now, Hope. You will testify in court at Biggers's trial, won't you?"

She wished that she never had to set eyes on him again, but she said, "Yes, I'll testify."

"By the way, I notified your family. Kate is on her way here, and no telling how many others. Hope, Kate said on the phone when I called that it was time you went home. She sounded determined, so I feel pretty certain that you're going to be pressured to leave here."

Remembering how wantonly she'd behaved with Matt, and how out of character that was for her, Hope winced. She'd actually been thinking about love, and since she was better equipped to read Matt's actions and reactions now, she was positive that the word had never entered his mind. Hopefully Kate would get there before Matt returned from Hawthorne; there really was no reason for them to ever see each other again, was there?

"That's fine," she said dully, and turned her face to the wall.

Chapter Fifteen

Kate had insisted that Hope stay with her and Brett, and every night one or more of their brothers would come to dinner. Their families, too, of course, and Hope relaxed a little more each day, surrounded by people who were fun and loving and so very, very glad that she had come through a dreadful ordeal relatively unscathed.

Through Rafe, the family learned that Randy Biggers had finally confessed his crimes. His excuse for putting Hope through so much hell? Revenge for what the Stockwells had done to the Johnsons years and years ago. He'd also been identified by Beth Johnson Stockwell and Jack Stockwell as the man who had threatened Beth at her own home months before, and who, indeed, had been a crony of her late first husband, Eben Johnson.

A date was set for the reading of Caine Stockwell's will, and the entire clan gathered at Caine's mansion near Grandview, where they learned that the massive estate was to be divided equally among his five children, Jack, Rafe, Cord, Kate and Hope. A collective sigh of relief among her siblings told Hope that they'd all been worried she might have been left out.

There was one surprise in the will: Caine had requested that four million dollars be placed in a trust fund, should any other children come forth and prove Caine's paternity.

"Obviously Dad thought it could happen," Kate said dryly. "But then he never was a saint, was he?"

The next day Madelyn and Brandon flew in from Massachusetts and another family reunion ensued. Good food, good company and lots of laughs. Hope told herself that since she truly loved her newfound family and because she had so much to be grateful for—considering that Biggers could so easily have killed her in that motel room— she should be ecstatically happy.

She wasn't. Behind her every word, gesture and smile lay a ponderous sadness. She couldn't stop thinking about Matt, and every morning she prayed he would phone her that day and every night she went to bed just a little bit sadder.

Madelyn and Brandon returned to their home on Cape Cod, and before leaving mentioned to Hope that perhaps she would like to fly to Boston with them. She told them that she wanted to stay in Texas a little longer, and everyone assumed it was so she could spend more time with Kate and their brothers.

It was partly true, although it wasn't Hope's main reason for staying. Something inside her rebelled at the thought of leaving Texas without seeing Matt at least once. If nothing else, she should thank him for all he'd done for her. And yet she couldn't pick up the phone and call him. As difficult as it was to face, Matt could have forgotten her the very morning she'd left the ranch.

Then she learned that Matt had refused the reward or

any other kind of money from the Stockwells, which angered her. She said nothing about his financial situation to the family, but it infuriated her that he would be so ridiculously proud and stubborn as to face bankruptcy rather than accept money that he so richly deserved. She almost called him that night, not to thank him but to give him a piece of her mind. It dawned on her a few hours later, while rolling and tossing in bed and furious over something she obviously could do nothing about, that she might as well return to Boston and resume her life. In spite of her immense wealth, she wanted a job and a normal life.

And why on earth should she hang around Texas secretly hoping that Matt would develop a conscience and phone her? In the first place he'd told her plainly that he would never again get caught up in a serious relationship with a wealthy woman. And since he'd known all along who she was, he'd also known she had money. She could conclude nothing else but that he never had really cared about her, not in a meaningful way. He'd had his fun, the cad, and was every bit as bad as Mark had been. Obviously she was attracted to unscrupulous men. It was a character flaw she'd do well to work on.

The very next day Hope was surprised by a visitor: Chuck Crawford. Kate brought him to the library, where Hope was sitting with a book in her lap and her eyes on the sunshine outside of the beautifully draped library windows.

"Hope, look who's here," Kate said.

Hope turned her head, saw Chuck and felt a rush of gladness. She put aside the book and hurried over to greet him. Instead of a handshake, he got a hug.

"Oh, Chuck, I'm so happy to see you."

"I'm happy to see you, too, miss."

Hope stepped back and smiled when she saw that her

effusive greeting had embarrassed the older man. "Come in and sit down," she said.

"Hope, would you like to have some coffee brought in?" Kate asked.

"That would be wonderful, thank you, Kate." Hope returned to her chair and Chuck chose one that was nearby. "So, what are you doing in Dallas?"

"I got a sister who lives about ten miles east of here, and I thought I'd spend a few days with her before I start looking for another job. Hope, you look very well. Matt said you had completely regained your memory. I had to stop in and tell you how happy that makes me."

Hope held up a hand. "Thank you, but back up a sec. You're going to be looking for another job? How come?"

Chuck fiddled with his hat, which he'd been holding since his arrival. "Hope, I didn't come here to upset you with bad news."

"Then again, maybe you did," she said quietly. "What's going on, Chuck?"

"He's losing everything, Hope. The bank is foreclosing and putting him out of business. Everything that isn't mortgaged is going to be sold by auction tomorrow. Hope, as long as I've said too much already, I'm gonna add one more thing. You're the only woman that ever brought so much as a ray of sunshine into Matt McCarlson's life. Don't get me wrong. He's surviving. He'll always survive, that's just the kind of man he is. But since the day you left I haven't seen one smile on his face. Even losing the ranch isn't hitting him as hard as losing you did."

She was so stunned that she could barely speak, and when she did her voice cracked. "Chuck, you must be wrong. He's never called, or tried to see me."

"Matt ain't got two quarters to rub together and he's a proud man. He doesn't have anything to offer you, and he'd plumb topple over and die if you ever got the idea that he wanted you for your money.''

She got up, walked to the far end of the room and came back again. Her mind had raced every step of the way, devising and discarding replies, comments and even possible solutions to what could only be described as an unnecessary, heartbreaking situation. Matt was too hung up on a person's net worth. Was money the only thing that had any value to him? The only thing he believed that *she* valued?

Kate came in then with a tray bearing a coffeepot, cups, sugar, cream and a small plate of cookies. ''Here you are,'' she sang out, then saw the taut expression on Hope's face. ''Enjoy,'' Kate said quietly, then made a discreet exit.

''Chuck would you please excuse me for a few minutes? There's something I have to do. Help yourself to the coffee and cookies while I'm gone. I'm sure I won't be long.''

Chuck nodded and said, ''Sure, Hope, you go ahead,'' which she barely heard because she was already out the door. Hurrying to another room, she shut the door and picked up the phone. After asking information for a certain number, she dialed it and said a pleasant hello to the woman who answered. With no hesitation at all, she continued with, ''My name is Hope Stockwell. May I please speak to your bank manager?''

She was back in the library with Chuck in twenty minutes. Seating herself again, she filled a cup with coffee and looked Chuck in the eyes.

''I'm in the process of buying a ranch, and I'm going to need an experienced foreman,'' she said calmly. ''Would you be interested in the job?''

Chuck's grin reached from ear to ear. ''Yes, ma'am!''

* * *

The following morning Matt saddled Dex. Unlike the other livestock on the place, Dex would not be sold at today's auction. Matt had raised Dex from a foal and wouldn't part with him for any amount of money.

Matt's personal belongs were already packed, but he'd load them in his truck later on, probably this evening. He'd take a long ride on Dex and have a final look at the land he loved so much. He would make sure that he didn't get back until the auction was over, for he couldn't force himself to watch the dissolution of the only thing in this whole miserable world that held any meaning for him.

That wasn't altogether true, he thought as he swung himself into the saddle. Hope meant more to him than he dared let himself think about too hard. It seemed damned unfair to him that the one woman he'd finally fallen for after years of self-denial was someone so far out of reach. The division of Caine Stockwell's estate was no secret. Matt had no idea how the media had come by the information, but anyone who paid the least bit of attention to the daily news knew that Caine's children were now wealthy beyond an ordinary working stiff's wildest imagination.

Besides that, Matt had read articles reciting once again the Stockwell family history. Caine had never known his youngest child, Hope LeClaire. She had been raised by her mother, Madelyn, and the man Madelyn had married, Caine's twin brother, Brandon Stockwell, who had changed his last name to LeClaire to make it harder for Caine and his snoops to ever find him. Caine and Brandon had vied for Madelyn's affections since their youth. It appeared that Caine had won out at first, for he and Madelyn had married young and then produced four children. Madelyn was pregnant with Hope when she left Caine and then vanished. Brandon, too, had disappeared, and Caine's explanation to the world was that his wife and twin brother had died in a boating accident.

Of course nothing could have been farther from the truth. After Hope was born, Brandon and Madelyn got married in Europe. Because of Brandon's innate ability to make money, Hope had been raised genteelly and with every luxury. She had attended the best schools and universities, and then had enrolled in the famed cooking school in London, Le Cordon Bleu, from which she had graduated with honors.

After devouring every bit of information he could find about Hope, Matt knew that she was so far above him on the social scale that there never had been a chance of a long-term relationship between them. He was darned lucky in fact, that he'd kept his true feelings for her to himself. At least he still had his pride.

Selling out to pay his bills didn't mean instant poverty for Matt; if everything sold for a fair price he'd have a little money left over, enough to get by on until he could make a new start somewhere else. It hurt like hell to think that way because he'd never lived or worked anyplace else. Regardless he'd take it on the chin and move on. What choice did he have?

Riding Dex up a rise in the terrain, Matt reined in and looked back at the ranch buildings. Men were still staying in the bunkhouse and maintaining the ranch—at the request of the bank officer who'd handled the foreclosure—so there were some familiar vehicles parked in their usual spots. Even so, the place already had a forlorn, deserted look to it, which tugged at Matt's heartstrings. He wallowed in sentimentality for a while, but when he felt tears stinging his eyes that was too much. Shaking off emotion, he turned Dex's head away from the compound and the two old friends went in another direction, leaving behind the only home either of them had ever known.

* * *

The day dragged for Matt. Even taking a last look at the land he'd grown up loving lost its appeal after a while. He was glad when four o'clock finally rolled around and he could start back. The auctioneer had told him everything should be over and done with around three, so Matt had timed his ride so that he would get back at five. By then, he was pretty certain, everyone would have hauled off his or her buys. He knew that his first look at the compound with all the equipment, vehicles and livestock gone would be a blow, but it was one he couldn't avoid.

At ten of five he rode over a hill and there it was—the compound. Gritting his teeth, bracing himself for what still lay ahead—the final chores of loading his pickup with his boxes and suitcases, and securing Dex in the one old horse trailer he'd been permitted to keep—he kept Dex moving toward home.

"Only it's not home anymore, old friend," he said to his horse. Feeling himself choking up again, Matt felt a hot surge of anger. He hadn't caused this, dammit to hell; a nasty little virus had!

It was small comfort for Matt to know that other ranchers in the area had been hit just as hard by that cattle virus and were paying the same awful price that had been exacted from him. He'd battled so hard, though, and had survived for as long as he had on sheer guts and determination. No one could ever say that he'd gone down without a fight, he thought wryly as he reached the compound's perimeter.

He suddenly realized that nothing was as he'd expected it to be. The tractors and haying equipment were still in the sheds, horses were in the corral—swishing their tails at flies and looking over the top rail at him and Dex—and he could even see trivial things, such as some harness leather hanging on a hook near the barn door. He pulled on the reins and mumbled, ''Whoa, boy.''

Hadn't the auction taken place? Puzzled, he nudged Dex into a slow walk toward the barn and then frowned deeply at sight of the brand-new white sports utility van—an extremely expensive model—that was parked near the house. It was so new, in fact, that it didn't even have license plates; it had a permit sticker in the front window.

After dismounting and caring for Dex, Matt turned him into the corral. The walk to the house took just enough time for Matt to work himself into a resentful lather. Obviously he'd have to go through the same unnerving exercise tomorrow, or whatever day the auction had been rescheduled for. It was damned inconsiderate of those auction people to cancel today's event without giving him at least the courtesy of a phone call.

Shooting the shiny new SUV a dirty look and wondering who was in his house—probably snooping around and trying to decide if they wanted to buy it from the bank—Matt pushed open the back door and strode in, all set for a confrontation.

He nearly fainted when he saw Hope in the kitchen, wearing an apron over her jeans and shirt, glowing with good health and giving him the most beautiful smile he'd ever seen.

''Hope,'' he said weakly. ''My God, what're you doing here?''

''Right now I'm cooking dinner,'' she said cheerfully. ''How does beef stroganoff, a green salad and strawberry chiffon pie sound to you? It's a simple menu, but I think I'd scare the men off with fancy dishes with French sauces, don't you?''

He felt sick to his stomach. She looked so healthy, but she couldn't possibly be, not if she was back here and reliving her weeks of lost memory and cooking for the men.

"Who knows you're here?" he asked gently, thinking that her family might once again be worried sick about where she might be.

Hope laughed. "That's a funny question." She kept grinning at Matt. "Are you trying to be funny, darling?"

Matt's stomach sank. "Something's terribly wrong here. Hope, are you feeling all right?"

"I have never felt better in my life. How are you feeling? A bit light-headed, perhaps? I've taken you so by surprise, haven't I, and that's not fair, is it, darling?" Wiping her hands on a kitchen towel, she tossed it on the counter and then walked over to Matt, where she boldly wrapped her arms around his waist then leaned her head back to see his face.

"I'm going to open a restaurant in Hawthorne," she announced. "It might be the only one, or it could be the start of a chain. However that turns out, there's a lot of work to do around here before I can concentrate on that project."

Matt probed her eyes for signs of insanity. "Hope, I hate being the one to break the news to you," he said gently, "but the bank owns the ranch now."

"You silly goose," she said with a delightfully teasing laugh. "The bank doesn't own the ranch, I do."

Matt felt the blood drain from his face. "You're not serious."

She rose on tiptoe and brushed her lips against his. "Deadly serious," she whispered. "How could you ever think that I would let anyone take your ranch from you? Or from me, for that matter. Matt, don't you know what this place means to me? What you mean to me?"

"You...have so much," he stammered.

"I do now." Again she leaned her head back to see his face. "That is, I do if I have you. Do I, Matt?"

He swallowed hard. "I'm nothing compared to you."

"You will always be my hero, Matt."

"Don't bring heroics into this, Hope. I'm talking about net worth."

"Oh, God, I had hoped with all my heart that those two words would not come out of your mouth. Matt, don't you know yet that you can't judge people by the size of their bank accounts? Or that the riches they have in their heart are far more valuable than any amount of money?" She raised her hand and adoringly touched his lips with her fingertips. "It's all right, darling," she said consolingly. "I'll teach you. After all, you taught me…so much."

Matt's breath caught in his throat. She was offering everything she was to him, and God knew he wanted to scoop her up into a fiery embrace. But however urgently she might want him sexually—and that's all it must be since neither of them had ever even said the word *love*— she still didn't understand him.

"Hope, I can't live off you. I'm glad you bought the ranch, because I'd much rather it belonged to someone who loves it than to a stranger. But every penny spent on every damned thing, even the food I put in my mouth would have to be paid for by you."

She looked into his eyes for a long moment, then said, "So I'm to do what now? Watch the only man I ever loved drive away and then try to make a life for myself without him? Is that what you're telling me?" Her voice broke. "Matt, don't you love me even a tiny bit?"

He had suffered so much of late that he could no longer lie about anything. "Hope, I fought falling in love with you for so long that I can't do it another minute. Yes, I love you. I'll always love you. But I'm a man, for God's sake, and I *can't* do what you're asking.''

Tears began spilling from Hope's eyes. ''You love me, but you'd rather go off somewhere by yourself than stay here with me and make this place into the finest cattle and horse ranch in the country. Matt, can't you hear how ridiculous that sounds? Do you have any idea of how much money I really have? What should I spend it on, for pity sake? Darling, think of the life we could have together. If you had money and I didn't, we wouldn't even be having this ludicrous conversation. Why should we be having it now?''

She rose on tiptoe again. ''Kiss me, you fool. I'm not going to take no for an answer, and if you dare to try and leave without me, I swear I'll follow you to the ends of the earth. The ranch will fall apart without either of us here, and someday, fifty or so years from now, we'll come back and weep together, because it will hardly be recognizable.''

He winced at that painful image and gave up completely. Lifting his arms, he circled them around her and brought her close. ''I've only been trying to protect you,'' he said unsteadily.

''I know, darling, I know. You've protected me from the moment you first saw me. Oh, Matt, I love you so much.''

A sob escaped his throat. ''I love you, sweetheart. I will till the day I die.''

''Me, too, Matt. Oh, me, too.''

Hope announced their engagement over the phone, calling each of her family members one by one. Kate insisted that the ceremony and reception take place at the Stockwell mansion, and by then Matt was so befuddled by love and happiness that he agreed without so much as a mild skirmish. The wedding date was settled upon, and Kate, Hope and their mother talked long-distance to each other numerous times every day to discuss plans. The sisters-in-law got involved, as well, and everyone was looking forward to the big event.

Matt was thrilled beyond words when Chuck returned, and they immediately hired more men and began the long process of returning the McCarlson ranch to its former glory.

About a week before the wedding Hope drove to Hawthorne and kept her appointment with Dr. Adam Pickett.

"Hope, you look wonderful," Doc said. "You only came by to say hello, didn't you?"

"Well…I think it's a little more than that, Doc," she said with an impish light in her eyes. "Doc, I think there's a very good possibility that Matt and I are pregnant."

Doc threw back his head and laughed. "You and Matt are pregnant, eh? Well maybe you should've brought Matt in for a pelvic exam."

Hope smiled. "Let's do mine first, okay?"

That afternoon Matt came into the house to clean up for dinner. He kissed Hope on his way through the kitchen, then whistling a happy tune he went to take a shower.

He had wet hair in his eyes when he heard the shower door opening. Shaking it out of his face, he grinned when he saw Hope, nude and incredibly beautiful, getting in the shower with him. He put his arms around her. "This is a nice surprise," he said before kissing her ardently.

She snuggled up to his slippery body and laughed seductively. "Uh-oh," Matt said. "Methinks you're up to some more devilry, Miss LeClaire."

"You're very perceptive, Mr. McCarlson. But first

things first. I've never made love in a shower before, have you?''

''Nope.''

''Liar.''

''Sex kitten.''

''Sex *what?*''

''You heard me. C'mere, sex kitten, and take a ride on this.''

She did, and as it always had been for them, it was again—hot, steamy sex that had only gotten better because now there was no holding anything back for either of them.

When their passion had been sated, Matt turned off the shower and they got out and dried each other off with huge soft towels.

He pulled her close for a tender kiss before they left the bathroom to finish the remainder of the day's chores. It was a particularly moving kiss, and when he raised his head he saw a beautiful glow in her eyes.

''I doubt if anything could make me any happier than I've been, but you're going to try, aren't you?'' he said huskily.

''I hope what I have to tell you makes you as happy as it does me,'' she whispered. ''Matt, we're going to have a baby. I saw Doc today and he verified— Matt! Put me down! What are you doing?''

What he was doing was dancing! Holding her in his arms and laughing and shouting and dancing, all at the same time.

''I take it you're not *un*happy about becoming a father?'' she asked dryly.

He let her feet slide to the floor. ''A baby. My God. A *family!* My family. Our family, Hope. Unhappy? If I went outside right now, I know I'd be able to fly.''

Her gaze slowly and deliberately washed down his body. "I wouldn't recommend it in your present state."

He glanced down to his "present state" and laughed. "Yeah, why waste this in a flight over Texas, right?" He reached for her again, only this time she backed away.

"I have exactly twenty minutes to finish preparing dinner before the men come knocking on the back door, lover. But I agree that we shouldn't ever waste anything so marvelous as that, so—" she smiled sweetly "—just put it on hold until tonight, okay?"

She swept grandly from the bathroom and Matt groaned. "You're cruel," he shouted down the hall. He heard her laughing while she got dressed in their bedroom, and he couldn't help laughing, as well. Life was unbelievable now. And to think of how hard he'd fought against being happy. Thank God she was a tenacious person.

Matt sobered when he thought of that word. If Hope *hadn't* been tenacious, and physically strong, she might have died before ever reaching the ranch that stormy night.

And if she hadn't been very, very clever in that motel room with Randy Biggers, she might not have escaped from that weirdo.

All things considered, Matt thought with overwhelming emotion, wasn't it a miracle that he and Hope had met, fallen in love and were now going to receive life's most precious gift—a child?

Everything within him sighed as the loveliest peace of his life enveloped him much as a soft, silken cloak would. There could not possibly be another man as contented as he; he knew that as clearly as he knew his name—all because of Hope, his sweet, wonderful, beautiful Hope.

* * * * *

Coming soon from

SPECIAL EDITION™

**gives readers the scoop in
her juicy new miniseries**

Catch the latest titles in 2001

THE STRANGER IN ROOM 205
(SE #1399, June 2001)

BACHELOR COP FINALLY CAUGHT?
(SE #1413, August 2001)

And look for another engaging title
in October 2001

Available at your favorite retail outlet.

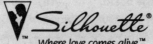
Where love comes alive™

Visit Silhouette at www.eHarlequin.com   SSEPRESS

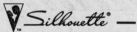

If you enjoyed what you just read,
then we've got an offer you can't resist!

Take 2 bestselling
love stories FREE!
Plus get a FREE surprise gift!

Clip this page and mail it to Silhouette Reader Service™

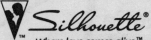